AMERICAN MOVIE
A Novel

PENELOPE BRINDLEY

Archway Publishing books may be ordered through booksellers or by contacting:

Archway Publishing
1663 Liberty Drive
Bloomington, IN 47403
www.archwaypublishing.com
1 (888) 242-5904

Because of the dynamic nature of the Internet, any web addresses or
links contained in this book may have changed since publication and
may no longer be valid. The views expressed in this work are solely those
of the author and do not necessarily reflect the views of the publisher,
and the publisher hereby disclaims any responsibility for them.

Any people depicted in stock imagery provided by Getty Images are
models, and such images are being used for illustrative purposes only.
Certain stock imagery © Getty Images.

ISBN: 978-1-4808-7091-8 (sc)
ISBN: 978-1-4808-7090-1 (e)

Library of Congress Control Number: 2018913025

Print information available on the last page.

Archway Publishing rev. date: 12/03/2018

for my children

Anne Elizabeth, Bartholomew Peter,
and John Brindley Hogan

One

It started the day Stephen Toledo came to audition students for his directing workshop, they camped in line for three days rehearsing scenes from box office hits because the Los Angeles Institute—known to intimates as Little Hollywood—didn't teach art, foreign film, or navel contemplation, Little Hollywood taught movies--the Industry way, the only way.

Sam's case was an exception, Little Hollywood didn't know she was at the Institute to do research for a novel ten years in the writing, her film scripts were intensely disliked by the writing professor—too internal, movies are external, movies are visual, movies move—yet when she made them into films he liked them and always asked if she'd really shot them herself.

After a year her money was gone so she wasn't a student the day Toledo came to Little Hollywood, still she had to see him, the man who produced his films independently, a crime in Little Hollywood tantamount to making art. Toledo's pictures were in the auteur tradition—the author as director and sometimes, star. Toledo the star. Arrogant and unburdened by experience as Sam was, she didn't like them very much—their limitless narcissism, their Hollywood character in spite of his much touted independence—but she thought Toledo the man might give her valuable insight for her novel.

The morning of the audition he was true to his reputation for being late, it was three hours past the scheduled time when a camouflage green amphibious car drove up to the sound stage door, Toledo got out dressed in white jeans and the ancient Navajo vest he was famous for wearing on shoots. His mirror sunglasses Sam remembered from the Vietnam film, and he took them off the same way he had in the first scene of that picture, pushed them up his nose and forehead into the wild corkscrew hair that flew around his eyes, their deep sockets with halfmoons under, black, still— that illusion of them looking directly at you. Students clamored around him but Toledo didn't notice, he was looking for someone, something lost, he squinted at the smog-filtered LA sun, the heels of his hands rose and pressed his eyes—also exactly as on film— his fingers continued up his forehead, knocked off the sunglasses, raked through his hair—the chaos of black curls—just as it was in the film, the *The Correspondent*. Several days of beard together with the raging eyes made him look hung over, doubtless from the ever present Courvoisier he was known to keep dangling from between his fingers during shoots. He looked as if he could use a hair of the dog now.

Media jocks spilled out of vans and trucks, as if they'd followed Toledo, with his terrible eyes looking past them, through the jungle of their microphones, as if it were all part of the smog.

One of the reporters stuck a mike in Toledo's face and said, "Is it true you're doing a workshop at Little Hollywood to find talent for your new picture?"

"What picture?" Toledo said.

"Everyone knows you're working on something."

"Ask everyone, then."

"Come on—give us a hint!"

"There's no picture," Toledo said, "and for that matter, no talent."

Stunned silence, even the students' mouths dropped open, "You mean talent is a myth?" one said.

When Toledo didn't answer, another jock said, "If talent doesn't exist, what does?"

"Nothing," Toledo said.

"Nothing!"

A laugh sounded shrilly through the new waves of media pros flowing from more vehicles, joining more students, workshop auditors, onlookers, former students screened out of production, looking for a way in, scrambling to get to Toledo yet parting like the Galilee for his boots, white with Malibu sand, driving through the breathlessly silent throng, up the stairs of the building that housed the sound stage—in a perpetual state of renovation, "Reincarnations to rival the Parthenon," Toledo was once quoted as saying. Now he stood at the door held open by students, turned to the crowd and said, "Who has an original scene for all this?"

Student faces paled, the media exploded in cacophony.

"Original?"

"What do you mean—for all this?"

"How can there be an original scene without talent?"

Students laughed nervously. "We were told to have a scene that works!"

Sam stepped forward and said, "Something so tried and true you can show it to investors—"

Toledo looked her way as a student cut in, "We were up all night!"

"Only one?" Toledo said, turned to Sam, said, "You have a scene."

Sam said, "I have."

Silence like atomic aftermath, the crowd parted around her—not reverently as for Toledo, but to avoid the contamination of her drop-out status—as nameless voices shouted.

"This workshop is for students!"

"We paid our tuition!"

Toledo stared through them at Sam, beckoned—and a hundred media techs turned their cameras on her, knees shaking as she climbed the steps—she with no scene, no idea at all of what she would do or why she'd brought this on herself, her lie ringing in her ears. Students snickered, stage-whispered.

"She doesn't have a scene, she has an inner state!"

"She has consciousness!"

By the time Sam reached Toledo, their laughter shook her more than her knees.

"Stephen Toledo," Toledo said and offered his hand.

"Sam Flannery."

Toledo's stare deepened. "I can see the Irish—all that hair and the eyes. My father's mother was Irish."

"I know."

"You do?"

"From *The Correspondent.*"

Toledo angled his head. "Do I know you?"

She started to say no then it came to her, what to do. "You remember?" she said.

"How could I forget?"

There were whistles and catcalls from the crowd, a video monitor, brought to the steps where they stood, showed a pan of the students and media then zoomed in on Sam's cutoff sweats, cutout sleeves, hair flying from its scarf, knobby feet bare because she'd shed shoes during the night of waiting for Toledo.

"What happened to your feet?" Toledo said, he squatted down and traced her crooked metatarsals with a finger.

"I was born with them wrong—"

"So what's different is wrong?" Toledo said and picked up her left foot.

"I could never play Cinderella."

The crowd shrieked with laughter—Toledo was on their side, he was playing with her, the video monitor showed her feet, Toledo's hands, "I'm not much of a prince, either," he said, "but I'll be damned if I haven't seen this foot before."

Sam said, "They've gotten worse since then—nursing, I think I had the wrong size shoes."

"Nursing—you?"

"It was after we—met—so to speak."

Toledo said, "When was that?"

"Ten years ago—more or less."

Toledo stood up close to Sam, pulled the scarf off. "The kind of hair they invented veils to hide," he said. The crowd noise grew, they cheered Toledo, jeered Sam, Toledo stepped back looking at her body and said, "A shape witchhunters like to burn."

Sam said, "That's a bit more drama than I had in mind."

"Ten years ago you were a teeny-bopper," Toledo said.

Sam shook her head. "New York—trying to get into theater."

"Was I in New York?"

"Yes—and broke."

"Always that—till I became a tax shelter—the Parthenon and I."

The crowd laughed and cheered, it was becoming a mob scene, video cameras and monitors were wheeled out of the Parthenon, carried up from the media trucks, stacked into banks like walls surrounding the steps that crawled with students and media, below the street was jammed with traffic, overhead media choppers circled like vultures, hundreds of video screens came alive with sweeping scenes of the irate students, media jocks talking softly into mikes, Toledo close-up—his face too round, too haunted for Hollywood.

The Improv Scene

Camera on-lights blink, the monitor picture zooms slowly out showing the Irish hair blowing across glass-blue eyes, cheeks round and white as porcelain—familiar enough to be Sam's yet not, she thinks. The actor's face.

Toledo's hands move into the picture, his fingers look as if they know work yet gentle, excruciatingly slow, tracing the lines of the porcelain face. "Don't look at the monitors," he says. His face is too close, searching, studying. "You paid more than tuition," he says.

She thinks he means the actor's face is haunted, too. She needs a Hollywood reason, says, "On my back, you mean?"

Startled, Toledo drops his hands and shakes his head, the terrible eyes rivet. "You mustn't blame yourself."

"Or you?"

He whirls away, laughs, plays to the crowd, glances at the monitors. "Do I have to tell you this is improv—this woman's raving at noble Toledo, Michelangelo of the flicker-addicted eye? Who is Toledo but a bit player in an empire of tax law?" he says, "No gigolo blowing oil magnate—not he!"

Sam the actor says, "Ten years ago you'd have called tax shelters and gigolos the same."

Toledo turns in a slow circle, his eyes pan the bank of monitors with the porcelain face and Irish hair, he comes close, lifts the hair, "Unveiled, the face is still a mask," he says, "—of Thespis?"

"I've been acting all my life."

"But never on your back—even for fun?"

"I didn't say that."

Toledo smiles, he turns the actor's face to the monitors, she yanks away, says. "Quit changing the subject."

"Subject?"

"Ten years ago."

"Ah—before your feet were beyond return to the laudable—if yawn-able—annals of normalcy—before your face became glass— and my vision turned to cash. Years ago, you say—where?"

"You know—the Paradise—" Toledo's laugh cuts in but the actor goes on, "—Hotel—remember?"

Toledo laughs again, says, "Delightful pathos!"

"You didn't think so that night."

"What did I think?"

"You said the Paradise sounded like a place that rents rooms by the hour—perfect for the movie."

"We met in a movie?" Toledo says, sweeps the Parthenon with his arm, "—my father's?"

"Does his money make it his movie?"

"That is the question! Let this Parthenon be the Paradise Hotel for today—Paradise of all the years of my father's money, years of forgetting and unforgetting you. Take me back there—where God still lived and men still longed for love," he says, turns to one of the media jocks, takes her camera.

"You wanted to hide behind the camera that night too," Sam actor says.

Around the camera on his shoulder, Toledo says, "Hide—how can a filmmaker hide? Even if his body isn't on film, his mind is."

"You weren't the filmmaker that night."

He says, "Who was I?"

"Actor—like me."

"At the Paradise with you—and no camera?"

"They had the camera."

"They," Toledo says, "—they who stole Paradise—and started the seed of that movie everyone thinks I'm making?"

"You're afraid of remembering the time you weren't behind the camera."

Toledo laughs—louder, sharper—and gives the camera back to the jock, takes the actor's hand. "Lead on, Flannery," he says, "—even without the twin companions of my fear—the camera and Courvoisier."

"You're so brave."

"The courage of the guilty—always guilty around women."

"And your father?"

"That too—Flannery judges me well. But then you have the advantage of knowing more about me than I remember."

They climb the steps into the Parthenon, into the jungle of

state-of-the-art equipment paid for by Toledo's father. "Why do you hate him?" Sam actor says.

"Hate who?" he says, leads the way through lights and cameras, banks of monitors, to a stack of risers, shadowy edges like the ruins of those postapocalyptic flicks, Toledo directs the students to drag the risers out to the center of the stage and pile them to form jagged steps that spiral up to a platform—the Paradise. It looks like a stage for theater-in-the-round or psychodrama. The students and media techs are completely in Toledo's spell, they operate cameras and lights or take up positions on an outer circle of more risers surrounding the steps to the Paradise. Monitors mounted in the sound stage at every position imaginable show the scene from all angles, Toledo and the actor stand at the bottom of the jagged stairs.

"It's darker," she says, and the lights go down to the yellow of flophouse hallways.

Toledo says, "You arrive before me?"

"You're late."

"You wait alone—in agony?"

Sam actor ignores the question, as if she can't think what agony means, says, "I'm always alone."

Toledo says, "You're always in agony."

The actor laughs to shake him off, the dim light changes the space, students and media jocks become shadows dissolving into the stains on the Paradise walls that rise and disappear into cobwebs.

"I've been here before—or in other hotels just like it—" the actor says, "all the dumps booking agents send you to—"

"And tell you they're quaint—the perfect ambiance for the audition," Toledo says, "—that the line?"

The actor laughs but it's flat, her skin crawls with damp nights in unheated halls, corners hiding drunks and junkies. She thinks, of course it's psychodrama, your mind creating the past in the moment, everything, everyone just as it was, that's how it works, theoretically, it's just psychodrama, except she doesn't know where or when, she's been here, but where is here? "Someone's throwing up in the can," she says, stares up the steps, shivers convulsively. "It'll be worse up there—the penthouse—they always call it that—"

"The top floor with no elevator?" Toledo says, gazes at the ceiling, "—maybe they're up there waiting—about three of them, lights, camera, Herr Direktor?" He looks meaningfully at a group of students, who start to move and pick up equipment.

"They're always late," Sam actor says.

"Always," Toledo says, "—you don't look like the type who'd know so much about always."

"What does the type look like?"

"You know—bleached—pushed up."

"How do you know I'm not in disguise?"

"Your eyes."

The actor jumps as if hit, says, "It's too dark in this hall to see my eyes."

"It's your first time," Toledo says.

"You were looking for a virgin?"

"Don't men always? But your eyes look like Magdalene's."

Sam actor laughs, says, "Making you..?"

"No—Christ," he says, "—you look like Christ."

"I'd rather be Magdalene."

The sound of a door opening: three men—students getting into the improv—with camera and lights, talking, laughing, not noticing anything, they shuffle up the stairs, Toledo starts up after them but Sam actor can't, no part of her body works, Toledo comes back to her, leans close, his eyes shine feverishly. "What did they tell you?" he says.

Shaking uncontrollably she says, "Audition—"

"You believed that?"

She tries to laugh but chokes instead.

"You poor kid—"

"I'm not a kid!"

Toledo mock-strikes a match, holds the actor's chin in the light. "A kid who's never been a kid," he says. "Listen, what do you say we forget this and go some place?" The match burns his fingers and he drops it.

"What place?"

"Get some food—you could use it."

"You going to pay my rent too?"

"Not like that," Toledo says, "but I do have a job opening."

"So to speak."

"No—a real job."

Sam actor hesitates. "We'll be too late—they'll leave," she says.

"Look, I'm just starting out but I do make movies," Toledo says.

"You too?"

Toledo rubs his eyes then reaches over, touches her hair, says, "I can see why they said I wouldn't believe this."

"Your first time too?"

"Yes—but why should you believe me?"

The actor walks away, Toledo comes running after her, grabs her hand, "Don't—"

"Will it be different with you?" she says.

"You're too young to be so cynical."

She yanks away, starts up the steps. Behind, Toledo says, "And I was afraid they'd tell you I'm not for real—just a film student doing research."

"Research," she says, meaning to sneer, but somewhere the word echoes, swirls her insides like a vortex. At the top of the stairs now, the penthouse bulging with the three men and their equipment, one man adjusting a camera, another putting up lights, the third pulling off his tee-shirt, wiping his pits. "You want to get cool too, dollface?" he says.

Toledo says, "She's no dollface!"

"They're all dollface," the pit-wiper says.

"Her name is Sam—and put your goddamn shirt on!"

The one at the camera says, "And what do we have here—the next Mrs. Goldwyn?"

"Sam is her name!" Toledo says.

"Oh, then you'd be Mrs?" the pit-wiper says.

Toledo takes two steps and with one stunt-blow, decks the pit-wiper while the other two shoot the scene. Sam actor checks to see if the pit-wiper is breathing, Toledo yanks him up again, stunt-slaps his cheeks till his eyes roll, and he sucks in his tongue, says, "Tell the boss no more sonny-boy!"

"Who's the boss?" Toledo says.

"What the fuck do you care? You get dollface and you both get to be movie stars—even paid—what you don't spend in damages!"

Toledo lifts the pit and glares at him. "Who's the boss?"

"You don't know?"

Toledo's face screws up in purple rage. "You're not going to tell me it's my old man!"

"No sir, I ain't going to tell you nothing."

"The fucking pimp!" Toledo says.

"Whoa, sonny, this ain't vice, it's Hollywood!" The pit raises his hands then turns to the other two. "Okay, we got a rewrite! Jack Hero here is undercover—playing the film student but he's no student, he's a cop on a sting, see?" The pit walks over and puts his arm around Sam actor, squeezing her to his cold stink. "Only dollface is too much for Jack Hero," he says, grabs her shirt and yanks. "Then right when dollface is fucking his balls off, Jack Hero's old man shows up for a piece himself—pure Hollywood!"

Toledo's fist stunt-drives into the pit's face, the pit drops, Toledo turns and doesn't even see Sam actor, frozen there as he smashes the porn camera, the lights. The other two rush and stunt-punch him down to the edge of the platform, they haul and push him as if out a window, but Toledo gets them off just as a scream goes up and slices everything—the fight grunts, sirens, the ambulance crew clattering up the riser steps. Sam actor realizes the scream is hers and stops but Toledo's war cries continue, something familiar at the edge of the actor's mind, almost physical—pulling, wrenching inside her head—like dreams that wake you then take flight and leave your memory exiled.

Sam actor kneels beside Toledo, his face white cold, the eyes pale yet warm as marble. "Come with me," he says, "I'll take you someplace wonderful—"

Sam actor says, "A nunnery?"

Toledo starts to laugh but chokes then grabs and crushes her against him. "A nunnery," he says, "—quick, before I fall!"

Two students once in the porn camera crew turn EMTs, lift Toledo onto a set door "stretcher" and haul him down the stairs, Sam actor follows into the ambulance—chairs arranged to size— and holds his hand, they sway as though swerving with the motion, his eyes never leaving her face. "Come with me," he says.

"I am."

"Not this—work with me."

"Doing what?"

"Acting—not skin flicks, real acting—what you were born for."

The actor hesitates again, Toledo hauls himself up on the stretcher, his eyes black. "Will you do it?"

"What will I tell my agent?"

"That he's a fool!"

"Maybe you're the fool. You think flattery will buy me?"

"I think nothing will buy you—and everyone will try."

"You're right," Sam actor says, "flattery will buy me. Everything buys me."

"What do you mean?"

She laughs, says, "I don't know. I don't know who just said that."

Toledo sits up, throws the stretcher-bearers off balance, everything collapses, he rises from the limbs and laughter, grabs her again. "I know," he says, "I know about things like this—trust me."

"Trust you to what?"

He shakes his head. "Stop talking—thinking—all that's in the past!"

"Why? What's happened?"

"Don't you know?"

"Just that you found out your father is the producer—"

Toledo's face flushes, he steps back, frowns. "Did he put you up to this?"

"What?"

"What did he do?"

"How would I know?"

"He didn't get you into this?"

"Your father?"

Toledo says, "Who did?"

"My agent."

"What's he look like?" Toledo says.

"I don't know—bald."

Toledo closes his eyes. "The only thing the old bastard isn't."

"You thought your father's my agent?"

"He knows all the girls."

"All the girls—"

"I didn't mean you," he says, shaking his head, pulling Sam actor's face into his cold neck. "Swear it!"

"What?"

"You think I'm crazy, but he's everywhere—believe it."

"He's not my agent."

"It doesn't matter—all these skintraders work for him," Toledo says, swaying as if about to fall. Sam actor gets him to lie down on the stretcher again.

"Where's *your* father?" he says.

The actor looks around to see who he's talking to, sees the exit sign. What to say, she thinks, what to say?

"You," he says.

"My father? I don't know."

"Your family?"

"I don't know—don't remember anything—except arriving in New York on a bus."

Toledo says, "You mean amnesia?"

"Not like Hollywood—I just don't remember."

"You don't remember—that's what kids say."

Sam actor searches for something. "I guess I got kicked out."

Toledo hears the lie, his face goes red, eyes cold. "Is this what you do with men—tell them anything?" He shoves his hand in his pocket, pulls out a wallet and tosses it.

So it's done. "Research money?" the actor says, dead runs, hears him from behind, wretched throat-sounds, his boots clattering after.

End of the Improv Scene

Two

Toledo shouted, "Cut!"

Still running, Sam crashed into the web of students and equipment, a hundred faces loomed over her, hands hauled her up and wrung her hands, incredible noise shook the Parthenon, the faces abruptly parted and left only Toledo's, Sam tried to look past him, to find the door, any door, she was a student here, she knew this sound stage.

"Sorry," she said.

"Sorry?"

"I crashed your class and messed it up."

"Who is this, now—lady gracious making excuses before leaving the tea party?"

"I feel like a fool."

"You didn't mess it up, you *mixed* it up—no work for a fool."

"And all this equipment busted..."

"I'll get more equipment, Sam Flannery," Toledo said. "How are you?"

Her mind raced. "How am I—late, I guess. I'm supposed to be somewhere."

Toledo laughed. "What the hell are you talking about?"

"You asked how I am. I guess I don't know."

"How about fantastic?"

"Fantasy I can relate to."

Toledo grabbed and squeezed her. "Don't you know you saved me today?"

He was joking, she tried to laugh, he shook her like a bad kid, this time she did laugh, he didn't. "Don't you know who you are?"

he said. She thought he was crazier than his movies and laughed again, he squeezed her tighter and said, "Just don't disappear."

"What if I have to?"

"You don't, you can trust me."

"Oh just like that—the scene," she said, thinking right, I can do that, the actor can.

Suddenly students and media were all over with cameras and mikes, all talking at once to Toledo.

"How many times did you rehearse the scene?"

"When's the picture being released?"

"Where have you been keeping her?"

Toledo said, "Sam, tell them what happened here today."

They shoved mikes in her face, she glared at Toledo for his desertion but he only looked bemused, her head ached in the blinking camera on-lights, lenses, mikes pointing, they could still be in the Paradise Hotel—Toledo's eyes still frozen on her. "Improvisation," she said.

The students and media jocks went on as if she hadn't spoken.

"Who wrote the script?"

"What did the property cost?"

"What's the budget?"

Sam said, "It wasn't anything like that—it was nothing. Toledo gave me an opening and I just played off it."

"When will he let the public in on it?"

"Who's in charge of preproduction?"

Toledo took Sam's hand and started driving through the crowd—Toledo making jokes, calling out the names of reporters he knew—they nearly ran down the steps of the Parthenon to the amphibious car, Toledo pulled students out of the jump seat, shoved Sam in, lunged behind the wheel and screeched off into the traffic with media vans hot after, LAPD motorcycles flanking, cops nodding and waving, practically saluting Toledo. "Check under the seat for my bottle," he said, and when she brought out the

Courvoisier, uncorked it with his teeth, swigged, passed it to her, said, "Where'd you get the idea?"

She held the Courvoisier like a flag. "What do you mean—me?"

"Come on, Sam, you must get the don't-I-know-you line all the time."

"Not on a sound stage."

"You've studied improvisation?"

"A little," she said, "mostly psychodrama."

"Psychodrama!"

"And then of course there's life."

"The 'I'm always acting' line?" Toledo took the Courvoisier again, drank, nodded to himself, said, "Okay, some lines are real, anyway it's Shakespeare, right, all life's a stage, okay," drank, nodded, said, "sound and fury, yes of course, okay."

Sam was delivered, it was like a scene from *The Correspondent*, Toledo playing himself in Vietnam, a journalist driving a jeep hell bent for any way out of the war, a soldier on a motorcycle catches the jeep, careens alongside while Toledo swills Courvoisier over a prostitute's head buried in his lap. "Come on, you can't do it all," the soldier says, they make a bet, the soldier's eyes rivet to the prostitute's head, her face comes up smudged mascara—Sam would never forget the look in her eyes, the first time she saw it she missed the next scene where the truck comes straight for Toledo's jeep, misses by a hair and throws the soldier and cycle into the dust, she had to see the picture three times to get it. She didn't know what it was about the prostitute's eyes, they reminded her of someone else's, she saw them in dreams. Now she realized they were like Toledo's eyes after he the journalist joins in a My Lai type massacre. She realized suddenly that his narcissism was self-revelation.

Toledo handed the Courvoisier back, said, "So you want to back off?"

"Back off?"

"The always acting thing."

"What do you mean, back off? You said it yourself, we're all always acting."

"Except that's not what you meant."

"Shit," Sam said, saw a motorcycle cop gaining, put the Courvoisier back under the seat.

"Don't worry about it," Toledo said.

"Do you pay the cops off in movie tickets?"

"Once when I was shooting a scene like this, we got stopped," Toledo said. "I was on the wagon and had straight iced tea in the bottle. My stuntman was wasted on coke, and I got the cop to do the scene. He must've told every badge in the state—I haven't had a ticket since. Get pulled over all the time, though."

Sam retrieved the Courvoisier, took a sip, it was no tea that slid down her throat like burning silk. Toledo said, "So it was hot for you, that's why you were so good. Do you always change the subject?"

"Part of the act."

He laughed, drove maniacally, leading the freeway caravan of motorcycle cops, media, students, motorcycle punks, trucksters with rifle racks, an Army jeep, overhead LAPD and media choppers, even one of the ill-fated Apaches, spinning its guns—whether to protect or intimidate—all of it hovering so close Sam thought she would stop breathing for the exhaust stink, all the way to the Burbank exit, to the airport where more cycle cops escorted them through a gate to the planes, Toledo stopped beside a helicopter painted in splotches like camouflage, but instead of jungle green, blood red, complete with drips. Sam said, "How did you get this effect?"

"Drugs," Toledo said, they were out of the amphibious car, racing to the chopper, one lurch ahead of the crowd. "Let's hope she's talking to me today," Toledo said, he tried the engine, again, again, lifted off just as the media vans screamed out onto the runway, camera operators shooting the six o'clock news from windows, even from the roofs of the vans. "Where did you do psychodrama?" Toledo said.

"Psych nursing."

He turned and stared.

"Why not?" she said.

"That's what you said in the scene—it's so far from acting."

"You think so?"

"I always thought of blood as one of the few realities."

"And acting isn't?" Sam said, she had it now, this could work, "—when someone's bleeding, you have to be able to act or you can't help. If everyone did what they felt, there wouldn't be any heroes and all the bleeders would die. We used to have code blue rehearsals because in psych they don't happen often enough to keep you sharp."

Toledo said, "So the blood is just a premise?"

"Sounds like you've been to graduate school, too."

Toledo nodded. "And on the faculty—which is worse. But the problem with all this is you're backing off again."

"How so?"

"Sam, you're collapsing distinctions. Act has more than one meaning—right? But what about the actor?"

"I think you've got it."

"*It*—as in, I think she's got it, my God, she's got it?"

"I've always wondered what it's like to be called Professor."

"Not much, I'll bet," Toledo said, "—or you'd be one."

"I was as close as I want to get today—Prof Toledo."

"Back there?" he said and shook his head, "—a professor has all the answers—she's memorized them. You don't find her in improvisation."

"She," Sam said, "her."

Toledo laughed. "I'm not above trying to blow your mind— mine will never be the same."

"But a studied answer—that's what they wanted back there?"

"The news junkies? They wanted entertainment—you as my succulent screenwriter-star—fucked instead of paid—imagine the lawsuit!"

Toledo pulled another bottle of Courvoisier out from behind the driver's seat, drank, asked if Sam knew how to fly, gave her a lecture on piloting while he snorted coke, drank, grilled her, drank. She saw how dangerous he was, this danger was easier though than the stuff about her backing off, for this they could just get killed.

"When did you start writing?" he said.

"I don't know—don't remember not doing it."

"I can see you pulling at your mother's tit and copping a look at the book she's reading."

Sam said, "Do I sound arrogant?"

"What's wrong with arrogant—girls shouldn't? Are you going conventional on me again?"

She watched the sky turn orange. "Isn't that what the scene was about," she said, "—what's a nice girl like you..?"

"Christ no—is that what you thought?"

She turned to look at his face, screwed up at her, almost red. "What, then?" she said.

"Men must fall for you all the time."

"Not really—"

"Don't shit me, Sam."

"They fall for the nice girl."

"Oh? Tell me about her."

"You sound like a shrink."

"No—that was my father—is, though I've divorced him. It was that or kill him."

"Sounds like you're been shrunk too," Sam said.

"Where did you grow up?" Toledo said.

She wasn't ready for the question, she usually was, her mind went blank, she reached for the Courvoisier to hide behind it till she could think of something, but nothing came. "Everywhere," she said.

The radio crackled, Toledo talked to someone about traffic around the Hollywood Bowl, Sam let the noise take her over—the radio and chopper—Toledo's voice, like a child in the back seat, riding somewhere with adults, thinking nothing, drifting through the reality of their power. Suddenly Toledo turned to her and said, "Everywhere is nowhere."

Sam stared at the nose of the plane, camouflage parody in blood. "That's the Army," she said, "nowhere."

"Your dad was Army?"

"Something like that." Instantly she knew she should've just said yes.

"What do you mean?"

She tried to think of a new lie. "My dad was a con—one step ahead of the law, you know?"

"Sounds like a bad script."

"It was."

Toledo's face was red-orange, almost the color the sky. "When did you go to New York," he said.

Again, she wasn't ready, was really slipping, "That was the scene," she said.

"You were playing yourself."

"That was you."

He said nothing this time. She said, "I was...teenage."

"How old is that?"

"I don't know—sixteen."

"Where in New York?"

"Different places."

Toledo said, "What places?"

"Manhattan, the Village..."

"Why don't I believe you?"

She drank more of his Courvoisier. "Playing yourself doesn't mean the plot has to be true," she said.

"Then why aren't you telling me something else?"

"What do you mean?"

"You know what I mean."

"What about you?" Sam said. "You think we actually met back then—when you were doing your porn research?"

"You stall like a frigging expert."

"And you don't?" she said. "Your memory isn't so good either, maybe."

"Shit—what filmmaker hasn't shot a skin flick?" He stared at Sam as he drank.

"I haven't," Sam said.

"Correction—what male filmmaker hasn't?"

San looked out at the burning sky, the freeway below that looked like a toy racetrack. "That's not what really happened, is it?" Toledo said.

"No?"

"What you said in the scene—you arrived in New York, not knowing who you were."

"You'd believe that—off stage?"

"What you mean about everything being improv—acting—is you really don't know who you are."

It occurred to Sam that she must have wanted him to know, usually she was so prepared, so careful.

"Tell me about it," Toledo said.

She shrugged, felt his hand on her arm, sympathy, always followed by nausea, she felt it climbing her insides, besides there wasn't much to tell. No, she'd had no identification, did not know her name, the police doctor said she was fourteen give or take, no one answering her description was listed as missing.

"What did you do?" Toledo said.

"Lived in a foster home for awhile."

"What was that like?"

"I had nothing to compare it to."

"That's not an answer."

"A couple with their kids," she said, "—the Brady Bunch."

"But you left."

"I wanted to be on my own."

"Your face looks like a fourteen-year-old runaway's," Toledo said.

"What does that look like?"

"Lies—a certain tension, as if you're trying to figure out what I want to hear."

Sam turned away from his gaze—too soft, too deep—cut to smog green sky, yellowed clouds that could pass for special effects—chemical bomb fall-out—and one distant shard of light. "Is that a comet?" she said.

"Yes—with Sam Flannery written on it. Tell me about the foster home."

She didn't remember his name, only the way the air would smell at night before he appeared, standing at the open refrigerator, drinking beer and eating, oblivious to whether the food was cooked or raw, the beer hot or flat, he didn't even seem to chew so much as to squirt it all down like gas into a car, his reddish eyes shifting constantly, seeking reaction, something to start a fight over, words to shout down or drown in his own choked laugh, he would whistle one line from a pop tune over and over, at first you could recognize this week's hit but after awhile it sounded like last week's, like all of them—his noise.

"Talk to me," Toledo said.

"There's nothing to say."

"What did he do?" Toledo said.

"Got money to keep me."

"No job?"

"I told you—he was a con."

"You said your father was a con."

"Did I?" She laughed, couldn't remember what she'd said.

"It's all lies, isn't it?" Toledo said.

"I have images of things that could be memories—"

"Or they could be stories like the ones you're always writing."

Sam looked out, studied the terrain down there, searched for landmarks, wondered where they would land, how she would get away.

"Ready to solo?" Toledo said.

His voice was warmer, softer, the way humanists talk when they want to project understanding, she could deal with it this way, his talking her through the piloting, even as they approached the Hollywood Bowl, swirls of traffic around it like nothing but special effects from this height, the air swarmed with traffic and police choppers, a sky-writer spelled out the words: SAVE A FETUS FOR JESUS! Toledo laughed, she thought he'd forgotten everything else, even that she wasn't a pilot, he seemed to have forgotten where they were, everything but the joke, it was a put-on he was sure, no one could be serious about a slogan like that, he laughed about it till she saw the sea on the horizon and asked where they were. "Malibu," he said and talked her through setting the chopper down into the sunset, on the roof of his villa, San Toledo, that rose from its pilings like ancient rock.

"Sea-battered coral shards," she said, "so *you*."

He laughed. "Took me three years to find an engineer crazy enough to build it," led her over a catwalk to what looked like a space ship on a launch pad, "my lighthouse," he said, slid open a glass door, walked out as if into space, a circular room with glass walls rising to a dome. He went to the center, under the dome, up three steps to a raised platform and said, "You ought to see the view from here."

"I can see it."

"The dunes—I had the sand imported—cost almost as much as the house—love dunes, I call them—come see."

"I see."

"Is this what we all do?"

"What?"

"Men."

Sam laughed, walked around the platform, into the outer perimeter of the glass room, filled with desks, tables, equipments.

"Have you been in a hundred glass rooms over the sea?" Toledo said.

"No—never."

"But you don't like it."

"I do—it's wonderful—reminds me of our scene today."

"At the Parthenon?"

"The way we had the risers stacked up—"

"The Paradise," Toledo said and laughed, "—a little too quick for men, are you?"

"What do you mean?"

"You think this is just about seduction."

"It's the...gestalt of it—way up here with the stars—and the platform..."

"Complete with mattress?"

She wondered how she could've missed the black-and-burgundy satin, "Ah, the casting couch," she said.

"Would you believe that no woman has been in this bed?"

She laughed, turned, walked around the platform, past a desk with a glass top and computer terminal, a video camera on a tripod, a telescope, the glass walls and dome connected by steel ribs hung with various shooting lights and cameras, background of sea, now black with darts of green moon-tipped foam—empty as the mirror of her mind, slashed by occasional light as if from naked bulbs in reeking rooms.

"True," Toledo said, "—I've been alone."

"Me too."

"Where are you now?" Toledo said, stood in front of her, inches from her face, "—still alone—back there—the life you can't remember and so it holds you captive?"

"Not really—just thinking about how the mind is like the sea—pulling everything down, then once in awhile spitting up something too bright to see."

"Is that what your mind is like?"

He touched her face, thick fingers odor of herbs or spice, she said, "Aren't you too quick for women?"

"So bitter—too much sadness."

He moved closer, she pivoted towards the desk, complete with computer and keyboard. "You write here?" she said.

"That was the idea. I built this place with profits from *The Correspondent*. When it was finished, I realized I'd built it because I couldn't write anymore."

"Why?"

"Nothing's happened since then."

"Your success has happened."

Toledo laughed. "There's the nice conventional lady again—what are we going to do with her?"

"It means something," she said, "—maybe not what you thought it would, but today was all about Toledo, the famous auteur, surrounded by media and students, a cast of thousands—it's not nothing."

"Come on, Sam—you know they're after media tricks, not me. It *is* nothing—the nothing happening inside—till today."

He was in front of her again, hands on her face, pulling it close. "Could you?" he said.

Mentally she retraced their steps, the position of the door, said, "What?"

"Work here."

She laughed, moved to step back but his hands still there. "In my fantasies," she said. He kissed her mouth, quick, barely touching it, then turned and charged out of the room and down the outside stairway that spiraled around the lighthouse, she standing surprised at the lightness he left, then running around the glass room to keep him in sight, to the spiral stairway, he in the distance transformed, silhouette flying like a child, his feet birds starting up from the sand—now one, now the other—rhythms of unrhythm, undancing till the moon exploded from its cloud-veil and cast Toledo back to his mortal form, he stumbling in the sand, arms flailing as he fell and rolled, pulling off his shoes, got up and ran again, over a dune where she couldn't see even his shadow, had to follow, down the cold steel steps, around and down into the cool sand on her feverish feet, sinking in the dune, its shifting mass, its top pulling her into velvet, the love sand, inching up her ankles, her eyes panning like searchlights for Toledo. Why was she following him? He was someone, a shadow she used to follow. Back there.

The wind shifted and rose, she thought she heard a faint, "Flannery," faint yet clear as in dreams where you hear your name just before waking, dreams she hadn't had since she could remember. There were no names in her dreams. No names back there. Flannery, what he called the actor in the scene, she could do this.

She started down the dunes towards the sea, red Frisbee rocketing at her, she howling, diving, grabbing the red, shooting back to the black waves where now she could see Toledo shaman-dancing, the wind spitting the Frisbee at shaman wings, shape-shifting to prehistoric bird, swooping into the vortex, plucking the Frisbee out, driving it back to the tornado's eye where the witch gazelle-leaped to catch, to stomp the triumph then fire again, Toledo, diving to catch, one-handed miracle scoop, popping it again before collapsing in the green froth, "Flannery," he said, tearing off his vest just in time for the next catch, a crazed pitcher now, winding up, driving the Frisbee into the wall of wind boomeranging it back, he plummeting flat on his back in the surf, arms stretched cross-like, legs jackknifing, stripping his pants, bouncing up, running naked, body arrogant as his mind, as if he'd stripped off more than clothes and needed nothing but to dive and disappear perfectly into a rearing wave, to leave nothing but its thunder and flash, its slow run up the sand to the flow crest then slipping back, parting like the Galilee, another Galilee, around his head then all of him, he flipping like a dolphin straight up, racing up the sand with the new wave licking her ankles, she witch-leaping till he caught her, they fell together, flesh slapped together, warm and cold, cold and warm.

He said, "You're shivering."

"I was coming to say goodbye—"

Toledo's laugh cut her off and his hand slid inside her shirt, her shivering turned to shaking, his vice arms rolled her up the wet sand, he kissing till she couldn't tell his mouth from hers. "You look like a child with cookie crumbs on her face," he said.

She said, "I need to go home now."

This time his mouth was soft with question. "I need you."

"I want to wait."

"For what?"

"So much has happened—"

"Everything has happened."

"I just can't think straight."

"You mean the conventional lady can't get control."

"I'd like to catch my breath."

"And run away—like the end of the scene today," Toledo said, "—isn't that what you do?" She turned from his eyes, his mouth,.

"How long can you keep it up?" he said.

She said, "Who is this nice conventional shrink?"

Toledo laughed and kissed again, said, "Some things are only simple if you don't wait."

"Some things are never simple."

"Why?"

"If I had the answer to that, would I be chasing a naked man through his imported love dunes?"

Toledo grinned, dotted her face with lip-puffs. "You're tough," he said, "I give you that. Okay, what do you want to do with your life? What are you here for?"

"To write."

"Only write—never publish or produce?"

"That too," she said.

"Will you stop running from it—stay long enough to remember yourself? Will you raise Toledo up from the dead?"

His kisses kept her till she had to breathe. "Tomorrow—even God got seven days!" she said.

Toledo didn't hear, he kissing and murmuring words too low, beseeching all, even the wind yielded, she surrendered, watched as if his mouth kissed someone else, his hands peeled clothes from a stranger's flesh, sucking, drumming, she still as a doll, he had to do everything, she only shivered where his skin didn't touch, his touch shivered her more, his tongue sang in her ear as the surf lifted them both, unfolding her, enfolding, making them one mindless, bodiless, impressionist splash like her dreams.

Toledo said, "Jesus Christ," he rolled this Flannery, sexed her up the beach, a breath away from the flowtide, whispered words she couldn't understand yet knew the song of her shuddering in the cold she could not feel for her own sweat, like whale oil, keeping off the cold, letting the sea fall like rain with all the unmemoried days—rushing into darkness, to wait for when she'll be back there.

"You're wonderful," Toledo said. "I'll get better—I've been celibate lately."

She laughed, he laughed at her laughing, the sea came higher, higher, almost reached her in his arms, he carrying her, staggering, falling on her, sexing her down to the wild foam, yanking her up, gasping for her, Flannery, Flannery, begging forgiveness, begging something, clamping her to him, mouth-smacking her neck, chin, nose, hands winding her soaked hair around their heads, against the flowtide slapping between them, wrenching their limbs, sucking abandoned clothes in its pool, the wind echoing his song, Flannery, Flannery, echoing him. Once in a dream a silhouette had stood over her then faded to the word hymn. Hymn. She'd wondered if they were the same—him and hymn—what that meant.

"You're the sea," he said.

"The sea is indifferent."

"And you?"

She said, "No."

"Do you want to be?"

"Yes and no."

"You know this is more than the movie," Toledo said, whirling her around like a dervish, "Flannery is more than movies—more than Hollywood—more than fucking—Flannery more!"

But Flannery was gone, Sam had slipped inside—where the sea seemed to boil harder than the rolling waves, she was afraid of what she would do and couldn't seem to get air no matter how she gulped. "I should go," she said.

Toledo said, "Why should you?"

"I'm out of everything."

Toledo laughed, she followed, they rocked together—she trying to breathe, to slow it all down. "Out of jokes?" Toledo said, "—do you think I require entertainment? Out of my arms—shall I hold you closer? Does closer exist? Out of my mind—could you ever be? I might—not you. Tell me, Flannery—more than Hollywood Flannery—what are you out of?"

"It," she said, "—you know—out of it—or is that too conventional?"

Toledo was suddenly silent, he thought she was copping out—wondered how many lies this was the first of. "Why don't I believe in you now?" he said.

"Because I'm lying."

"Why?"

"I don't know—don't know what the truth is—why I want to leave—run—mostly run—the whole Malibu beach without stopping—till I drop."

"Running can be a drug," Toledo said.

"Want a hit?"

He was a mad runner, in ten minutes almost out of sight, when she thought she'd lose him, he'd reappear, running backwards, letting her catch up, they'd talk for awhile as they ran, he didn't seem to require air, even yodeled for awhile, then off again under the fogged moon, into the cool wet, wearing it on his nakedness, the passing moonwalkers didn't even notice, it was Malibu, she didn't see her own bare skin until Toledo's back reappeared again and he said, "Do you know that you are the nakedest of women?"

They ran together back up the beach to his lighthouse, the courtyard of tropical plants, San Toledo, silhouette of Spanish Mission stark against the dusk, up the lighthouse steps to the glass room where he disappeared into an archway of mirrors.

"Do you have a control panel for the spotlights?" Sam said.

She heard Toledo's laugh, he reappeared, gloriously colored fabrics spilled out of his arms. "Those spots?" he said, nodding at the stars. "You know, I never used to—they'd hang up here doing whatever they damn pleased—no matter how I yelled at the stage-hands. All that's changed since Flannery."

"Now you can yell at me?"

"Now they just see I'm with you—and fall to their knees."

"And you?" she said.

He tossed the fabrics and fell to his knees, pulling her belly to his face, she fell on top of him, they rolled again, this time in his red and yellow velvets, purple feathers and white silk. "To cover my nakedest nakedness?" she said.

"Never—not even to decorate—only frame it."

She tossed purple feathers onto his head, from under them he said, "Be warned, I have this insulting little scene on camera—" He tapped his head through the feathers. "I have light so subtle, so sensitive it captures every image perfectly. My sound equipment records your most silent—" Toledo broke off to sneeze, the feathers went flying, he frowned ferociously, said, "So beware—these indignities you create!"

She said, "Do you have hidden cameras—outside your head, too?"

Toledo picked up the white silk and draped it on her head. "All truth is hidden," he said.

From behind the silk she said, "Is that a yes?"

He shook his head in mock despair. "Will Flannery ever trust?"

"Damned if I know," she said, "she doesn't let me in on much."

"Flannery is the one inside who remembers everything—and trusts no man?"

"I know a zillion shrinks who are frustrated artists. Now I know an artist who's a frustrated shrink."

"—that you don't trust," Toledo said, "—and laugh at."

"I?"

"Veiled laughter is all the more cutting," Toledo said. "Didn't your mother teach you how to protect a man's ego?"

"Guess I forgot that with everything else."

"I didn't mean to joke about that," he said.

"I don't mind."

"Does Flannery?"

Sam blew off the white silk, noticed the room light—soft, so subtle she wasn't sure where it came from—lighting Toledo's face now almost perfectly—just enough to see its angles, there were even dots of light in his eyes—as if reflected from a private star, programmed to follow his gaze. "How on earth do you get this lighting?" she said.

Toledo said, "Is that a red herring?"

"Were we talking about something?"

"Flannery—whether she minds jokes about amnesia."

"Oh," Sam said, "she doesn't mind anything."

"How accommodating—but are you sure?"

"I'm not even sure who she is."

"But do you know she's brilliant?"

Sam threw yellow velvet at him, then the red, the feathers, the silk—pummeled him with the colors, softnesses, over and over, and with each toss he moved closer to her, crawling on hands and knees, colors hanging off his head, sliding off his backside, when he was close enough to touch her he said, "Be gentle, this fool hasn't been in love since twenty-one—"

"Tell me about her."

"Ah," Toledo said, "do I have Flannery's attention—at last?"

She sat noticing him as he stood up and the fabrics tumbled, even without eye-lights his eyes had the sparkle they were created for, his body the Malibu tan that looked like he lived in it. "You don't look naked," she said.

He opened a drawer, glanced at her. "You do."

"You said that."

"Would it help if I had an erection?"

"I don't mean sex—you just seem more...I don't know—real."

"Could it be the rags you keep pelting me with?" he said. "All that hostility is what feels really real?"

"How does it feel when *you* do it?"

"Sporting. Are you going to be one of these women I have to treat as if equal?" Toledo said. "Name the author!"

"John Fowles," she said. "You read too."

"I read too."

Toledo was setting up lines of coke on a glass square, he brought it to where she sat, squatted down with it, did a line, offered the glass, Sam shook her head and noticed it was throbbing—she didn't do coke, that was all, but the headache was something about Toledo, his skin or the way he moved, the way he breathed, even after the coke, though she avoided cokeheads. "Why do you do it?" she said.

"Have you ever?"

"No."

He laughed and shook his head. "You are contrary about everything—is that it?"

"Just about."

"Flannery—or the conventional lady?"

"What makes you think they're different?"

"Because you use the third person—don't you listen to yourself?"

"I guess I'd rather listen to other people."

"Men?" Toledo said, he was starting up with the coke, his eyes glistened, skin glowed, there was something so strange about being next to him, as if they were kin—not that she knew anything about kin.

"Let's talk about the movie," he said.

"What movie?"

"You know—ours."

She said, "Of the hidden cameras?"

"Those aren't hidden—" He pointed to the cameras on the beams."

"Touché."

Toledo stood up again, reached for her hand, pulled her up, said, "I'm too high to eat, but you must be starved."

She wasn't, he decided they would go to the kitchen for some champagne, he pulled one of the white silk fabrics over her head, "Vietnam pajamas," he said, he'd brought them back for something, he couldn't remember now—not some*thing*, some*one*, she thought. "For our movie," Toledo said, each Spanish mission room he walked her through was for "our movie," he'd built it for something, he couldn't imagine at the time because Flannery hadn't come yet, he turned on all the lights as they went, "Here she is," he told each room—mostly long, simple, many with no furniture, as if waiting just as Toledo said, there was no point in asking what movie he was talking about, he thought she was in his mind, heard everything, felt everything he did. "It has to be just as it is with us," he said, "no false characterizations—don't you think?"

"Cinema vérité?"

"Something like that—a structure solid enough to be dramatic yet open for improvisation."

"Shoot in video?" she said.

"Film, too—for the structured sequences—I can't give up film—could you?"

"Not if I could afford to shoot it."

"You've shot film?" Toledo said.

"Sixteen millimeter."

"Black and white?"

"Yes."

"Black and white for the script scenes—color for the improv—shit, can you see it?"

"I see your armor of nakedness," she said.

"Armor!"

Toledo shadow-boxed his way to a sculpture made of mirrored glass, an abstract figure that could be man or robot, "Damn, if the woman ain't right again," he said then stood staring into the glass, saying, "Black-and-white film for the script scenes—video for the vérité."

"Wouldn't Little Hollywood hate it?" she said.

"Sweet revenge—so you'll do it?"

She was thinking. "You know Jerzi Grotowski's work?"

"Something about a theater..."

"*Towards a Poor Theatre.*"

"Right—" he said, "I read it years ago. Improvisational repertory...very stark, wasn't it? Probing—more ritual than theatre?"

"Stripping off the masks."

They were entering a room with a fireplace decorated in tiles that looked handpainted—primitive designs, aboriginal shapes and colors, she took a taper from the fire and lighted all the wall sconces, also surely handmade—ornate motif yet almost abstract in execution—a baroque design in one of a group of three candlesticks, segments repeated in the other two, she walked slowly around the room, studying the sconces, back to the fireplace tiles, Toledo watching, his eyes on every inch of her, under the Vietnam silk her skin felt his approach from behind, the wind of his arm—swinging, now his hands lifting her, she an extension of his body, a doll he danced with his legs, sang to, "She's got it—by God, she's got it!" he chanted, laughed, sang it over and over, at last set her down, his eyes pale, shocked, "You're tough," he said, "—none of that Hollywood soft shoe and sweet old sexism—even if I were a hunk and could dance?"

"You can dance," she said.

"Can you fall in love?"

She felt the word, love, like a something physical—a touch? "Yes and no," she said, "—I'm not sure I know what it means anymore."

"Yes and no—you and Flannery."

"Maybe," she said, "What about you?"

"We'll find out—in the movie. We're already in it, you know—cameras or not. I can't think of anything else."

"I think about my book," she said.

"Book!"

Toledo was shocked, she thought he might keel over, he laughed and slapped his forehead, said, "Of course—I'm not usually such a jerk—no, cancel that—I'm always a jerk—you've been writing all your life—of course, a book!"

He grabbed her hand and they nearly ran through more rooms, one that she wanted to stay in had a skylight ceiling and was filled with exotic plants and flowers, the kitchen was skylighted too and large enough to feed an army—or film crew—the table a glass sculpture, curved to follow the contours of the center cooking area, Toledo liked to cook during production conferences, the whole house was a sound stage, he'd started it that way for tax reasons but then the idea had taken over the entire building project, it had become an engineering nightmare, did he have footage of the construction? Of course, they would use it for the movie, it had been germinating in him all that time, waiting for Flannery.

The champagne cork hit the skylight, "Do you know champagne?"

"Cordon Negro."

"Film school champagne. I've gotten fat—the tastes of corrupt politicians. I tell myself they don't really taste the difference—but I do."

Toledo poured the champagne, gave her a glass, touched it with his, said, "To Flannery and Flannery's book!"

Sam said, "To Toledo, Toledo's movies, and a day I'll never forget."

"To our movie?" he said.

"Our movie—whatever it may be."

"Believe in us, Flannery," he said, wound his arm around hers for the toast, "nothing happens unless you believe."

"Now that's Hollywood," she said.

Toledo laughed, they spilled the champagne on the Vietnam silk and his tan, drank what was left, he poured more and led her to the glass table, leather chair, to sit and watch him do another line of coke then cook—for Flannery—he wouldn't take no for an answer, it would be something light, his groceries had been delivered today, there was fresh shrimp, if she didn't like that, filet—though of course, she was a vegetarian, all California women are vegetarians, he had fresh vegetables too, a veggie pasta or the shrimp, and while he cooked he wanted to hear about the book.

She said, "Do you use coke every day?"

"Only when I'm working—gets the juices going—want to try?"

"Are you working now?"

"Damn straight—this is going to be the movie to end movies—feel it, Flannery?"

"I feel drunk," she said.

"Making movies is the greatest high!"

"How can you tell whether it's the movie or the drug?"

"Take away the movie, all you've got is chemical euphoria—45 minutes, an hour and you're crashing. A movie keeps you up—like love."

Toledo looked up from the shrimp, she wanted to ask how he tells the difference between a movie and love, but wasn't sure she wanted to hear the answer. Toledo wanted to know about the book. "A repertory theater group that becomes a film and video co-op making a movie about California politics," she said. "They shoot on location and become a media event that eventually turns political."

"Art becomes reality?"

"Is it sophomoric?"

Toledo didn't seem to hear, he left the shrimp and rushed to her chair, grabbed her up and turned in circles till she reeled, "It's too simple—that's why I never thought of it!"

"So I'm a nice, conventional, *simple* lady?"

"Not simplistic—not easy, baby," Toledo said. Simple is the hardest of all—truth."

"Why do I feel like I'm in a Little Hollywood story conference?"

"You do?"

Toledo stopped dead, she must have reeled again because he held her unromantically, held her up, it was the champagne. She said, "when I was in school, they always talked in seminal statements."

"Seminal statements!"

"Ten-word theories of the universe."

"Of genius too brilliant to be heard," Toledo said, "so they had to teach?"

She wondered at him. "Of course I always wanted to be a genius—but believe me, none of them suggested it."

"So they'd give the speech about what movies are and then bash your script?"

"Something like that."

"Come back when you have it right? You must have scared the crap out of them."

"So I tried to tell myself but it wasn't much comfort."

Toledo sat her down in the black leather chair, kneeled in front of her, said, "Only because you don't believe it. You will. Listen, do you have a screenplay of the novel?"

"How many do you want?"

"All of them."

She laughed, reached for the champagne and made as if to pour it on his head. "Go on," he said, "it won't change anything." She poured, Toledo didn't blink, "Scare the crap out of yourself too, don't you?" he said, sprang up, poured more champagne, went back to cooking the shrimp, humming as he worked, Mozart, the *Jupiter*, then abruptly broke off, saying, "Have any early drafts—unfinished—before you changed it from a repertory theater to film co-op?"

"All that years-ago stuff?"

"When you were reading Grotowski."

"I thought you were reading my mind."

"Would that be okay?" he said.

"If I had enough champagne."

"The screenplay—do you ever work out scenes with video?"

"In a rudimentary way," she said. "Mostly haven't had the actors or equipment."

"You have now. What about the early drafts?"

"All the repertory work is in novel format."

"That's okay," Toledo said, "we'll go get it after supper."

"Tonight?"

"It's either that or make love all night—which would you rather?"

He wanted her to smile, she did then said, "But I'd rather you didn't call me baby."

"Shit—did I?"

"Awhile ago—about it being too simple to think of."

"That's what put you back in Little Hollywood—a jerk twice in one day—don't let me get away with jerkism."

"It's sexism."

"Now wait—I'm not that bad," he said, "—am I?"

They carried the shrimp and another bottle of champagne to what he called the bath, a Romanesque pool with steps all the way down to more handmade tiles, pieces of an abstract scene of lovers on the bottom of the pool, the sides, even on the retractable stained glass privacy screen surrounding the pool and the skylight where strobe colors played like hues of changing sky, over a center fountain shooting water up between two more lovers, connected at the groin, sculpted from one piece of marble, "Takes my breath away," she said.

"You take mine," Toledo said just before the phone rang, he ignored it, took her hand, they walked down into the water, colored from the lights above—another stage, "It all seems garish now," he said, "I hadn't met you yet—I'll start over—we will," the phone kept ringing, he pulled her down to the shock of his skin again, his entering every opening of her, even the pores of her skin, the corners of her eyes, tears, hers or his, sobs racked him, she held him, he said, "Let me," another spasm took him, his throat let out a howl that sounded ancient yet child-like, "Come with me, Flannery!"

She was watching again, somewhere above the fountain where the water rocket lifted off from between the lovers as she had from Flannery's body, from Toledo, who sexed her till her throat sang as he howled, her flesh quivered, her bones shuddered echoing his, he said, "I've never had a woman like you—are you coming?"

"The phone's ringing," she said.

"The phones don't ring—it's all on voice mail."

"Something's ringing."

"A computer probably—is it bringing you down? Want some coke?"

Sam heard something else, boots on the gravel courtyard. "It was the doorbell," she said, "—someone let them in."

"No one's here."

Fists banged the stained glass screen, "Stay behind me," Toledo said, and raised his voice, "Okay, out there—it better be good!"

A man's voice said, "Stephen Toledo?"

"Never heard of him."

"Mr. Toledo, your wife—"

"Not married," Toledo said.

The voice said, "Andrea Soledad—"

"My ex—tell her I'm busy."

"She's in the hospital—"

Toledo sighed. "What is it this time?"

"She's critical!"

"That's Andy."

Sam grabbed towels and said, "I'll go with you," the fists started again, Toledo said, "I can't put you through that—it's probably some media stunt—I'll be right back."

"I'll leave my number," she said.

"I can't think of you anywhere but here."

"I'll come back."

Toledo didn't believe, he turned and lumbered out of the pool as if she weren't there, retracted the stained glass screen, half a dozen motorcycle cops surged in. "What the hell are you talking about?" Toledo said.

"We'll tell you on the way."

"Tell me now!" Toledo walked back to the house with the pack of them following, all but one, a Black woman.

Three

Sam rifled Toledo's drawers and found some sweats, looked like a stuffed toy a child dressed up in everything too big. She rode home on Jan the policewoman's cycle, it was against the rules but Jan was going off duty and would take the chance, she said Andy Soledad had taken an overdose of something, no one seemed to know whether she was an addict or anything else about it. Sam couldn't imagine Soledad an addict or OD-ing. That was Jan's problem too, it didn't make sense, a strong woman like that, she'd passed for White all her life till she met Ray Soledad and turned it upsidedown, she jailbait when they met, he Black as they come and ended up the way everyone said he would—shot through the head by one side or the other.

When they stopped at a light Sam said, "Do you think someone tried to murder her?"

Jan didn't answer, said, "Will you give me a statement about Toledo's whereabouts today?"

It was kept from the media, Jan took the statement at a quiet precinct in Santa Monica that looked more like a UCLA hangout than a police station. Sam asked what hospital Soledad was in but they wouldn't say. Jan drove her to the Parthenon to pick up her car, told her to be careful about the company she kept, left her staring at the sound stage where it all had started only a few hours ago, only a lifetime. Sam went up and tried the door—open for some reason, students shooting late or the cleanup crew—yet inside only a couple of spots interrupted the windowless dark, scattered risers from the set they'd shoved together, cameras still in position with on-lights blinking as if they'd only stepped out for a moment, tape in the cameras, the monitors were on too, with her image looking too bright-eyed, flushed.

"How much would you want for it?" a man's voice said.

Sam said, "Hello?"

A tall, broad shadow moved through the lights and tripods. "The tape," he said, his voice deep and smooth, an actor surely, he reached the light and loomed bigger than his shadow, football shoulders in a camel suit jacket and jeans, white mane just above his eyes, hazel with blue streaks—watching Sam as steadily as if he knew her. In fact he looked so familiar she stared. He smiled, extended a thick, long hand, golden as his face, "Forgive me—I've seen you so much on tape, I feel as if we're friends," he said, his hand warm, grip strong, just long enough, "Richard Toledo."

She was suddenly dizzy, plunging backwards through a tunnel, wondering what he'd actually said, what she imagined.

He went on, "The famous one's father."

"I had the feeling I'd seen you before," Sam said, relieved, "—your picture in the papers after you built the Parthenon."

"Paid for it, you mean."

"But I can't imagine meeting you here. Didn't I read that you aren't interested in movies?"

"Just tax shelters—I think it goes."

"Oh—your media image?"

"It was my son who told you that," he said, "—you know families."

"Were you here for the scene?"

"Unfortunately, no. I came in as the two of you were making your exit. My son has never been so excited—I had to find out why. Since you ran off and left your tape, I took the liberty. Do you mind?"

"Yes—"

"You'd like to have seen it first," Richard said.

"It's rude of me."

He shook his head. "It was rude of me."

"I don't know why I try to fight this fishbowl culture."

"You're a powerful fighter, Ms. Flannery," Richard said, "—let's talk more over a drink—are you free?"

Soledad's suicide came back, she asked if he knew. "Not about this one," he said.

So she had tried it before, Toledo must have kept it out of the media, a second attempt was more serious, "Do you know why?" she said.

"Stephen thinks her melancholy is about the condition of Blacks—our fault because we're The Man. But his mother was a Jew, and she did it, too."

"Killed herself?"

"He was ten or eleven," Richard said. "He repressed it completely. If you ask him about it, he'll say it's a lie."

"Do you think he remembers?"

"He acts it out with Andy—trying to save her."

"And if sometime he should fail?"

"It could cure him."

Sam was stunned. "Cure him?"

"The act of suicide is an attempt to control someone else. When the actor—or actress—succeeds, the game is over."

Right, the psychiatrist. "But if it's a game," she said, "what about the other player—or players?"

"Only imagined by the suicidal fantasy."

"Do you think struggles for power are always fantasy?"

"Now that is a very big question," he said, smiled, Sam wasn't sure whether he was patronizing her or showing real interest. She should leave—would, as soon as she got the tapes.

He waited while she got them and shut off the equipment, walked with her out in the night too smoggy to be dark, even the birds were fooled and made their dawn musics overhead, the street empty except for the tow truck driving away with her car, Richard delighted to give her a lift in his grey Jag with red interior, its only sound the whisper of leather and Richard's deep voice on the phone, arranging to have her car delivered, he would come up to her apartment just until the car arrived then persuade her to come out for that drink, he had many things to discuss, he insisted on taking her key to unlock the door. "You're too young to have seen those old Hollywood movies where men did such things, and I'm too old to forget them," he said, put the key in the lock but the door wasn't latched and swung open, her apartment yawned—empty except for a rug crumpled in a corner, the chair leg that always came loose, a yellowed lamp shade. She felt oddly warm as if in a familiar place but not her apartment. It seemed such a coincidence that Richard was here, that he had been at the Parthenon and now here, as if he were involved, even arranged this emptiness. Sam walked around and touched each remnant as if it could tell the story, Richard would not let her stay there, she must go with him, she sat eyes closed, head resting back, listening to the deep, smooth voice call again about her car, he didn't seem like an actor now, even the cashmere jacket over a white shirt of such fine cloth she couldn't imagine what it was, he seemed sincere as he made call after call to locate Toledo and Andy, finally gave up and pulled off the road at a small cafe on the beach that looked like a private home, he was greeted familiarly by the maitre d' who led them to the table in front of the fire—just as the wine steward arrived with champagne. "Why does this feel staged?" Sam said.

"Would you rather have something else?"

"I didn't mean the champagne. "But of course he knew, he was deliberately misunderstanding—or was he? Was she being paranoid? She said, "Is this your place?"

"An old friend's."

"That's why it seems staged—like they were waiting for you." She was relieved again—though not sure what about—proof she wasn't crazy? Familiar relief—not that she'd ever really thought about it that way. Or had she?

Richard said, "I do come often."

"I can see why. It's wonderful."

Richard's tanned smile seemed too perfect, even the wrinkles only gave him a worldly look. "When was the last time you ate?" he said.

She told him about Toledo's spiced shrimp, uneaten on the edge of the pool, Richard's eyes changed, he looked down, "Another of those movies you're too young to remember," he said.

"The one where they get married before she goes to his place?" she said.

"I suppose you think I'm a chauvinist."

"If morality is the price men pay for beauty, chivalry is the one they pay for chauvinism—I saw it too—on the late show."

Richard said, "Of course—you've seen all the pictures I grew up with—do you ever think about that?"

For a moment she thought he was asking whether she thought about him. "You mean the culture of feedback," she said, "—no history, no time—just time-slots—the paradise of the technogods?"

He said nothing for a minute, then, "Are you really as cynical as you sound—or is that a defense?"

"You're a psychiatrist—that's where Toledo gets it."

Richard laughed and excused himself to call about Toledo again, seafood delicacies arrived, Sam couldn't taste any of it, even the champagne was wasted on her, Richard returned without word of Toledo, worry-crease between his eyes—a nice effect, she thought. He talked about the tape, wondered whether she would consider a movie, perhaps with his son, the only time they had anything to do with each other was when Richard was permitted to back one of Toledo's movies, there was no explaining it, no understanding it, some fathers and sons were like that, could she understand a father's wish to give the one thing his son would accept?

She told Richard about the movie Toledo and she talked about, he wanted to know every detail, the property, for instance—would they have to acquire it, or was she working on something really fresh, like the scene they'd done for the workshop? Sam suddenly flashed on her empty apartment and realized the novel was gone. She pretended to have to use the restroom so she could hide, didn't cry, hadn't since the bus to New York—finding herself there, not knowing why but knowing something was lost, something terrible, whether what was lost was terrible or the loss was terrible, not knowing if there was a difference, not knowing anything. Then she'd cried hysterically until she'd stopped, it was pointless to cry, she had to think what to do.

The café was the same, Richard looked concerned, so attentive she once again had the sense of an actor and asked if he'd ever done any, only in high school, he said, when he'd beheaded Joan of Arc.

"Do I seem insincere?" he said.

"I don't know—"

"You're saying sincere interest in your work must be an act."

"Am I?" she said, "do I sound starry-eyed?"

"No, you're an artist—you question everything. But you can question yourself too much—be too introspective."

"Never get the work out there?"

"You're going to get your work out there," Richard said.

She laughed. "Of course it doesn't matter now—it's gone."

"Gone?"

"The novel—it was in my apartment."

The concerned look turned darker. "You don't have a copy in a safe deposit box?"

She laughed again. "No, but I read that novel—the protagonist who was writing a novel about love and kept running to the bank deposit with his pages—*The Tenants*, I think, by—who was it— Malamud? He was refusing to leave this condemned building, he and a Black guy who was also writing a novel—better, fresher, but the White called it neo-Joycean. Something like that."

Richard said, "The novel was about love?"

"Yes—of course he knew all about it, so he thought. But everything he thought was about him."

"To play the devil's advocate—isn't everyone's life about himself—or herself?"

"Now that is a very big question," she said.

I mean the tape you made today, Stephen was very smitten with you. But wasn't that about him?"

"Which takes it to a more personal level."

"Too personal?"

"You're alike."

"My son and I? He couldn't agree less."

Sam said, "What about you?"

A guitarist began tuning up, Richard poured more champagne. "My son has developed my few good points," he said, his blue-streaked eyes steady, "for example, his taste in women has taken an incalculable leap forward today."

"You are alike," she said, "but surely you admire Andy Soledad." Richard's eyes reacted, "Sorry if that was tactless," she said, "I just can't help wondering why a woman of her talent and beauty would attempt suicide."

Richard leaned back, "Andy knew my daughter, Rachel, first. That's how Stephen met her—and became obsessed with her— perhaps because she showed little interest in him—you know what fools we men can be."

"Women too," Sam said.

"An honest woman is a rarity in my life—an honest beauty is unheard of. But here I am, a chauvinist again. If you believe it, I was worse back then. I kept after Rachel because she stayed away from men. I had no idea why until her suicide. She left a note—not for her family, for Andy—her lover."

They sat in silence broken only by the guitarist who walked from his place in the corner to their table as he played the Rogers and Hammerstein, *Are You Beautiful Because I Love You,* Richard sang along.

"From Cinderella," Sam said.

"You were a kind of Cinderella in that scene—"

Sam interrupted, "Does Stephen know?"

"No—please," Richard said, "this is our secret."

"He was pursuing Andy without knowing about her and Rachel?"

Richard looked puzzled then said, "I thought you meant does he know about this moment."

"This moment?"

"You're somewhere else?"

"Oh, he's very good," Sam said and looked for the guitarist, nodded at him.

"Or are you trying to obfuscate?" Richard smiled, shook his head. "You remind me of when I was a young man and decided to forsake beautiful women."

Sam wanted to say she didn't like being called beautiful, even the idea of beautiful women, it all made her want to puke, but she didn't say it, maybe she was kidding herself, maybe she did like it, the whole hype. "Why do I think I should leave that alone?" she said.

He laughed. "Beauty is always in control."

"Of what?"

Richard laughed harder, his face flushed, "Of admirers—and unlike pretty women who use it—beauty is oblivious even to being admired."

"So the myth goes," Sam said, "was it that way with Andy— when Stephen pursued her?"

Richard's face flushed more deeply but this time he didn't laugh, he signaled the wine steward, drank nearly a whole glass then said, "Andy is darkly pretty—in the sensual way of such women. Even after Rachel's death, Stephen pursued her. A grieving man needs sex to feel alive—and sex has never been easy for Stephen..." Richard paused pointedly but Sam was definitely not going to touch that. He said, "Andy was the driving force—determined not to lose her hold on him—in fact she got him to marry her less than a year after Rachel had died for love of her."

Sam thought how ugly it was, what he was doing to his son— saying these things to her. "Died for love," she said, "—what was it Shakespeare wrote—something like 'Men have died and worms have eaten them, but not for love?'"

Richard fixed her with his eyes, she dizzy again but couldn't look away, "You think love is a spiritual feeling?" he said. "Rachel was not a Christian—neither of my children were subjected to religious indoctrination—neither Jewish, as their mother wanted, nor Catholic, as my mother wanted."

"What do *you* think love is?" Sam said.

He looked surprised then raised his newly refilled glass, "The question of the ages, isn't it? Your Shakespeare wrote of passionate friendship. We thought we could trust him, but now we learn he was homosexual."

"What do you mean, trust him?"

Richard laughed. "In a few seconds you want a definition of love and trust."

"I suppose that could sound intrusive—I just like to know what people think."

"The constant writer. Tell me, do you have men friends?"

"Sure," she said.

"Heterosexual men—who don't desire you?"

"Yes."

"Only because they're afraid of your rejection," Richard said, "—or because they're waiting for the right conditions?"

"I thought you said I was the cynical one."

"There's a difference between cynicism and acceptance of

reality," he said, "cynicism preserves the fantasy—holds it in anger. That's Stephen's problem with Andy. He can't face who she really is."

Sam said, "Who is she really?"

"A fortune-hunter."

"Because she married Stephen?"

Richard said, "As Rachel's lover she had nothing."

"Might you have felt the same about any woman who married him?"

"Now *that's* cynicism," Richard said, "and you feel nothing on learning about Stephen's sister and his ex-wife?"

"I feel moved."

Richard reached across the table and touched Sam's hand, she pulled it back, he said, "Do you have any idea what my question meant?"

Sam was dizzier, maybe the champagne, he looked so ugly now, she wanted to check the room for exits. He went on, "Abnormal sexuality doesn't upset you?"

She laughed. "Abnormal—didn't that go out—even from psychiatry—in the Seventies?"

Richard stared, the streaks in his eyes seemed to move without his eyes moving, "You have a strange innocence," he said.

"What do you mean?"

"Knowledge without corruption."

Sam said, "So to you, knowledge and corruption are synonymous?"

"Simultaneous," he said, touched her hand again, she pulled back again, he said, "Don't mind me, I suppose I'm too old for your New Age enlightenment."

"No one is too old for enlightenment."

Richard raised his glass for a toast, said, "To Sam Flannery—my fountain of youth."

The steward filled Sam's glass too, Richard held his until she raised hers, he drank, she wetted lips. "You don't trust men," he said, "is that what your novel is about?"

Again she laughed. "Oh my lack of trust goes way beyond men."

"Ah—meaning?"

She felt her face flush, shook her head. "Sometimes I just say things, I don't know where they come from."

"Your unconscious."

"Spoken like a shrink," she said, hurried on, "But the novel is about filmmakers making a movie."

"And this movie—will you talk about it?"

"It might be too radical," she said.

"Because I'm, as they say, a senior?"

She laughed, "Because you're rich."

Richard said, "Would you rather not talk about it?"

"No, I'm just getting used to being the only one where I'm sitting who still thinks about freedom."

"Political freedom?"

"Okay," she said, "the novel is about people making a movie in which the world is controlled not by governments but media conglomerates—reality producers who compete and make deals to produce the economy, jobs, resources—survival. Buy-outs, mergers, all forms of consolidation have created a kind of economic totalitarianism. The conglomerates cooperate with each other in the service of mutual profit. War is obsolete. Nation states are obsolete. The only conflict expressed is terrorism."

Richard said, "The futuristic world that's really the present?"

"I think of art as a metaphor—which is sometimes the only way to—in your words—face reality."

Richard raised his glass, "Please go on," he said.

"One of the conglomerates, Medialennium, is staging a California governor's race—"

Richard said, "Staging?"

"Politics remains in this world as a kind of essential illusion—like, in an earlier world, the personified God."

"You *are* cynical."

"Participatory politics as a kind of religious ritual that reaffirms the basic power relationships."

"Interesting premise—titillating," Richard said, "so this governor's race?"

"One of the candidates is the incumbent—a progressive—throw-back to the Sixties liberal—complacent, drinks too much, drugs too much. The other is a Chicano running on a platform of California secession."

For a split-second, even the guitar was silent, through the windows, the sea rolled restlessly, Richard's streaked eyes and perfectly creased brow pondered, "Like Quebec?" he said.

"Well, not really—they want to join Mexico."

"Mexico!" Richard said, "Against the US?"

"More like a reunion with their own tradition."

"So they're Mexicans."

"Mexican Americans," Sam said, "—feeling like America doesn't include them the way it did European immigrants. They're joined by some Black Americans, other Hispanics, some Whites too."

"And all this is but sound and fury?"

"At first, but the realism of the ritual, as it were, creates a kind of alchemy."

Richard closed his eyes, "So art becomes life," he said, opened his eyes and rose at the same time, went in the direction of the telephone again, returned and sat, "I hope I'm not being impertinent but did my son make you an offer?" he said. As a humorous interlude, she thought, and laughed, but Richard didn't, he reached for her hand again, said, "Forgive me—I know not what I do—but has he?"

"He wants to work together."

"I meant cash."

"For what?"

Now Richard laughed, shoved his chair back, Sam had never heard anything like the sound but the maitre d' had, so had the wine steward, the waiters, the violinist, the sound was nothing to them though it shook glasses standing on a tray, tables, the crystal chandelier. "You're more intoxicating than champagne," Richard said, "and you know it, don't you?" The blue streaks in his eyes sliced the hazel, he shook his head, stood up and said, "I'm determined not to bore you with an old man's obsessions."

"Obsessions?" she said.

"All this and grace, too."

"I'm not being graceful."

"You're pretending not to understand. I suppose that's what lets you keep your options open?" Richard laughed, put out his hand— she thought to say goodbye but he moved around the table, "Come," he said, "maybe my son hasn't told you about his profligate father."

"Does he know?" She was playing now, stalling for time, her eyes sweeping the room for exits.

Richard's laugh ended in a coughing spell and deep flush, the maitre d' supplied snifters—more expensive than Courvoisier, Sam thought—Richard sipped with slightly trembling lips, Sam swirled hers, Richard led the way out on the small, private dock where waves chased between the piles like a caged cat pacing, "Weather out there," he said, nodded towards the sea, "—come," and led her up an outside stairway to a room over the cafe, fireplace, antiques, Persian rugs, what looked an early Matisse, small kitchen alcove, another room filled with a king-size brass bed.

"Your apartment?" Sam said, sure it wasn't.

"Occasionally, when I'm in town. I want you to have it."

"Have it?"

Both stunned, they stared at each other before Sam broke out in nervous laughter, bit it off, said, "Sorry—"

"No—it's for me to apologize. What could you think of such a proposal? What I'm trying to say is, you've been robbed and until you find another place of your own, this is yours. I have plenty of other places to stay—please."

Her empty apartment, this fully loaded apartment, she thought. This paranoia. "Thank you," she said, "I'll speak to Toledo—"

Richard said, "No—it's the one thing I ask, that you keep everything—even the fact of our meeting—between us. You know my son and I don't get along. I made a disaster of fatherhood and I refuse to interfere with his work."

"I thought you funded his work."

"I do—he tells me what he needs and I give it to him. I never see the scripts—even the budgets."

"Is that what he wants?" she said.

"He's afraid I'd corrupt him."

"Would you?"

"Undoubtedly."

The phone rang, Richard answered, there was still nothing on Toledo and Andy, "Maybe she's all right and was discharged," Sam said, not believing it, Richard squeezed her hand, he had to go, he hoped she would consider staying the night in the apartment, although if she intended to meet his son at San Toledo, her car had been delivered, there were clothes in the closet, hopefully her size, the maitre d's wife had taken care of it, there was no need to feel obligated, the hope of funding a movie Stephen and she might make would more than repay everything, a number where he could always be reached was on a card by the phone, the key roo, Stephen must not see it though, he must know nothing, he was convinced that Richard would never fund anything experimental or artistic, nothing Toledo—the name she obviously preferred to call him— nothing he would be remembered for, could Richard trust her with his secret desire to give Toledo the one thing he wanted? He didn't wait for an answer, Sam didn't give one—meaning he could?

At the door, Richard took her hand, held it for a moment in both of his then turned it over, his streaked eyes watched her, he opened her fingers and planted wet lips inside, she pulled away, nearly gagged, felt the wetness long after the door closed and his footsteps on the stairs faded, felt the wetness, her gagging, the knowledge that something was wrong—in some absolute way that could neither be reasoned with nor changed, she walked around the apartment trying to shake the feeling, seeing everything as if through a distorted lens that made the rooms appear like a Victorian doll's house, closet with doll clothes—running tights, jeans, what looked like a designer evening gown, all ln her size—and in two colors. Except for the fancy and cost, it might have been her closet—she always bought two of everything, one for you and one Flannery, Toledo would say, but it was no comfort, she shot out of the apartment, drove her Bug like a maniac to San Toledo, dark with Toledo's absence, the double front doors intricately carved with shapes she thought at first were conquistadors on flying horses but on closer examination she couldn't make them out at all, nor had she a key, something she hadn't thought of, yet as she started to turn away the door opened and Toledo's recorded voice said, "Hi, you probably know that your image has been entered in the security system and now acts as a key to the house. You wouldn't be hearing this if you didn't know where things are, so come in and make yourself at home." So there were hidden cameras, she thought, searched the door area for signs, the hall of Mexican baroque—but they gave up no secrets, nor did the sculptures of the glassed garden, and beyond, the pool, it was all different without Toledo, he was right—a slightly garish museum with no poet to say its history, a haunted theater—dark until further notice.

Sam walked through every room, none of them the same as last night—except the lighthouse, the glass stage under stars, now fading as the dawn fog rolled over the incoming tide—changed, as if their love-making had left an irrevocable mark.

She called every emergency room in metropolitan LA—none

of them had treated Andrea Soledad in the last 24 hours, it was no use trying the psych units, they wouldn't confirm or deny, she didn't know why she was doing it anyway, there was nothing but to wait and lie dizzy on the stage bed under the smog-puked clouds, wait for a phone, a car engine, footsteps, any sign of deliverance. Deliverance? Jesus, what was she doing here? She told herself she had nowhere else to go, no money, no alternative, but if she did, would she take it?

Overcome with a sense of inevitability, familiarity, she watched hypnotic clouds become a child's face—pale eyes, closer, closer, then deep, sea blue or the color of space—of nothing—the void—surrounding her as if she'd entered the child's eyes and plunged down where the color turned hot and parted like curtains revealing a knife, small with worn teeth and puce tip—no, rust or dried blood, just a smudge of it, as though from a slip while cutting steak—she laughed at her horror-flick fantasy dissolving into a steak-eating accident.

This time the Bug headed for her apartment in Hollywood, she had to see it again, to walk through the space where her things used to be—things of no value except the memories contained in their flaws—plaster holes where the photographs had hung, prints going back to when she got off the bus in New York, each carefully dated to prevent more lost years—as if knowing the date were the point. Except the novel—but really, of what value was that? With the overhead light on she could see drag marks in the dirty mustard carpet made by her file cabinet, the paper and thumb drives of her novel, dragged out—for what conceivable purpose? A thrill went through her as she thought maybe her novel was stolen to be published by someone else—she the fool who didn't take a copy to the bank. She laughed at the ridiculous thought, wondered whether she'd forgotten to pay the rent, been evicted, and her possessions junked—she would take action—sure. Her mail box was empty, she drove to the closest ATM and the receipt told her she had $5000—another impossible play on reality, the landlord didn't answer so she left a message and gave Toledo's number, drove to Santa Monica and visited a couple of clothes shops she knew, nothing looked right though, besides she couldn't spend that five grand and her plastic would probably bounce, she kept thinking of the clothes in Richard's flat, if she borrowed a few things just till..?

The cafe was almost as quiet as last night, the maitre d' hurried over and bowed, she said she wasn't coming in, just going up to the flat, he said if she required anything, anything at all, he was at her disposal, "Anything hell can offer," she said, "is that it?" The maitre d's face froze, she apologized, "Major stress—I hardly know who I am, let alone what I'm saying," she backed out, charged up the stairs to the flat, the fire casting violent shadows as she opened the door, he's here, she thought, but Richard wasn't, she tore off the sweats, put on the first thing her hand hit—silk shorts in a color they might be calling tangerine this year, a rayon vest in patina with three little buttons she worked on all the way down the stairs—silly as a commercial for aging nymphets. It occurred to her she would never have bought these clothes, only the bought one would. She was becoming her own fiction.

The maitre d' was standing on the dock. "Shall I have some things delivered to another address?" he said, Sam shook her head and rushed past him, she thought he said, "Anything at all," again, but didn't look back, even the Bug's rear view was angled so she saw nothing behind, only her face she barely recognized though it was familiar, naked, younger, even freer, she thought, was it the loss of her possessions, even the photos and the novel, had the weight of them somehow led her off the track, sent her searching for some ghost of security? That was over now, the eyes in the rear view looked out as if from someone else's face, someone she had known once, her presence, the warmth spreading through her, she wondered—was this sensation feeling?

Four

Andrea Soledad had taken enough Prozac to kill a horse, Toledo put it, but she didn't die, she stayed in a private psych hospital for a month, Toledo went to therapy sessions and received calls in the middle of the night to go to the hospital and talk to her, he was worried she would try it again because of her bitterness about therapy for Blacks, normal was White, she'd tried normal all her life before Ray Soledad, it hadn't worked then and was no better now. Toledo thought the problem was lack of meaning, she no longer believed in political activism—all the real radicals were dead—she'd lost a baby just before the suicide attempt, her second miscarriage in two years, Toledo was trying to interest her in the movie, she'd always been his fund-raiser, every scene he took with him to the hospital, Sam didn't mind because to be honest, she thought the movie was a pipedream, the script might as well be used for something, Soledad had contributions too, there was a part for her, the Medialennium bureaucrat who hires Flannery—broke artist who specializes in theater combined with video feedback, hired as a Medialennium agent to change Toledo's image for the re-election campaign in a political climate lurching to the right.

Soledad would be a double agent, working underground for the campaign of the Chicano, Jesus Cahero, she would have a few singing numbers too—she used to sing with a local combo. Toledo had already talked about an original jazz score, musicians were working on it, Soledad knew them, she was a great cultural ambassador, without her Toledo would never have built San Toledo, it was as much hers as his.

One night after he came back from the hospital, they took the hovercraft to Toledo's imported dunes, the love beach, skinny dipped and made love in the sand, "Why did you and Soledad get divorced?" Sam said.

"We fought," Toledo said, "I was always The Man—White as her skin, she'd say, though she isn't that white—but no one knew she was Black till she started letting her hair go Black, she'd say bullshit like that all the time. We couldn't even have sex without a summit complete with manifesto."

"Was it that way from the beginning?"

"Pretty much—I was just guiltier then—and hotter for her, she would say."

Sam said, "True?"

"What's the real question?"

"I guess I was just wondering what happened to the marriage."

"Christ," Toledo said, "I don't even know if you've been married."

"I thought I should find out who I am first—serial killer or Snow White." Toledo's eyes were rivetted to hers, shining as if holding back tears, "I wasn't serious," Sam said.

"You're the most serious person I've ever met."

"All in all, I think I'd rather be a serial killer."

"Now you're not serious. But why the extremes?"

She thought for a minute. "I don't know—my verbal armor, I guess."

Toledo nodded. "Verbal armor is good. Would you rather be a serial killer than married?" Toledo said, he stared at her face as she laughed—a terrible choking sound—then put his arms around her. "What have men done to you?"

Sam said, "What do you mean?"

"The way you stand like a statue—as if you're holding the world together."

The statue part stung, Sam stepped back.

He said, "I didn't mean it like that—"

"What then?"

"Like archetypes, they hold myths together—our sense of reality. When I was studying philosophy I used to walk around mentally juggling constructs. I'd wake up at night panicked because there was nothing in my mind—nothing real, just the jumbled images of dreams. I hadn't been holding it all together, I might be dying, everything might be. I'd lie for hours in a cold sweat trying to reconstruct—to see with infinite precision—the exact nature, for example, of the relationships between Venus de Milo, the physics of light, and Hamlet's soliloquy," Toledo went on, winding his way into his past, he had forgotten it shooting *The Corespondent*, forgotten everything, sometimes on location where they all slept in bunkers to get the realism he would think if it was real he'd try to get back his past, to see the Sistine Chapel, hear the *Jupiter*, feel paint on his hands, hear Olivier as Lear, close his eyes and feel the space of Isadora Duncan's hands, it didn't help, he'd lost it all except bits, fragments, sometimes he'd cry with the agony of trying to find enough to put one image together, it was part of his transformation to the soldier, one night after they'd smoked hash and drunk the company moonshine, Toledo had danced *Sacre du Printemps*, the next day he hadn't remembered it until one of his buddy's had called him the mad fag, it had stuck so hard the next time they'd gone to Saigon Toledo had bought a whore, hadn't fucked her though, had never been able to with whores, kept thinking how they must hate him—all men."

"Mostly themselves," Sam said.

"How do you know?"

She flinched.

"I didn't mean *that* that way, either," he said.

Sam didn't know why she flinched, said, "I suppose I've been bought—not in the standard way—"

"In what way?"

She faked it, said, "Oh something innocuous—dinner followed by the hit—too guilty to refuse."

Toledo studied her. "I don't believe you, I don't believe that's what you meant."

"I don't know what I meant. I just think selling yourself—however you define that—makes you hate yourself," she said, "hating men is a way of kidding yourself."

"So only women sell themselves?"

"No—of course not. I guess it's just when we do, it's to men."

"Or The Man—maybe that's what's got Andy."

"I think power gets everyone, though," Sam said, "—just in different ways."

Toledo nodded, said, "Listen, I noticed something you do and I've been studying it," he put on a videotape of them in the Roman bath.

"The hidden cameras you don't have," Sam said.

"Hidden only in the sense they're designed not to be intrusive."

"Not to be intrusive or not to seem intrusive?"

"Right—all research is intrusive."

"Research," she said, the work struck her as so odd, as if she didn't understand it.

"In a way this is research," Toledo said, he turned back to the tape, they were splashing around, clowning, Toledo pulled her under the water, she came up gasping and sputtering, "Don't you know when a man's in love?" Toledo said on the tape. He froze the frame, "Here—look at you when I say the word 'love'—" he said, he pointed to her face, "Did you know the word 'love' makes you wince?"

Sam said, "Bullshit—we were splashing each other!"

"Watch again."

Toledo studied her as she watched the tape, she did wince a bit, he was so romantic sometimes, he was over-interpreting a nose-wrinkle, "What are you rubbing your hands for?" Toledo said.

She looked down at her clasped hands, said, "I'm freezing."
Toledo said, "You're lying," his voice was low, "tell me."

"Tell you what?"

"You really don't know, do you?"

"The love thing?" she said, "well, love is a power word, you know, all that Hollywood stuff."

"What d'you mean, power word?"

"You want it, it's in you like the candy you ate watching the movies."

"You want it?" he said, pulled her on him, "take it, Flannery," rocked her like a baby, she giggled and went along, thought he was benevolently sexist—the sweet persistent pressure you get tired of fighting—and she liked his arms, love songs ran through her mind, songs she had no idea she knew, they came out whole—melody, words, second stanza—as if playing off a record, when she caught it she freaked, told herself she knew what happened to Romeo and Juliet but her mind went on spinning the records, Toledo went on, even when he wasn't erect, whispering he had to do it, had to get through it, the not doing it she supposed, and she too alone with his necessity—but as if he couldn't stand her loneliness, she had to pretend for him. She'd take off like the dollbird and watch them, Toledo and Flannery, movie sexing, writhing, whimpering, sometimes crying her tears but she could feel them, taste their salt, hear Toledo chanting the lies in her ear, she was beautiful, she was art, she was time, she was eternity, she was love, the way he held her felt like floating on wings of swans or some ethereal being, unbound.

"Let the tears come," Toledo said.

Sam said, "I thought you said this is theater—not therapy."

"People cry in theaters too."

"And afterward—at home in bed?"

"Especially then," Toledo said, "if we're any good."

She said, "I hate it."

"Hate what—crying?" he said, "I know—reality might wash away with your tears."

"Did you really forget who you were—shooting *The Correspondent?*"

"For a while," he said.

"When you told me it felt like being there."

"We did the same thing—but yours hasn't ended. You forgot because of something about power—someone crushed you—your father, probably. Who has such power but a father?"

"Like yours?" Sam said.

Toledo didn't hear, said, "Your novel is a kaleidoscope, the pieces of you, I'm always turning it with whatever light I have, seeing you—a million fragments of Flannery," he said, started to kiss but Sam was going to throw up, tore away and ran for the toilet then didn't throw up, sat thinking about a road she'd seen once, Toledo came and said words she didn't remember long enough to get to the end of the thought, she nodded as if understanding, his eyes didn't believe, "I have to go to the hospital now," he said, she didn't mind, wanted him to go, loneliness was different now, the hard edges gone, her mind would play the songs and she'd think of Toledo, Soledad, he would come back—Sam was generous now, and wanted him gone, this—gone, it was too—something, she didn't know what.

They lived constantly in the movie whether tape was rolling or not, ate, drank, made love, talked, thought, made love, wrote, dreamed, made love—all in the movie, all of it working on the official opening of the vérité shoot, scheduled to take place at a Mardi Gras party in honor of the arrival of Jesus Cahero, the cinematographer who had shot several of Toledo's movies, Toledo thought he had Jesus in the bag to shoot their movie and play the role of the Third World Party candidate, "He was born for it." Sam hardly recognized her novel in the screenplay they were writing, Toledo would laugh at that, take her to a mirror and say, "Do you recognize Flannery?" It was true, the change in her appearance continued, she lost ten pounds and the body that emerged was one she'd never seen—gaunt, anorectic as a vogue model, Toledo photographed her wearing clothes he'd worn in high school and college—which his sister used to wear.

"Was she gay?" Sam said.

"Rachel—no, just a tomboy."

"Where is she now?"

"She was a musician—into drugs and booze," he said, "—she overdosed," he began sobbing then swore and said this always happened—five years and he still couldn't believe she was dead. Sam knew she should believe Toledo but wondered whether he or Richard told the truth—or whether either of them did, she was doing research too, was there anything else?

The morning of the Mardi Gras party, Toledo left to pick up equipment, the caterers arrived, the combo arrived, the media set up camp on the outer perimeter, guests descended in costumes that framed rather than covered their flesh, body and face paint in lurid colors, masks that covered more than their clothes did, they filled the pool, the house, courtyards, beach, horizon, Sam shot video of them drinking, dancing, running, swimming, one couple trying to make it standing in the surf against the passionate sky, she shot the vans pulling in, production assistants unloading equipment in the dark that seeped into everything, the smell of booze and sweat, music heating up, dancers hot now too, under the sudden shock of carbon-arc lights.

Toledo materialized in Bavarian shorts and bare chest, hands grabbed for him—partiers, media jocks, all like one animal— wanting a piece, Toledo l'auteur clowned for the cameras, took one and pointed it at a tall brown man striding through the crowd, also with a camera and sound recordist running to keep up, "Jesus Cahero," Toledo said, using the Spanish pronunciation, "the greatest camera of them all," he said. "Let the movie begin!"

The crowd took up the chant, "Jesus, Jesus, Jesus!" some in Spanish, some in English, others stood speechless, gawking—his Aztec face, gold skin, body that should be too tall for grace yet turning, swinging through the crowd as he shot with the dance-like movements of an athlete. A truck rolled into the courtyard carrying the biggest video monitor ever, big enough for the Hollywood Bowl, "Look—" Toledo said and pointed to the picture, "the only man alive who can walk with a camera and get a picture that steady!"

Jesus turned his lens on Toledo, said, "What other lies have you told about me?"

Toledo said, "Better ask Flannery."

Jesus turned his camera towards Sam, the monitor picture panned to her face—still round in its thinness—as a child's before the person emerges, ancient and new at once. "You're always on time," she said, "never disappear, and you'd rather shoot a movie than...almost anything."

"He said you were shy," Jesus said.

"He lied."

"You're the liars—both of you," Toledo said, "What I told you is you'd fall in love with each other."

Jesus smiled, handed off his camera, he and Sam took each other's hands, stood grinning like fools, he said, "I've got to talk to some people and then let's get out of here," they dropped hands, Jesus stepped back and turned to the crowd, instantly all over him again—he had everything they lacked and weren't supposed to want—brown skin, native features, self-confidence—no, charisma, they wanted to feed on him, consume him—become him.

Sam turned and ran into a production assistant who said, "There's a dress Toledo wants you to wear," and when Sam didn't answer, went on, "we got it on Rodeo Drive." Her "we" pricked, Sam watched Toledo, his lips moving into to the ear of a woman with the most beautiful thick hair and cheekbones so high they rivaled Jesus'. Sam's jealousy made her laugh, she realized it must be Soledad, he brought her over and introduced, Soledad nodded gamely, held Sam's hand with cool fingers, said, "Don't believe anything he says," laughed, turned into the crowd.

Toledo looked meaningfully at Sam, said, "How are you?"

"Jealous," she said.

"You?"

"I never realized that before—research, huh?"

"I'm dazzled," Toledo said, touched her shoulder, "I brought a dress for you."

"I heard."

"You don't have to wear it," he said, put his arm around her waist and began walking her through the crowd, towards the lighthouse stairway, beside it a scaffolding being raised to hold lights, Toledo's arms waved like a candidate's at the crowd, they whistled and catcalled, the Hollywood Bowl TV screen showed them—Toledo waving, Sam hanging behind him like a rag doll—till they were inside the glass door and the carbon-arc light receded, "God, I missed you," he said, tackled her and pulled off her shift, even without light she could see the crowd down there—a few were climbing the stairway, they might already see—Toledo pulled her face around, said, "Stop worrying."

"I don't want to fuck with an audience." Actually, she didn't want to anyway, it was for the movie—as if the other times weren't.

"We'll simulate," Toledo said, laughed, kissed, laughed more, wrenched off his lederhosen, "Now I know how Germans stay chaste. Did you know it's better to be a German Jew?" he said between kisses and muzzling her.

"I give up—why?"

"Ah—it's one of the finer points I didn't quite get—blood, I think."

"Are you a Jew?" Sam said.

"So they tell me—it's a matter of blood—the mother's."

"Your mother was a Jew?"

Toledo said, "Was?"

She should have said is, not her first slip about Richard, she hated the lie—the only lies she didn't mind were the ones she told about her past. For a moment she thought she would tell Toledo, didn't know how she could keep it up, "You don't talk about her," she said.

Toledo said, "I don't want to talk about my mother," and covered her mouth with his, covered all of her, as if peeling her skin, the slightest pressure of him floating her free, bodiless as in dreams, watching from a great distance, Toledo and Flannery, she becoming part of him, doll in his hands, extension of his sex, her life but waiting for him, red dollbird waiting to fly so close to the sun it could always be the last, her apocalypse, every time, closer, closer, his rhythm faster, faster, as if speed would keep him in her, speed would be his apocalypse, his face red as sunset, looming over her, zooming in, out, all rhythms, in, out, till she slept. From above Sam saw her sleep too, doll-size, floating in blue light that flashed on and off like a neon.

She must have dropped off, Toledo woke her, ready again, he'd done more coke, "Can we talk?" Sam said.

"Give me ten minutes—I have to work this out."

"Work what out?"

He covered her mouth again, screwed into her hot rawness, she flew up again, prayed for him, watched them, he in some wild dance, Flannery singing like Circe till he said, "I'm coming—Christ, baby—oh Christ!"

Toledo lay spent, arms, legs still around her, face smoother, younger in rest, nearly translucent with sudden light darting across the glass walls, "You're not the only one who was coming," she said, "—in fact they're almost here."

"Terrible pun," Toledo said, "but what about you? Will you ever come?"

"They're still coming!" she said.

"I have a gun—can you shoot?"

She wrenched away, to the shower, he followed, "What did you do today?" he said.

"Went crazy."

"Alone?"

Toledo picked up the soap and traced her with it, she said, "Sure—with that circus out there?"

"It was awful with Andy," Toledo said, "she lost it in the therapy session."

"What happened?"

"She said I made her abort."

Sam was stunned then for some reason thought about Soledad saying not to believe anything he said.

Toledo went on, "How could I make her abort?"

"I don't know."

"She kept 'forgetting' to use something."

"You mean when you were married?"

Toledo stopped, the first loss for words, flushed. "Yeah," he said, "that miscarriage."

"You're still having sex with her?"

"No—not now."

"But recently enough for her to be pregnant by you?"

"I don't see how she could be pregnant by me."

Not an answer, Sam thought, he must like her being jealous, what difference did it make anyway, it was a movie, beyond them now, they'd argue again, take care of it that way, she put on the dress he and the production assistant had brought, red satin with a black bra, panties, garter belt, the return-to-the-Fifties look, black hose too, tiny patterned seams, Toledo dancing around her, "Are we re-enacting the porno audition piece?" she said.

"Wow—is that what it feels like?"

She didn't know what anything felt like, the red on black pushed her up, she looked like one of the guests—dressed naked, straight out of the movies, aesthetically lurid, "Flannery of Medialennium?" she said.

Toledo said, "Isn't it perfect?"

She had to admit it worked, wanted to argue about him doing it without her though—or something, she wanted to argue about something.

She said, "We're still co-producers, okay?"

"You, me, and Jesus—the triumvirate!"

Toledo turned her to face the mirror, her image murky, as though the shower fog had settled on the glass to stay, "Welcome to our movie," Toledo said.

"So this is your opening sequence?"

"For the improv part, nothing's planned—remember?"

"Except you planned this."

Toledo said, "Not like script."

"Did you plan the sex too?"

"I thought about it—wasn't sure what would happen—just like life, you know, you want to have sex, you think about it, not sure it will happen."

He was looking at her intently, sweetly, the trust-me look, he had a red sequined purse to go with the dress, inside a lipstick the same red, she laughed, red-slashed her mouth as light burst through the glass walls from the scaffolding outside, cameras were going to shoot as they walked down—she still barefoot, Toledo had forgotten shoes, not that she ever wore them if she could avoid it—the lights were eerie with the fog drifting around, like a movie she saw once, so much light the cons went crazy from lack of sleep, but there was something comforting about it, like a cocoon.

By the time Sam started down the stairway, Toledo had disappeared, she saw nothing but intense, steamy swirls of light she was descending into, the red dress and inferno's steam, the scaffold lights turned to the courtyard, jumping with dancers, strobe beams bathing flashes of flesh, colored thighs, shoulders, a cheek, a breast.

She thought she saw Jesus, she pushed through the crowd almost desperately, as if lost, hearing his voice from a great distance, she broke into a near run and crashed into a circle of media cameras and mikes. A reporter was saying, "...about California seceding from the U.S. to join Mexico?"

"The character I play is running on that platform," Jesus said.

"What do you think about that—as a Chicano?"

"Interesting idea."

"What can Mexico do for California?"

"Bring it home," Jesus said.

"But is it home—any more than, say, Europe is home to European Americans?"

Jesus said, "Mexico and California are the same land."

"But is it land that makes a culture?"

"You agree with anthropologists who tell us Mexican culture isn't genuine—just a European copy?" Jesus said.

Uncertain laughter broke out, the reporter said, "They mean it as a compliment."

"The way you whistle at a woman before hitting on her?"

Breathless moment, applause, whistles, cat-calls—first friendly then turning scornful, derisive. Sam moved through the crush of near naked bodies now beginning to feel like a mob, said, "Don't anthropologists—like other observers—see in mirrors?"

Laughter escaped like air from a balloon, Jesus, the camera still on his shoulder, mikes surrounding him, Hollywood Bowl monitor showing his image, captured by one of the media jocks, just as his face moved away from the camera, deep eyes, dark shadows under. Media jock with the waxy look of a facelift stuck a mike at him, "How big is the movement?" she said.

Jesus said, "Movement?"

"For secession."

"I haven't finished reading the script."

"Could there be a real movement?" she said.

Jesus raised his brows, "You think so?"

"But don't illegals cross the border to work? What would happen to the farms?"

"What do you think?" Jesus said.

"Who would run them?" the jock said. "Wouldn't sanctions be imposed on US business in California?"

Jesus said, "US business is all over Central America—at least."

"The government would just sit there and let California go?"

"I don't know what they would do but I doubt if business would stop. Maybe it wouldn't be US-owned anymore."

A hush caught them for a moment, then another jock said, "Are you talking Mexican nationalization of US businesses?"

"I'm talking too much," Jesus said, the mob hooted, the jocks shouted questions but Jesus turned away, laughing, moving through the faces, hands that reached for him, towards the Hollywood Bowl TV now showing Soledad dancing like a pro, her black satin hips shimmying in the up-tempo swirls of strobe light, the picture moved out, caught her dancing with a man wearing a white tunic and pants, his face painted like a clown's, eyes bright with beautiful pathos— like Jean Louis Barrault in *Les Enfants du Paradis*. Soledad danced circles around him, vanished in the gyrating background of other dancers. The clown danced alone, stopped every woman to search her face—wrong face—in despair hurled away to the next one, his movements faster, more frantic, eyes changed from pathos to anger, his hands yanking the men from their partners, dancing with the women, dizzying turns, hip jabs, dip-tapping their heads on the floor, wrenching them up, down up down up, like furious sex-thrust, faster, faster, he lifted one woman—blond with a body-double build, her legs around him, he shaking her like a dog does a snake, her legs loose, he dropping her on her feet, whirling away, alone to the center, spinning like a top—whirling dervish or maniac—careening through the mob, Hollywood Bowl TV showing an edge of red, Sam's dress, then the clown—spinning towards her—Toledo, of course—she'd known it yet couldn't imagine him this way, he always the super macho director, hard-ass adventurer, journalist, never the artist—the master of intricate emotional expression—clown-face changing with every step towards her, movements slowing with fear—not of losing the contest but something indefinable, some dream he'd cast her in. His eyes returned to the brilliant pathos, stopped in front of her, absolutely still, looking as if for the first time then opening his arms, combo playing a waltz—of all things—they waltzing to old ballads gradually moving off to jazz, "I'm fucked," Toledo said, "—in love at last."

His eyes said he meant her. "Flannery?" she said.

"Didn't you see how I searched for you?"

"I've never seen anything so beautiful—or sad."

"Sad—because you don't love me?"

"Because I'm your statue, as you put it—"

"But don't you see—that's love? That's what we're doing. I've never done it before—felt it like that—it's you!" he said, began kissing, out of the corner of her eye she saw a man—boy, really, another dancer, Toledo must have hired a troupe, this one was costumed like a forties mobster, zoot suit, shoulders out so far it looked like he would fall over, he wouldn't though, he dervish-whirled, around and around Toledo and Sam, his face hidden by hat brim, his spins and kicks so fast Sam thought he'd knock them down, "I'll handle this," Toledo said, dropped away, turned to the zoot suit, he a clown again, winding up to attack the zoot, the zoot deftly turning, kicking, Toledo sprawling, lying motionless, the zoot dancing over him, towards Sam, the wide-on-wide shoulders over the narrowest hips shimmying around her in tightening circles, gloved hands spinning her, zoot hips rounding her—Soledad tearing off the hat, tossing it, shrugging off the jacket, black dress under hardly crumpled, tossing the jacket into the steaming mob—clapping, stamping, catcalling—as she dances faster, unzipping the trousers, kicking black-stocking legs free, running to the clown's fallen form, sinking down to cradle his head—the Pietà unfolding from drag.

Even the mob was stunned by her, Sam thought of the Saigon whore in *The Correspondent* who'd danced with a mask on—of course it had been Soledad, Sam remembered the credits and how they'd been criticized for her nudity. This time she looked nude, danced nude even though she wasn't, they were incredible together, how could he say he'd never felt it before? Sam tore out of the circle forming around the dancers and searched for signs of a camera, saw one and took the distance at a dead run, "I'd like to shoot," she said to the operator but he didn't seem to hear, just kept watching the Hollywood Bowl TV, shooting off it, "Excuse me?" Sam said.

The operator said, "Not now," the way it's done with costars— the talent.

"I'm a coproducer," Sam said.

The operator glanced sardonically, as if she were one of those pathetics who accost passers-by on Hollywood and Vine to tell the story of the part they almost had in a blockbuster, she looked wildly around for Toledo, found him on the big TV screen, he and Soledad dancing close as lovers, she moving her head back, saying something in his ear, her face all photogenic cheekbones and eye sockets, and Sam without a camera, she headed straight for them, her legs felt like a wind-up doll's, it occurred to her that she couldn't stop them, they belonged to someone else, she marched past the media jocks and their questions, danced around the mob of dancers, the men who reached for her, ignored them too, kept marching till she reached Toledo and Soledad, dancing as if they had done it together all their lives, Toledo's glance moved past Sam as if in a dream, "There's your star," Soledad said.

Toledo said, "Look at her!"

Cheekbones sang, "You stepped out of a dream..."

Toledo said, "How do you like your movie?"

Sam started to speak, her eyes ached, she went on anyway,

"You're the dream," she said, "—you two—if I could get my hands on a camera!"

Toledo stopped dancing, Soledad continued to dance around him, between him and Sam, he tilting his head around her, saying, "Jesus has the shooting covered."

Sam said, "I want to cover it too."

Toledo stared. "You all right?"

"When I get a camera I'll be all right."

She heard her voice quivering, Toledo did too, he opened his arms but she dodged, "I'm no one here," she said, "a costar—we're never all right—just what you make us—hysterical talent—"

Toledo's laugh cut her off, "Fabulous!" he said, "you're right at dead center—as always."

"I don't want to be right—I want to shoot—"

"Now wait—how far can you ride this? It's your screenplay we're producing. You really are the star. If anything, I'm the co-star here—what do you want?"

"A camera."

"Why can't you leave the shooting to the operators? Do you have to do everything?"

"I'm not talking about shooting the script," she said, "just the documentary—we said we'd all shoot the improv."

"But that's the point—it's part of the movie, not a separate piece," Toledo said, "the camera work isn't making the movie—it's a technical element."

Now it was Sam's voice that belonged to someone else, "The medium of the artform—just technical?" she said, "—is that what you said about Jesus' camera work?"

"It's nothing to get upset about."

"I'm not upset, I'm trying to get through to you!"

"Let go, Flannery," Toledo said, "let the artist create."

Soledad danced between them again, her angles like knives in the whirl of the strobes, her black satin thighs vibrating with the same rhythm as the fire rushing up and down Sam's spine, "Artist?" she said.

Toledo's eyes moved back and forth between Soledad's thighs and Sam's face, "Jesus is in charge of the cameras," he said.

"For the script scenes—"

"For the movie."

"You want me to ask Jesus if I can shoot?"

Toledo shook his head as though dealing with someone hopeless, Cheekbones pirouetted like a top between them, "Thanks, Andy," Toledo said, stopped her spin and kissed her.

Soledad looked at Sam, said, "Your screenplay blew me away."

"She's killed herself getting the backing," Toledo said.

Soledad smiled at me, "Has a real way with words, doesn't he? Good thing you're the writer," she said, smiled again even more photogenically and swung away, through the crowd that gushed open for her—one of the stars of the movie being shot right in front of their eyes. Cheekbones, Sam thought, that's her name.

Toledo said, "The dress is right. I see your hair streaked though—give you more contrast with Andy—don't you think?" He pulled Sam close and held her in a vice of his arms, his lips on her ear, "Why'd you stay away so long?" he said.

"The dress should be green—to match my jealous bitch bit."

"Jealousy can teach you a lot."

"My lesson for the day?"

Toledo looked at her with eyes she'd never seen, "Don't change the subject," he said, his voice soft as his eyes.

Sam said, "What was the subject?"

"That I love you, fool," he said, and took her earlobe in his teeth, mock-growling.

"For the cameras."

Toledo said, "I told you it's more than the movie—but it's also the movie—is that all right?"

A strobe washed across them like a searchlight, Sam closed her eyes and saw an image of a stone rolling toward her, so vivid she nearly stepped back, said, "I want to know why you changed our agreement. We said we'd all shoot the video—don't pretend you don't remember."

Toledo turned his head to the side with his chagrined smile, "I know I'm terrible—listen, we'll talk—not here, we'll leave separately and meet at love beach—remember the night you named it?"

"I did not—you did—before me."

"Did I? I don't remember before Flannery."

She laughed in spite of herself and thought of the dunes—lazy hours of love and talk, love and dream, wake up and love, still she hesitated—love beach was hardly the place to settle power issues—but Toledo was already off and running through the crowd, now open for his escape, now chasing him like the groupies that follow film shoots—sports fans, fire-chasers, news junkies—a mob they'd never be free of, like fugitives forever running, whether they were there or not, the feel of them always there, Toledo was right, love beach was the only place, they were all hot on his heels now, it was easy for Sam to get through the house to the garden house, in its screen of bushes, up to its roof where the hovercraft was, easy to lift into the shadows over the crashing surf, unbroken by anything but moonglow, she could see Toledo sprinting ahead of the chasers who spread across the dunes like ants.

Toledo was high-stepping in the surf just as Sam reached him, he climbed in, they flew over surf and sand, Toledo kneeling beside the pilot's seat, kissing her arm, "Have I mentioned that I'm helpless with you?" he said, in this dream they glided down the beach to the large dunes, "They'll never find us," Toledo said, they set the hovercraft down, Sam wondered how they could talk business in this ethereal light, they stripped and ran into the surf, Toledo chasing till she dropped, sexing, lying in the dunes listening to the surf-lick under the neon stars.

She said, "We have to talk."

"I'm all yours."

"Unless I can shoot I'm nothing—a costar."

"Tell me what that means," Toledo said.

"Like just the talent—tits and ass—I don't know whether a man can understand it." Toledo raised himself to an elbow, his eyes moved romantically around her face, if it weren't impossible in the dunes, her paranoia would say there must be a camera on him, he planned all of it, down to this moment, "Is this what you want Flannery to be?" she said.

Toledo said, "It's not that I want her to be anything, I want to know who she is—why she feels this."

"The Toledo I know left this morning and a stranger came back."

"Really? Say more."

"Your grand entrance with Jesus and Cheekbones—"

"Cheekbones?" Toledo said.

"Soledad—all that photogenic bone structure."

He laughed, "Cheekbones—I like it," he said, "so, somewhere beneath that porcelain mask lies a heart as hot as Flannery's flesh?" He lay back and pulled her up on him, "It's only the beginning, darling—don't take every surprise as betrayal, okay?"

"Could I surprise you?"

"You just did—I feel like a god!"

"But could I surprise you with some action, a sequence I plan and keep secret?"

Toledo said, "How about this one—the love beach sequence?"

"You wanted to come here."

"But in response to your summit invitation."

"You mean my demand."

He grinned and said, "How about seduction?"

"My seduction—which you set up by leaving, staying away till everyone would be here and you could make a grand entrance—"

"You're saying I set you up," Toledo said.

"Thank you."

"Welcome to Medialennium—where all images, all myths are controlled by the board of directors. As director of the movie, I—why do I have to tell you this?"

She said, "You want to control even the improv—be meta-director!"

"Meta-director—good—yes."

"Why?"

"Have you ever seen cinema vérité without a director?"

"But it takes you out of it—makes it your master game—not an exploration—don't you see?"

"A director's just a leader, baby, he's not out of anything—especially when he's acting in it."

"Don't call me baby!"

"Okay—don't you attack me!" Toledo said, he rolled over and sat up, grabbed his pants and pulled his coke box out of his pocket, stomped off to the lee side of the dunes so the wind wouldn't get more than he did, Sam ran down to the water, eyes welling up, furious welling, wanting to drown them in the sea and disappear, was what he wanted too, he could have it all his way, no more attacks from her, no more co-stars wanting to shoot, she was turning into a jellyfish anyway, "Don't go in—it's shark feeding time!" Toledo yelled from behind, she hadn't noticed she was walking out, green foam running up her ankles, still she couldn't stop the march of the feet no longer hers, heard Toledo behind, "What do you think—is this the opening? Listen—fade on Flannery driving some company car—Maserati, a Medialennium perk—she's just signed on—sold out, to her—she feels trapped, she drives the car like from hell—maybe she does it white—"

"No coke," Sam said and walked farther out in the surf.

"Honey, you can snort baking soda if you like—"

She loved that he gave her this. "Don't call me honey," she shouted, "—or baby or darling or any of those generic put-'em-in-their-place tags—is that an impossible request? Is this Hollywood?" She stepped off a sandbar into swift current—much stronger than she'd imagined—had to struggle to surface.

Toledo was walking out too, barely looking at her, still musing about the opening sequence, "Listen, the Maserati rockets off the road," he said, "—straight down the sand and into the surf—about here." He lifted her from the sea just as headlights came around the dunes—jeeps carrying equipment, partiers, media, Toledo ignored them, held her so tight her flesh burned, his arms and legs trembled violently as he carried her through the hammering surf, when they reached the sand he stood like a statue except for the trembling, his voice so low she could barely understand, "Don't you ever pull another stunt like that!" he said.

"Did you think I meant to keep going?"

"How the hell do I know what any of you are going to do?"

Toledo plopped her down in the sand, with the mob all around and in the glare of lights from the jeeps, it was like Coney Island, even ghetto blasters in the distance.

"All honeys act the same?" Sam said.

"At times."

"Because you throw us to the wolves—one way or the other," she said, she could see some movement out of the corner of her eye, Jesus with his camera, on-light blinking, and a towel—he handed it to her in silence, the mob hushed and everything was silent except the ghetto blasters, she put the towel around her nakedness, the sound returned—explosion of boos and hissing—she said to Jesus, "Will you give me the camera?"

"Hasn't he told you?" Jesus said.

Toledo said, "I had to go union shop—not just for the film. They said if the footage was going to be used in the edit, it had to be union."

Meaning only union operators could touch a camera, not even

directors or directors of cinematography. "Why didn't you tell me?" she said.

Toledo said, "I didn't have a chance."

"Too busy softening me up—"

"If you weren't so paranoid I wouldn't have to!"

Sam looked at his face and didn't know whether its redness was the color of his skin or in her eyes, turned to Jesus, "What about you—you're shooting, aren't you?"

Jesus opened his mouth but Toledo said, "I got an exception for Jesus and me because of the special nature of the work—the investors wouldn't go for you because you don't have feature film experience."

"So the reason isn't union shop, it's your exclusive little deal," she said, "—what investors—?"

"What difference do names make?"

"That's why you came back like a conquering hero," she said, "you didn't tell me because you wanted it for this—the love beach sequence."

"I wanted it to be part of the movie," Toledo said, "tell me what's wrong with that?"

"Manipulation!" she said.

"So directors are manipulators—aren't writers—isn't that what art—"

Toledo broke off at the sound of a helicopter engine, it was his Vietnam jungle-hopper coming in low just above, Cheekbone's voice came over a megaphone, "Soledad to Flannery—did you call?" she said, the ladder dropped, Sam took off the towel and threw it at Toledo who laughed and shouted for a camera to get the flesh climbing up out of his love dunes while his mob whistled, clapped, catcalled, chanted—all in strip rhythm—and Sam climbed, careening, up into the chopper, then looked down and saw them as if through the lens of an aerial closing shot—zooming out till all detail, everything, was lost in the sea.

Five

Cheekbones looked down at the disappearing love dunes. "Fools," she said, "look at Toledo strutting around—thinks everybody likes to flash their stuff the way he does." She had brought Sam's clothes—the black lingerie and red dress—even the sequined purse. "One thing I'll say for them, they really did try to get you on the camera crew," she said, "can you hear Toledo giving one of his lectures on art as the salvation of western civilization? Flannery's eye is as good as Cahero's and better than mine.'"

"Toledo said that?"

"'One more genius lost between the ears of investors who want glory without risk.'"

Sam said, "The man with the golden tongue."

"You have this effect on people of making them think," Cheekbones said, "for investors that's a contradiction in terms."

Sam laughed, "I just want to shoot," she said, "—video, not their precious guns."

"You understand the essential symbolism of the male," Cheekbones said, "which is to the point of whether Toledo can control you."

"Am I that dangerous?"

"Truth—which is what your script is about—is, they want it more fictionalized—futuristic—special effects, you know."

"Over my dead body," Sam said.

"Art—which equals reality—versus realism—which equals entertainment," Cheekbones said, "—Flannery versus Toledo."

"I never thought of it that way."

"Toledo as entertainment or Flannery as art?"

Sam said, "Art's a big word—and I'm not even sure I believe in it—though I use it."

"You've had a number done on you."

"Who hasn't?" Sam said, "I mean, I like Toledo's movies, but some of that stuff on the Independent Film Channel buries me."

Cheekbones laughed, said, "Thank you. Still you say who hasn't had a number done. well *they* haven't."

"White boys? I don't know—rites of passage to the fraternity is a kind of number."

Cheekbones nodded, "The cost of membership in the power trust is mind."

"Why can't I remember that?"

"That's what they're good at—forgetting and making us forget."

"And I always bite," Sam said, "—thanks for the rescue."

"I owe you."

"You do?"

Cheekbones said, "What say we set down for a drink somewhere?"

She landed the chopper on a penthouse heliport, courtesy of We the People—The We, for short—a group of international financiers, kind of a brotherhood of economic power, this was their watering hole in Beverly Hills. Cheekbones had a key that let them inside the penthouse, museum of priceless antiques and art, in the elevator she trembled visibly, "This place is everything I want to burn," she said.

"It does have an aura of Rome."

"Toledo told me he talks to you about my shit."

"That White therapy doesn't do much for you?"

The elevator opened in the garage, Cheekbones led the way to a grey Jag, Richard Toledo's, Sam supposed she should have expected it.

"Car of the day—I never know what I'll find," Cheekbones said and looked at Sam, "what's wrong?"

"Wrong?"

"You look like you've seen your dead mama."

Sam's mind blanked the way it always did when someone spoke of parents as if she, like everyone, had them. Cheekbones said, "Sorry—Toledo told me about your past—I didn't think."

"It's just this car," Sam said, "wheels like this make me feel as if I've stolen them."

For a minute Cheekbones said nothing, as if she knew Sam had lied—knew about her meeting with Richard and had brought her here as a test?

Cheekbones went on, "Cars like this speak to me. I even believe if you run fast enough you'll be free."

"Now you're talking my favorite myth," Sam said.

On the freeway Cheekbones drove as if there was no danger of cops, she was as expert with the Jag as she'd been with the chopper, "Toledo wants to open the movie with me driving a Maserati," Sam said, "I've never even been in one."

"The We has a red one."

"Will you teach me to drive like this?"

"You're a natural."

"But will the Maserati know that?" Sam said, "and Toledo—is he in the We?"

Cheekbones laughed, "If he knew you asked, he'd shit," she said. "No, but theoretically he would be when the old man kicks off. Richard won't though, he'll live forever just to keep the boy from getting his loot." Cheekbones took the Watts exit, on the ramp she lit up, "Ever been to the Circus?" She offered the joint.

"No thanks," Sam said.

"Come on—medicinal purposes only—it's light."

Sam took it, even before the smoke was in her lungs felt the euphoria of anticipated relief, though from what she wasn't sure, "What circus," she said, "Barnum and Bailey—or San Toledo?"

Cheekbones laughed, said, "The Circus Bar—Toledo didn't tell you? Wait till you see the scene—you'd think he grew up under the big top."

"I believe it," Sam said, leaned her head back, the weed was hitting, "that's why the clown dance—you were sensational."

"It was all for you."

"Me?"

"Not saying I didn't get off on it," Cheekbones said, "but Toledo was after you."

"And wasn't I cool?"

They laughed like potheads, passed the weed again, "I mean, how do they do it?" Sam said.

"Two broads with steel trap minds befucked by the same fool."

"If this were Hollywood, the next line would be about those minds between our legs."

"Steel ball-busters?" Cheekbones said, they laughed hysterically again, Cheekbones stopped the Jag outside a square building, its Spanish porch strung with tent flags, she turned off the engine, the weed had gone out and neither could light it.

Sam stared at the Spanish porch, "I have this love-hate thing about circuses," she said.

Cheekbones said, "Love the animals and hate the truth of cages and tricks?"

"Well said."

"True confessions," Cheekbones said, "you're a real psych nurse?"

"Was."

"What do you think about therapy?"

"I used to believe in the myth of normalcy," Sam said.

"Myth?"

"As a consensus of values and beliefs at the heart of a culture—in the west, tradition of normal being White—or playing it—profitably. Therapists as priests—like the churches, doing well by doing good."

Cheekbones said, "So science it ain't?"

"What's science except our current religion?"

"You don't believe in anything?"

"Not as absolute, only as value," Sam said, "—you shouldn't get me stoned."

"How do you stand it when you're not?"

"I don't—I revise reality—you know, write."

Cheekbones said, "You do that," she relighted and passed the joint, "You keep it—I need something else," she said, opened her hand-bag, pulled out a box of coke, said, "Toledo tells me you won't get down with him."

Sam said, "Do you use as much as he does?"

"I was free-basing when I damn near blew my lights out."

"Toledo told me it was Prozac—a suicide attempt."

"The official story," Cheekbones said and did two lines.

"But cops came for him that night—didn't they know?"

Cheekbones put away the case, took out her make-up and expertly repaired everything from smudged mascara to tiny lines under her eyes, their sockets even deeper in the garish phosphorescent street light, her cheeks more hollow, "Everyone goes along with Toledo," she said, "and he takes care of everyone."

Sam said, "But you could've been killed."

"I don't free-base anymore."

"Aren't you afraid you could again?"

Cheekbones stopped fixing her hair and touched Sam's arm, her eyes had coke-pupils, black holes like sea night with no stars, no smog reflection, no neon aura of technogods, "He's in love with you," she said.

"Love!"

"I've known him for ten years—he's in love."

"You're braindead from all that coke," Sam said.

"You know anyone who isn't braindead?"

Sam laughed. "Taking drugs the effect, not the cause?

Maybe—maybe the cokeheads get treated so they'll take prescription dope instead—to keep up the mythic appearances—till boredom sends them back to the coke-edge."

Cheekbones leaned across Sam and opened the door, "You're just like he said," she said, "—for the first time in ten years, I understand the man. Just don't leave."

She let Sam out and went to park the Jag, Sam stood on the curb and watched the Mardi Gras masks and costumes, people walking arm-in-arm, talking, laughing, Sam as always fascinated, trying to memorize the rhythms of their movements, as if their belonging with each other were a matter of some ritual choreography, the way they approached the corner, for instance, the way they paused at the bus stop where a child stood motionless under phosphorescent brilliance, the way the partiers looked at her—her costume of a fake sheepskin car seat-cover pinned around her—the lamb mask that dangled from her hand. The partiers hesitated, wondering why the child seemed to be alone, decided she must not be, she must belong to one of the others, the area crowded with them now, they stepped off the curb to the potholes and tarred street, crossed in front of the child—too young to be alone, she was surely with someone, her face needed no mask, her gaze cast slightly down, unblinking, frozen as her arms and hands, the slump of her shoulders, all of her—expecting nothing. Sam was too far away to see these things yet saw them as clearly as if through a zoom lens. Maybe the child's picture had been on one of those supermarket posters or milk cartons or the endless postcards advertising lost children, Sam had to find out, at least get close enough to really see her face, the street was suddenly full of cars going both ways, when Sam got around them the bus stop was empty, the bus must have come and gone, but maybe the child hadn't gotten on, maybe she was still here in the shadows of the street leading away from the light.

Even before Sam saw the man—Black—sitting on a high wall beside an alley, she felt him, his legs swinging, his face lost in the shadows above a crumpled white shirt open to the waist, cuffs open too, hanging above thick wrists. As she got closer she felt rather than saw his eyes, she thought of crossing the street but there was no one else around, the insult would have been too cruel, instead she went up to him and said, "Have you seen a little girl in a lamb costume?"

The Black didn't answer, his eyes reflected light from a passing car, but like the child's, didn't blink, his hands on the wall lifted him off, he jumped down and landed, his face inches from Sam's, she thought he was smiling but then realized it was an illusion created by scars, he reached with both hands and plucked the red sequined bag from the crook of Sam's arm—with infinite care not to touch her—a loud scream went up, he jumped as if struck then turned and ran, Sam after him, accompanied by the screaming, other shouts and footsteps, all chasing the Black into an alley where he dropped Sam's keys—the only thing in the sequined bag—then dropped the bag, Sam didn't stop to pick it up, she ran after him, even when he was out of sight, she ran, exhausted, passed other runners, her legs keeping on for reasons nothing to do with her purse, nothing to do with anything she had the slightest idea of, till the shriek of brakes, the sound of metal hitting flesh, gasp of silence punctuated by cat screams.

A white Continental burned back, turned, squealed away from the heap in the street—the white shirt turning red. Sam dropped beside him, said, "I'm a nurse—may I help you?" The Black's eyes glistened, his lips worked soundlessly as she pulled the shirt away from a rib that stuck out through his skin, the hole a geyser of blood. "Call 911!" she yelled.

The Black wheezed violently, his eyes brilliant with pain, Sam's fingers searched for the bleeder, she thought the gush slowed but he breathed as if through water, "What you doing here?" he said.

"Quiet—save your strength," Sam said.

The scars rearranged themselves in a smile that deepened the pain in his eyes, "Beautiful," he said, began to cough, gagged, quit breathing, chest heaved then collapsed.

Sam yelled for a CPR partner and started working on him, someone dropped down on his other side, they worked together till the EMTs appeared and took over with their cardiac needles in the heart no longer his, bag to breathe the lungs—not him, the cut-down in his ankle because he had no usable veins anywhere, even in his groin. If he didn't bleed to death first, they would keep his flesh working like a machine till some mother or wife could prove she had the right to bury him.

"Let's get out of here," a voice said—the CPR partner Sam hadn't looked at till now, it was Jesus—which should have surprised her but somehow didn't, pathetic paranoia, or maybe she half-hoped this was the movie, Toledo would yell cut and the Black would roll over and get up, didn't happen though, Jesus said he'd guessed Soledad would take Sam to the Circus and had arrived just as the screaming started. "Why did you run after him?" he said.

"I don't know—I knew someone like him once," she said, "— shot on a Friday night in east Baltimore. When he died an orderly had to tell me not to put the body in the White morgue."

"You grew up in the north," Jesus said.

"I don't know where I grew up but I couldn't understand, I thought I'd walked into a really bad movie."

"How old were you?"

"Sixteen, seventeen—"

Jesus said, "Didn't it get easier?"

"No," she said, "I suppose that's one of the luxuries of being White, you can be endlessly enraged without having to live it."

"Oh, you live it."

The ambulance screamed off, Sam went around like a maniac asking people if they got the license plate of the white Continental, till an undercover cop appeared, flipped his badge, he was the driver, he and his partner—patrolling the area when they'd heard the screams.

"Undercover—in a Continental?" Sam said, she wanted to hit him.

"A lot of drug deals go down here," the cop said, he wondered why Sam had nothing in the red sequined bag except keys. "What was your relationship to the perpetrator?" he said.

"He grabbed my purse."

"Before that."

"We're both human."

A crowd had gathered, cameras and mikes appeared, the media must have followed Jesus—it would be like this from now on—the cop drew out his scene, made them go to the precinct to give statements, not even Toledo's name would get them out of it, maybe they were just being overly cautious, Sam didn't believe it though, she kept seeing the Black run from the alley into the street where the white Continental stood waiting for its target. "You were in the area," Sam said to the cop, "but how did you know where he was? Who made the call?"

The cop laughed and said, "You did, lady. We just followed your screams."

"Mine?"

So she'd been the one screaming—the one who'd killed the Black. Her eyes started to burn, she shook her head to secure the dam, if she hadn't gone up to him, belying her racism, offering herself as a target—and him as a victim. Jesus put his arm lightly around her shaking, she told him about the little girl, hoping for redemption, his presence stopped the madness inside. When the cops let them go they went back to the Circus to look for Cheekbones, a man dressed like a barker stood on the curb in front of the bar, "Welcome to the Circus," he said, "—steal your car?" He knew Jesus, they talked and laughed together, everyone who passed knew Jesus.

The Circus door was fine mahogany with relief carvings of animals—not caged and circus-trained but wild, running free. The foyer was dark, filled with jazz, they passed through a narrow corridor with a high ceiling of stars that looked far enough away to be real, at the end a canvas flap opened to a lounge with a tent ceiling complete with holes and stars peeking through.

"Made from a real big top?" Sam said.

Jesus said, "Real is Toledo's trademark."

"He built this?"

"He was looking for a location when the owner went belly-up, and he bought the place."

"A location for what?"

"The same with his house in Malibu," Jesus said, "he built it to shoot a film in someday. Locations looking for a script—found yours."

Sam said, "The novel was mine. The script I hardly recognize."

"If you're writing it, it's yours."

"I'm not sure I am writing it," she said, "have you ever been taken over by something you're working on?"

"Yes."

"So there's life after?"

"But different."

Jesus led her through the lounge filled with masked dancers leaping, gyrating almost as one, a sax blowing under blue light, bass and piano standing by through the solo, smoke drifting among the shafts of spot light, curling around the dancers winding their way between booths—replicas of circus cars set at angles to frame the dance floor—Jesus moved through the scene like a master choreographer, again everyone knew him, wanted something from him—a handshake, a word, a turn around the dance floor. Sam saw how perfect he was for the movie role, a leader created not by his own ambition, nor even the ambition of others—something between him and people, as if part of him belonged to their deepest needs and they belonged to something he inspired in them. If Toledo were here, as earlier at the party, she wouldn't have seen it, Toledo's energy was different, he was ego, the crowd's persona. Jesus was someone else—the one within, beneath the masks.

Above the lounge was a balcony with several doors, one opened as Sam watched, two figures emerged, the light too low to see their features but even their silhouettes were familiar, the taller wore not a costume but a sport jacket of impeccable tailoring. Whether it was the jacket or the man's figure in it, Sam was so sure she knew him she almost waved, he stepped back into the room beyond the door and closed it in the face of the other, whose entire body stood rigid as if to keep from trembling. This one wore a Mexican poncho and silver-studded boots and hat, he looked as if he were shouting but the music was too loud to hear anything else, he hurled away from the door and down the balcony stairs with such power and grace Sam knew he was a dancer, the other dancers opened ranks and took the Mex in to their gyrating limbs and masks, Sam tried to keep the poncho in sight—if only she had a camera she could have moved inside too, no one questions a camera. When there was no sign of him a terrible sadness gripped her, as if the mugger were dying in the street again.

"Guess who," a voice said, the tone husky and strained as if to sound deeper, Sam turned towards the sound and there stood the Mex, his face covered with a black satin mask, thick black hair tumbled down to his shoulders.

"Zapata," Sam said, "—no, Pancho Villa!"

"I'll answer to either—and you?"

"The Treaty of Guadalupe Hidalgo—Gringa for short—except I have no mask."

The Mex laughed—a short, scornful sound Sam was certain she knew, "Au contraire—your mask is the best—you're sure to win the prize," he said and began to dance around her, pulled her into the rhythms of the other dancers.

"I'm out of my league in this crowd," Sam said.

"There are no leagues or levels here, Gringa," the Mex said, "just who you are."

"And if I don't know?"

"Then you're here to find out."

The music became frenzied but the Mex didn't miss a step and somehow pulled Sam along into the intricate sensual movements of the other dancers, now unmistakably a group. It became difficult to see any one dancer, even to tell which body part belonged to which constellation of music-fused flesh, till the final sax run tore off into shattering silence, the bodies froze like statues.

The Mex's arms were fast around Sam, she standing still as the other dancers, unsure whose heart pounded her ribs—no man's though, the silver-studded hat came off and landed on Sam's head, "I need a hit," Cheekbones said.

Sam tried to laugh—how could she not have known, took a step and reeled, Cheekbones grabbed her around the shoulders, "You can lean on me, for Christ's sake," she said, "I sure need to—like the little package of therapy Herr Direktor said he sent—with you?"

"Therapy?"

"Not with you—shit," she said and pulled Sam up the stairs.

"I saw you up here with a man," Sam said.

"Who?" Cheekbones said, as if she had forgotten it, she opened the door—the same one they'd stood in front of—to a huge room filled with gaming tables, a winding corridor leading to small rooms, almost cubicles, with a narrow bed and sink, "Not monk's cells," Cheekbones said.

Sam said, "Don't tell me Toledo's in the business."

"Only the movie business—though some wouldn't see much difference between that and skintrade."

"This place gives me the creeps," Sam said, "—reminds me of that improv scene we did at Little Hollywood—"

"That happened to you, didn't it?"

"The porn audition?" Sam said—to buy time.

"You don't have to make things up for me," Cheekbones said, "I'm not Toledo."

"Okay—then the answer is, I suppose something like that did happen—I just don't know what... This place, though—" Sam broke off, shook herself, said, "The man I saw out on the balcony with you?"

Cheekbones didn't look at her, said "Just some old fart hangs around here," walked away with a new set to her shoulders—studied, cautious.

"What about the package you expected from Toledo?" Sam said, "what was it?"

Cheekbones waved a hand, "I guess he didn't catch you—so to speak."

"Why did you call it therapy?"

"Figure of speech—medicinal purposes..."

"There is no therapy, is there?"

Cheekbones looked shocked for a minute then recovered her mask of satire and said, "The only reason you don't recognize the therapeutic benefit of coke is you never tried it."

"And when Toledo told me he was going to your therapy sessions?"

"He was supplying me."

"And you did the coke together."

"Not like that—all he talked about was you," Cheekbones said, her eyes reminded Sam of the mugger's—same brilliant pain.

"When he's with me, he talks about you," Sam said.

"He thinks he owes me—is all."

"Why?"

"Because I was falling apart when we met," Cheekbones said. "I fell into marriage with him—he said it would be the glue to hold everything together but I never stopped falling."

"And that's why he pulls himself together," Sam said, "to take care of you?"

Cheekbones said nothing, only checked her watch and looked at the door she was still expecting him to come through.

"Do you want to kill yourselves?" Sam said, "or each other?"

"What will kill him is if you leave him."

"And what will kill you—drugs—or being his mission in life?"

Cheekbones rushed over and hugged Sam then turned and ran out, Sam called after, cursed herself for what she'd said about therapy, for what she hadn't said. From the balcony she saw Cheekbones weave through the Mardi Gras partiers, if only she had a camera with a zoom—but by the time she was down the stairs, Cheekbones was gone, no one would admit to having seen her.

Jesus reappeared with a camera—and a Toledo Productions crew—they hadn't seen Cheekbones either, "Do you know she's a cokehead?" Sam said.

Jesus kept the camera in front of his face, "Toledo likes drugs," he said.

"Meaning I must be a cokehead too?"

Jesus moved his face out from behind the camera, "No," he said, "I didn't figure it that way."

"You just wondered what he did want with me."

Jesus smiled. "No, I didn't wonder that."

Sam felt a drip on her cheek and thought the ceiling—the big top—was leaking or some special-effects, it took her several moments to realize she was crying, the dam had a leak, after all the work she'd put into not doing it, not being the woman. Jesus led her to one of the booths, gave her a napkin, she bawled more, Jesus sat opposite, put the camera down and ordered something from the waiter costumed in gold lamé loin cloth, mask, wings, and garland of thorny roses—who gave Sam another napkin and kissed the top of her head. When she could talk she asked Jesus whether he knew Cheekbones had nearly died free-basing.

"Recently?"

"So it's happened before."

"With Andy, everything has happened before."

"Why didn't Toledo tell me?"

"Maybe he was afraid it would put you off," Jesus said.

"He told me she took Prozac."

"You're a psych nurse—didn't he tell me? He might have thought you'd accept that."

Sam said, "So truth is a matter of what I'll accept?"

"Maybe he thinks keeping you is."

The waiter brought brandies, "To one hell of an opening night," Jesus said, and they drank the velvet numbness.

"Where will Cheekbones go?" Sam said.

"You know where she'll go."

"Toledo?"

"She'll try to score on the way."

"But always ends up there," Sam said, "she lives with him, doesn't she—it's only because of me she's been staying somewhere else."

"Andy stays where she stays."

"That's not an answer."

"They've never lived together for more than a few months at a time."

"Why?"

"They don't do home—they do drugs."

"Maybe they do drugs because they can't do home."

"Something you can relate to?"

Sam slid out of the booth, said "Restroom," and felt Jesus' eyes studying as she left the booth. At the same moment, the tent flap to the corridor exploded with white uniforms like ones she had seen in a movie, she thought, or in a dream, helmets with face shields, M-16s at the ready as they circled the lounge and weaved through the dancers, Sam thought it must be a Mardi Gras gag, but Jesus got out of the booth, pushed the camera at her, said, "Make a movie," then disappeared.

Sam zoomed in on the white uniforms, their helmets decorated with American flags, hands wielding the rifles like sticks, driving through the crowd, hitting people, knocking them around, breaking furniture, Jesus appeared at the mike in front of the band and held up his arms, "Show your warrant!" he said.

In the split second of silence afterwards, Sam moved in to get a better shot, something hit the camera, the lights went, gunshot rang out, spotlights came up directly on the uniforms—all grouped at the entrance now, "Next time we shut you down!" one of them shouted, they backed out, rifles still ready, like bank robbers in a made-for-TV flick, except for the white uniforms.

Jesus was in charge now, he spoke to the freaked crowd, invited those who would to meet at the Circus the next night, to discuss the incident and make plans, now they must leave the Circus, get off the streets, go home—and above all, don't panic, tomorrow they would work together to find out who these people were and deal with them, nothing could be accomplished here—nor anywhere else tonight.

It took over an hour to empty the Circus and the parking lot, and finally get back to the Toledo Productions van Jesus had driven from San Toledo. "What do you think is happening?" Sam said.

"They weren't LAPD."

"Looked straight out of Central Casting to me. You don't suppose Toledo was up to some more improv?"

"The scene was too unbelievable to be staged."

"Publicity?"

"That's Andy's gig—but this wasn't her style."

"Besides, where was the media?"

"I wonder," Jesus said, "they could've been there—in costume. It wouldn't have to be planned, they follow us around on shoots—you have that tape you shot?"

Sam told him about the flags on the helmets.

"Now I know Toledo didn't plan it," Jesus said.

"And where was the punch line? I know his bag is realism, but this went beyond—would even Toledo tempt fate that much?"

"When I first knew him, I thought he *was* fate—the Whiteman-god thing," Jesus said, "I thought he could do anything—fix anything—like the union shop problem."

"Meaning I can't accept the fact that he can't fix it so I think he doesn't want to?"

Jesus said, "You're doing all right."

"What hit me hardest was the way he told me—on camera with a cast of thousands."

"I saw his side of that. It might be easier to work without an audience, but it wouldn't be your movie."

Sam said, "I just felt so stripped."

"That's what it takes to create a role. Then with your improv element, it's bound to get tough."

"I guess this was amateur night for me."

"How much acting experience have you had?"

"My life—a little summer stock and psychodrama—if that counts."

"Everything counts."

"Stages always seem like home to me."

"That's the way it is with actors," Jesus said, "which is what makes your script hard. It's not just acting, the role we have to learn and develop with technique is our own mask."

"Can it be done?"

"I don't know."

"I feel like a jerk."

"Before this is over we'll all have our turn at embarrassments. Intimacy does that."

The traffic was rush-hour pace, "I never thought about it that way," Sam said, "how did you learn stuff like this?"

"Mostly workshops—Chicano repertory."

"Where did you grow up?"

"Brownsville, Texas. My father was from Mexico City and thought the Gringo were gods—especially the French," Jesus said, "he spent years trying to prove there was no Mexican blood—meaning Indian—in the family. We were Spanish with a flavor of French—not as good as pure French, but better than Indian, especially Central and South American tribes. Apache would have been acceptable, but Mexicans were too passive—exactly the lazy drunken halfwits Texas Rangers created to justify the border wars."

Sam said, "So your father helped the Gringo teach you self-hate."

"Not hate—survival—the kind he knew."

"Of course—it's Whites who teach self-hate."

"Something you know about?"

"Do I?"

She wondered if he hated her then realized she was proving his point. The traffic moved like a giant worm bouncing off concrete, a few people got out of their cars and walked around, but it wasn't like the days before the freeway shootings when gridlock was nothing but an excuse to party, this wasn't the usual freeway crowd either, they wore polyester and visor caps. "Do you think they're all together?" Sam said.

"They do have the same tailor."

There was something else about them, a pinched intensity at the same time lacking resonance, the ones outside their cars went between the other cars as if they were checking for something but didn't know exactly what—or who?

Sam wanted to know everything about Jesus, asked him incessant questions. He'd studied in Paris for a couple of years, his parents had worked through the church to get him a scholarship, and he'd wanted to believe his father's fantasy, so decided he was French Apache for a couple of years, then during an exchange year at the University of Mexico studying archeology, he'd found out who he was. "The poverty tore me up," he said, "but I was home."

Sam said, "I envy you."

"Isn't that what the movie is about for you?"

She was too surprised to answer, the traffic worm started crawling again, motorists hurried back to their cars, "When I started the novel it was a complete fiction. Now it's turned into this screenplay I don't even recognize."

"Sometimes you're too close to home to see," Jesus said, "it'll work out."

"I never realized I'm such a coward."

"That's the last thing you are."

"Then why do I feel like I'm about to jump out of my skin all the time?"

"Fear just means you're alive. You have the guts to act in spite of it."

"I hope," Sam said. "When did you meet Toledo?"

"Mexico—taking cinematography—he gave a seminar about documentary film—very Gringo—and by then, I was very Mexican."

"Worthy opponents?"

"We did get into it."

"And the rest is history," Sam said, "I love the way you shoot film."

"I've got a camera for you—if anyone asks, say you're doing shot preview for me."

"Thanks—I really am a fool."

"Real fools never feel it," Jesus said. "Where are you staying?"

She didn't hear the question until the silence after, then wasn't sure what the question was, parried, "I thought we were all staying at San Toledo." The traffic slowed again, just when Sam needed speed, Jesus' eyes rested on her for a moment then jumped away.

"How is it there?" he said.

"Loony tunes—preproduction—you know."

"Toledo says the two of you talk about everything."

"Oh we talk all right." Sam had a sudden image of herself standing somewhere with an audience, lines forgotten, mind blank as now. "We've both been in therapy and all those seminars about communication—got the techniques down, you know—we only fight when we understand each other."

Jesus laughed, the sound felt like a waterfall in the country, she wanted it to go on, "Toledo didn't tell me you were funny," he said.

"I've always thought of myself as tragic."

He laughed again. "Since the amnesia?"

"Do you suppose all theater people are like shrinks—a joke never a joke—what're we going to do for laughs?"

"Laugh at the truth."

"Or lock ourselves in closets to see if it feels as claustrophobic as this script?"

"Truth is seldom comfortable."

"I used to think I wasn't really as stupid as I sound," she said, "—guess I'll have to off that fantasy too."

"Not knowing something used to make me feel stupid too."

"Why do I think you're going to tell me that's ego?"

"Maybe it's what you tell yourself?"

"Oh shit."

Jesus said, "Do you have flashbacks?"

"More like flashcuts."

"What about the therapy?"

"I basically flunked," she said, "—kept running away."

"You mean not showing up?"

"We lived together. He wasn't really my shrink, he just thought he should be. Every time we had a problem he gave me a new diagnosis—and I left."

"Left him?"

"I felt trapped—he'd buy me flowers or girl clothes when he

didn't want to talk about something. Sometimes I could barely breathe. He always had another diagnostic point."

"For you to admit?"

"You've had therapy too."

They laughed, she thought how easy this was—too easy. "The time you didn't go back," Jesus said, "why was that?"

"He ran out of his own diagnoses and sent me to another shrink who told me I had a father transference and the only way he could cure me was if I left home."

"And moved in with him?"

She wasn't sure about being so easily understood—as if Jesus had read the script and was coaching her—she *was* paranoid—like Toledo said. The car behind barreled into the van, they got out to check the damage—she still thinking how odd it was talking to Jesus, as if she'd known him for years yet had never known anyone like him, she was paranoid because he had the very insight and sensitivity she longed for but didn't know how to trust. There wasn't any damage but the other driver—who looked like a discount shoe salesman wearing a baseball cap and new teeth—offered a flyer and a bumper sticker, "You need to park," he said.

Sam said, "We do?"

"Aren't you going to the Bowl?"

"Who's there?"

"We are," he said and handed her a bumper sticker.

"SAVE A FETUS FOR JESUS—VICTIMS VIGILANT," Sam read aloud, "where have I seen that before?"

"We're having a membership campaign," the other driver said and flashed a smile that could stop an FX monster, Sam remembered the sky-writing Toledo and she had seen flying over the Bowl, realized the bumper sticker was also on the car ahead—and most of the others in the gridlock. The flyer was about a rally at the Bowl, neighborhood citizen anticrime groups launching a national movement—complete with TV show, "I wonder who's paying," she said.

Jesus said, "Someone who can afford the Bowl."

"Want to find out?"

"Toledo didn't prepare me for you."

"I could say the same."

This exit was the Bowl, they swung around the traffic, went ahead to the next and circled back to the parking lot, the security guard looked at the bumper sticker sitting on the dash and waved them through, Jesus took two cameras from the back of the van and they joined the Bowl crowd—very White, down to the baseball caps with American Flag emblems. Jesus found a moldy Oakland A's relic and a white jacket in the van. "In a scene like this, most people don't look beyond the costume," he said.

Nearly everyone carried a Victims Vigilant sign, there were a lot of cameras perched on the polyester shoulders, Sam and Jesus had no trouble getting past the security checkpoints, all the way down to a front row seat, just in time for the National Anthem—country rock style—while a spotlight over the podium swung out and picked up a large, silver-haired man, white tails flapping as he ran down the aisle, waving his arms at the cheering crowd. He looked like Richard Toledo but Sam couldn't believe it, she zoomed in and caught his face just as he reached the podium.

"Good evening, Victims Vigilant!" The cheer became deafening, he jabbed his arms high again and called out, "You are the ones who should be cheered!" The crowd grew louder, the look-alike waited, finally raised his arms and when it was quiet, said, "I'm a man who usually sits in his counting house counting out his money. I have bodyguards protecting me day and night. I have more investments than I need. When you came and asked me to be Master of Ceremonies for this rally, I wondered what Dr. Toledo—not even the famous Toledo—could have to do with Victims Vigilant. Then I was introduced to some of the members of your movement who told me their personal stories—and shamed me with the suffering I had been blind to."

Jesus and Sam looked at each other, "Toledo doesn't know?" he said.

"Not unless he's keeping it a secret—and I'm sure I saw Richard earlier at the Circus too," Sam said—too late realizing she'd used his first name—and longed to tell Jesus about meeting him.

The crowd noise was so loud she wondered whether recorded sound—like canned studio laughter—was being fed through the system, Richard gestured for silence, "First, let me thank you for opening my eyes!" he said, again the noise took over till Richard raised his arms. "This is happening because you sent in the money to rent the Hollywood Bowl! Victims Vigilant is proud to be in the tradition of genuine grassroots movements of the United States of America—the greatest nation in the history of the world!"

This time Richard let the crowd and the electronic cacophony go on for over a minute while he marched slowly back and forth like a revivalist preacher—complete with sweat-beaded face radiating charisma as bright as the spotlight, "What's it all about?" he said, "why do we have to be here instead of at home with our families and friends tonight? Why must the victims of crime band together for protection? Where is law and order? Is it on the street when the rapist is released after therapy to find out why he did it—and nothing to keep him from repeating it?"

"And he's a shrink?" Sam said.

Jesus said, "Do they believe in therapy?"

"You really are hung up on truth."

The noise went on for a couple of minutes this time, Richard continued his slow march back and forth, head bowed as though thinking deeply, next he stopped the frenzy with a slight gesture as though to demonstrate his control, then closed his eyes and threw back his head like a crooner, "Not that I would put myself above anyone," he said, "I condemn no man. Even Jesus Christ knew sinners because he knew himself. But if we sin in our minds, if we understand sinners, forgive sinners, even pay taxes to have them rehabilitated—does that mean we deserve to be their victims?"

"Sinners rehabilitated?" Sam said, "he believes this?"

Jesus said, "He thinks they do."

When the echo of Richard's words stopped, the silence was louder than their cheers and stomping had been, louder than the electronic cacophony, Richard's voice dropped nearly to a whisper, "Did Jesus Christ deserve to be crucified?" he said.

The crowd vibrated with angry shouts, clapping, stamping feet, the entire Bowl shook, Richard was triumphant, "Who should we call on for help?" he said, "should we petition the Communist-infiltrated Congress that tells women to kill babes in the womb?"

Someone in the crowd screamed, "Save a fetus for Jesus!"

"Thank you, sister," Richard said, "do you think Communism is dead? I've been called a neo-McCarthyite looking for Communists under beds. But could there be neo-Communists—hidden terrorists—*in* the beds of lawmakers and judges—while America sleeps?"

The crowd was erupting again but Richard's raised arms checked them, "Who shall we petition?" he said, "—the courts where the Communists sit hiding in the robes of democracy—dumping murderers and rapists—immigrant terrorists—into our streets?"

Above the noise of the crowd a single scream rose like the song of someone crazed and finally tore off in jagged sobs.

"Yes," Richard said, "we are in pain! They've taken down the Berlin Wall—the Iron Curtain—now they're everywhere—in our neighborhoods, in our schools, in our workplaces, secret cells of neo-Communists—Muslims, immigrants, terrorists—"

A voice in the crowd shrieked, "Terrorists!"

"Terrorists!" several of the crowd shrieked together, then the whole Bowl took up the chant, the crowd was larger now, and men in work clothes stood beside the pale ones in polyester suits—in fact, surrounded them. "Get them! Get the Terrorists!"

After a few minutes Richard broke in, "Shall we write a petition about the Terrorists *to* the Terrorists in Congress? Tell the Terrorists about themselves?" The crowd continued behind Richard like a chorus, he went on, "Shall we petition the Terrorists? Or shall we petition the American people? Shall we petition each other? Shall we hear from the American people who came to share their stories and the victimization they rose above to be here tonight?"

The crowd cheered like Romans at the games, Jesus no longer beside her, Sam moved into the aisle, camera rolling, zoomed in on the crowd faces of rage close and sharp, Richard's face too—the mouth more sensual than she'd seen before, his eyes with the blue streaks almost neon. For some reason she wondered what it was like for Toledo, Richard as a father, she shivered violently at the thought.

A second spot came up at the side of the stage, a man walked shakily into it, Richard dancing in from the other side, shaking the man's hand, sticking the mike in his face, the man as if he would fall, round face beaming under plastered-down hair, voice halted, stuttering, saying how last week he'd been happy, his wife expecting their second child—his only son—but when he'd arrived home from a business trip, his wife had been in bed—struck dumb, his house robbed—thieves had rolled up a van and cleaned it out—left him nothing but his pregnant wife.

The crowd cheered furiously as if the victim had won a prize, he stood with tears on his cheeks while Richard pumped his arm and thanked him for sharing, the man told the crowd they could sign up to be members of Victims Vigilant, ushers arrived in the aisles with sign-up lists and baskets for donations. Richard led the victim off-stage and brought on a woman, polyester and blue hair, she'd been mugged, had her collarbone broken, right outside her house, crowd rising rageful, Richard holding up the victim, she in a near swoon, spots up on the ushers again, their forms and donation cans, woman victim led off, next a teenage boy—crewcut letterman from Berkeley High, who'd been with his girlfriend after a school dance—parked in his dad's car, maybe they shouldn't have been but they were only talking about their college plans, when they could get married, then a group of hoods had squealed up on motorcycles and surrounded the car, broken the windshield, slashed the tires and took his girlfriend—never to be seen again, the boy spit it all out in a gush then stood staring blankly, sweat rivers streaking his made-up cheeks, dumb silence, as if he couldn't remember his speech.

"Terry here believes his girlfriend was kidnapped because he failed her," Richard said, "what do you think?"

The crowd shrieked, "Terrorists!" Terry stood wringing his hands, waiting for punishment till Richard led him off.

The crowd transformed into a twisting beast straining its chains, a man broke loose and rushed up to the front of the stage, he waved his arms crazily at Richard, said, "I hope you are Joe McCarthy raised from the dead!" His friends rushed up and flanked him, whether in support or to cart him away. Richard came to the edge of the stage, leaned down, shook the maniac's hand, said, "I feel what you're feeling, brother!"

The man shrieked, "Joe McCarthy—"

"I'm not Joe McCarthy," Richard cut in, "but I think I understand him. If you haven't joined Victims Vigilant yet, I want to welcome you in advance. We need you, brother—I need you!"

The man said, "I'm going to give you everything I got—" broke off, reached for his wallet, a spotlight on him now, his face turning dead white, he staring blankly at Richard.

Richard said, "Friend—are you all right?"

"My wallet—it's gone!"

The crowd surged into the aisles as the man screamed, "She was next to me—"

The crowd screamed, "Terrorist!"

Another spotlight swung out into the crowd and picked up a

young woman with olive skin and black hair. The din rose, crowd swelled like a tidal wave, the woman's mouth opened, eyes froze as a purse was raised, a hand grabbed a wallet out of it. The crowd was in a lather now, it seemed to roll the woman and the maniac up on the stage, dozens of hands tore at the woman, she squatting down, covering her face, the shouting one continuous growl till a gunshot reverberated throughout the Bowl, the stage stormed by white uniforms and helmets—the same as earlier at the Circus, again their white-gloved hands held M-16s ready.

The crowd panicked, Richard shouted into the mike but his voice was lost in the roar, the dark woman was pulled down, her screams cut off as she sank into the bowels of the crowd, Sam tried to push through but was squeezed off, the woman disappeared, Richard's voice came back, louder, "Join hands—join hands!" Most did, country musac whined through the sound system and the crowd swayed to it in a weird caricature of a protest demonstration.

Richard came back to the mike, raised his arms, palms spread, hushing them, trying to speak but still not heard, trying again, finally shouting, "I've just received word that the men you see in white are called the Citizens," he said, "—ordinary citizens tired of the impotent LAPD. They say they're here to protect innocent people from Terrorists who have more protection under the law than law-abiding folk—I understand their frustration! Still I want to say for the record, friends, I deplore any violence—no matter what side it's on—please, join Victims Vigilant and render violent defense unnecessary!"

As Richard talked, the Citizens seemed to increase in numbers, the crowd was mesmerized, "Press!" Sam said, held the camera high, pushed her way out.

The van was standing at the gate, Jesus behind the wheel, "Ten o'clock news," she said to the security guard, climbed in the van, and when they were back on the freeway, Jesus said he'd seen the Citizens arrive, they had police radios.

When they got to San Toledo it was still almost as crowded as earlier, Jesus drove the van up the road where they always parked it, they sat in silence for awhile—Sam thinking that in spite of the madness of the evening, she hadn't felt so relaxed in months, Jesus said he left her in the Bowl in order to get better shots of the action, when the Citizens came in and he saw what was going down, he stayed out because his presence would only have made it worse.

"They would've killed you," Sam said.

"But if you hadn't come out, I would have come after you," Jesus said, "I wanted you to know."

"You shouldn't—"

Sam broke off because Jesus turned so sharply toward her, said, "It's not about that," leaned across the space between them and softly kissed her cheek, "Bring the tape," he said and got out of the van.

Sam sat shuddering, whether with his warmth or the horror at the Bowl, wondering what she would have done if they'd gone after Jesus the way they had the woman with the olive skin, if he'd died there?

Toledo was pacing around the courtyard with a cell phone and a bottle of Courvoisier, his eyes bloodshot, hands shaking, Cheekbones on another phone, Jesus with his camera, on-light blinking, talking about the Citizens—and Richard. Toledo said he knew, he'd seen it—the whole party had—on his cable channel, Playback, the cameras fed directly to it, "I saw everything you shot—at the Circus and the Bowl," Toledo said, looking at Sam.

She said, "Playback—another director's prerogative?"

"I didn't want to tell you till I was sure it would go through."

Cheekbones said, "He wanted to tell you on camera."

"We have to talk," Jesus said.

Sam said, "It changes everything."

"I don't know what I'm going to tell the investors," Toledo said, "but we're cutting your footage into the movie."

Playback was the only channel that carried the Bowl story, viewers called the channel phone number and asked if they were watching a movie or what? Radio news said nothing about the Bowl incident—the woman who went down in the crowd—it might never have happened, like the things that happen every day and go unreported.

"Media defining reality," Sam said.

Toledo said, "That's why we got Playback."

"So we can be the definers—what will be the difference?"

"Art isn't about definition," Toledo said, "it just reveals what hasn't been seen."

Sam said, "Like the sculptor reveals the form in the marble."

Toledo said, "Yes!"

"But we have no control over it—or responsibility if it's misused?"

"Can't put the genie back," Cheekbones said.

Sam said, "What about that woman at the Bowl? What if our revealing was part of what happened?"

Jesus said, "You felt responsible for the mugger and now the woman. Do you feel responsible for everything that happens around you?"

"You mean like paranoia?"

"You know what I mean."

She did. "Maybe not responsible *for* but definitely *to*."

"That's what we're doing, isn't it?

"Being responsible *to*" Toledo said, "—brilliant!" He bowed and started to back away, said, "mademoiselle l'auteur."

Sam said, "I've got something I want on camera, too. Why did you tell me Cheekbones took Prozac?"

Cheekbones said, "Oh-oh.," got a camera, said, "are we on Playback?"

Jesus said, "No."

"Why?" Sam said to Toledo.

"Because I didn't want to have this conversation."

"What is this conversation?"

"Truth—right? Andy and I get high together."

"And she almost dies—but you just go right on?"

"We're not—no more free-basing."

"How long do you think that'll last?"

"She's been in treatment," he said, "—it's called harm reduction."

"You mean you supplying her?"

"That way I know how much she's using."

"How much does it take to kill yourself free-basing?"

"This is about something else, isn't it?"

"What it's about is I want you to stop—both of you."

"Stop?"

"The coke."

Toledo laughed, said, "Anything else you want us to stop?"

"Meta-directing."

"Aren't we all doing that? Andy rescues you in the chopper, you and Jesus go to the Bowl, now you want to stop us using coke. Who defines meta-directing?"

He was right, Sam said, "I'm afraid about the coke."

"Are you afraid about Andy and me?"

"No."

"That's what I'm afraid of—that you don't care."

"I didn't say that—but how would I know? I don't know who you are—what's you and what's the coke. You test me on something I don't have the answer to."

Toledo was silent, pacing, finally saying, "This is exactly right—you're Flannery now."

"He means you've got him by the nuts," Cheekbones said, "so where's the shit?"

Toledo said, "Now wait a minute, I didn't agree to that."

Jesus said, "That's what I heard."

They covered every inch of San Toledo, looking for his stashes,

Cheekbones was merciless, every time he would say that was all there was, she'd go on, he had it in every room, even the bathrooms, when Cheekbones said they had it all, they went outside where the courtyard was still full of people, Cheekbones said, "We can't burn this stuff, everyone'll get wired," they took the chopper instead, Toledo piloting, Jesus shooting, Cheekbones and Sam cutting open the bags, sending it all out to sea.

When finally they slept, Toledo woke Sam to tell about a dream, Mozart's *Jupiter*, music was often in his dreams but this was different, his father was humming it the way he used to when Toledo was a child, "Weird," he said, "—my father is a bastard and I hate him as much as I love Mozart—how could a man like him have Mozart?"

"Is that all the dream was," Sam said, "—music?"

"He was shouting at me the way he used to when I wouldn't fight—he hated me for that."

"Wouldn't fight who?" Sam said.

"School boys—macho rites of passage."

"You mean boys tried to fight with you and you refused?"

"I was afraid I'd kill someone."

"I know the feeling," Sam said, "tonight when they attacked that woman—if I hadn't had the camera to show me how useless it was, I don't know what I would have done."

"You would have fought to defend her," Toledo said, "—even to the death?"

"I might have died trying."

"That's the saddest thing—to feel you could kill. If anything had happened to you tonight, I'd have gone after him till one of us was dead."

"Your father," Sam said, "—you think he's involved with the Citizens?"

"Damn if I know. He's gotten more rightist over the years, I never thought he'd go this far, maybe he has Alzheimer's."

"Sure he just didn't want to be in the movie?"

"Christ! He's always wanted that—I always said no."

"Now you've got a movie anyone can get in."

"We," Toledo said, "we've got a movie everyone can get in."

Sam said, "Right—but are we ready for it?"

"Shit, I feel like a kid again—never knowing what he'll do, getting through everything just thinking about leaving, when I could do that and be rid of him. The first time he offered to fund one of my movies, I was afraid of this but I thought I could control it."

"Sounds like you did—till now."

"Did I? Today made me ask that question. I did the Vietnam movie because it made him furious—and then it took my soul—just what I was afraid of with him."

"Took your soul? I thought Vietnam took America's soul."

"Same thing."

Sam said, "When the correspondent joined the massacre, that was us—observer as participant—right. But owning it—isn't that getting it back?"

"I guess that's the question."

Sam lay awake thinking about Richard, how he might have her novel, not that Victims Vigilant or the Citizens were in it literally, just the part about everyone can get in, she let him in, she didn't even tell Toledo he could have her novel, she had to tell him.

Six

Playback became hot, they had to hire a staff to handle the calls and mail, the problem that rapidly came to light was location shooting, it could be a mob affair, they thought about going outside LA but couldn't bring themselves to sacrifice the realism—there's only one LA. The Saturday they were to shoot the first script sequence, there was grid-lock on the Santa Monica by 4 am, a battalion of CHP in cars and cycles and another in choppers overhead, Sam thought they were waiting for a permit violation in order to shut down till she saw them jockeying for position like everyone else, production crew went around and told the spectators they could see everything better from their TV sets, the crowd laughed and applauded— wasn't this the movie? They didn't want to see, it would be replayed and replayed, they wanted to be in the movie, they played to the documentary cameras, didn't tolerate being butted out or blocked, motherfucker was the only word distinguishable from the noise, a blond bodybuilder climbed up on his car and stripped, it caught on and clothes flew everywhere.

When light began to seep through the smog, it brought along the broadcast media and cable channels—not to be outdone by Playback. Toledo said it was a first—a hit before shooting so much as a foot of film, "If the crowd doesn't make it impossible to shoot," Sam said.

"Don't worry," Toledo said, "I have a way with the CHP."

Jesus said, "Yeah, they know who we are—but do they know who they are?"

"The Citizens," Sam said, "or is that the LAPD?"

Cheekbones had it covered, of course. "The investors are talking about requesting the National Guard for security on location," she said.

"Holy shit—that's it," Toledo said, "it's what Sam wrote, it's the novel—Medialennium a totalitarian order based on the economics and politics of information control—right? The middle class as we know it has disappeared—Medialennium the new feudalism—the new company store that provides all basic needs—company-owned housing, transportation, food and clothing from the corporate chains—you charge against your pay—entertainment at corporate theaters, discos, restaurants—where you also charge, no real money—no need of it because you can only spend it in company facilities anyway—there aren't any others. Move your money around with a voiceprint—more secure than a credit card—and it means everyone is printed, everyone is controllable—shit!"

Toledo was beside himself, he went on, "Medialennium the new corporate read old corporate-owned—economy. If you don't work for Medialennium, you don't work," he said, "the only other choices are the military—privatized so also corporate-controlled—and crime—also organized and owned by Medialennium. Here's where the National Guard comes in—we couldn't buy the kind of military state atmosphere they'll create just by being everywhere we shoot. In Medialennium the Guard has become the domestic security force—ostensibly to keep the public peace and check any activity against the state, but really to carry out more repressive measures than Medialennium wants to be identified with— Victims Vigilant—shit, we could bring them in as the front for a Medialennium-owned vigilante goon squad—like the Citizens, only with different uniforms—brown, if we dare, and red helmets with black sentry decals—call them the Sentry! They stage terrorist activity to justify repression and keep the level of fear high enough to make opposition suicide—what do you think?"

Sam said, "You mean bring Victims Vigilant into the scripted movie? Suppose the organization *is* a front for the Citizens?"

"If true, we'll find out."

"And then what?"

"We don't even know who or what Victims Vigilant is," Jesus said.

Sam said, "Except Richard was there."

"But we don't know how involved," Toledo said.

Cheekbones said, "We know he's a funder—part of the We."

"How?" Sam said. Cheekbones raised her arm, of course, she always handled Toledo's funding, Richard always funded Toledo's movies, why was she being so unreasonable about this, she said, "So do you think there's a connection—his being a funder and at the Bowl tonight?"

Toledo said, "I'll find out."

"Find out if they can take direction," Sam said.

Jesus said, "Who would direct the National Guard?"

Toledo said, "Point—but if they want to be in the movie—like everyone else, we direct them."

"We," Sam said, "or you?"

Toledo said, "Meaning you still don't trust me?"

"I don't trust them—I don't trust power."

"Okay," Toledo said, "you're two and I'm one—if I get out of line—or thrown into the brier patch of power, you two veto me—I swear!"

"That'll be three vetoing you," Cheekbones said.

"Christ," Sam said, here she'd been scrambling for her piece of the power and it never occurred to her they'd left Cheekbones out altogether. "Thank you," she said. Cheekbones smiled like she knew, of course she'd known all along, but her smile wasn't bitter or superior, it was a welcome, welcome to the reality behind the White curtain.

"It's a lot of people and a lot of different programs to juggle all at once," Jesus said, "we could still lose the movie."

"Or make one of the greats," Toledo said, "suppose we research it and then look at the options."

Cheekbones would talk to the investors and set up the liaison and communications about the Guard. Toledo would take on his father. Whether it was that prospect or just the shoot, he was different today, his face light-filled, voice low, body in constant motion, Sam wondered if he'd used the coke to slow down, even shut down some essential spring in himself, some pain, though she didn't know why she thought that, again he reminded her of Jean Louis Barrault, every movement fit, as if he didn't need vocal language, it was merely accompaniment, she was fascinated, he got a squad of CHP to set up a road block so they'd have enough room to shoot the freeway sequence. Sam was to drive a white Ferrari—the red Maserati was too macho for Flannery, Toledo said—Flannery wore femininity like a costume, but that was only the first layer and like Salome's veils, it was designed to hide—and hint at—the next, "This broad knows her stuff," he said.

Sam said, "A manipulator?"

Toledo stopped, studied her. "What do you think?"

She was stunned. "You really want to know?".

"I'm making your movie of your novel, Sam, talk to me," he said.

She bit her tongue to keep from saying I thought *we* were making the movie, when she could she said, "She's playing a role—the one she has to play for Medialennium—but there's more to her."

"Okay, she's Medialennium's instrument of power—what else?"

"A kind of innocent."

He moved around her, turning, holding his head, "Ingenuous," he said, "—no inherent guile—only the requirements of the role?"

"Or maybe that's how she thinks of herself."

"Because..?"

"Does there have to be a because?" she said.

"You know there does."

She did. "Because to think she is the role is too terrifying."

"Is she the role?"

"No."

"So another kind of power beneath the Medialennium power."

Another kind of power, the words riveted, "I have to tell you something," Sam said, not knowing what she meant till she blurted out, "I met Richard."

Toledo moved away, left the room, ran to the beach, they followed him, he charged into the waves like that first day, shadow-boxing, lost, sprawled in the foam till Sam went, told him about meeting Richard at the Parthenon, her apartment with nothing in it, the dinner, the room over the restaurant. "So he has the movie," Toledo said.

Sam knew it was true for the first time, she was hollow, scraped, her insides ripped out, over-reaction of course, she covered with, "The novel's not the movie."

"But the movie is the novel."

"How can you say that—you never read it?"

"I'm not talking about the plot, we may have changed some things, I'm talking about the interior—you."

Sam said, "Why does that feel like flattery?"

"Because you don't believe in yourself—or me. Don't make me him!"

"Him?"

"You know what I mean—Richard!"

"How could I do that when I don't even know him?"

"Goddammit, quit playing the innocent!"

Sam countered, "Maybe it's because you keep playing the director! Yeah, yeah, we're co-directors, but really it's you. You know how to direct, I know how to write, Jesus knows how to shoot, and Cheekbones knows how to deal with the real world. You're the director."

"So I can play benevolence but I still get the rage for the worst tyrant?" Toledo said.

"What you don't *get* is the rage—as you call it—of being controlled."

Toledo's face went dark. "You think I don't know about being controlled? What about Richard?"

"What about him? What did he do to you?"

"You saw him on stage—the way he distorts everything, uses everyone for his games—used you!"

"I should've told you about him," Sam said, "I don't know why I didn't—except he asked me not to—like you wouldn't let him help if you knew. I guess I wanted his help."

"Why didn't you accept his offer?"

"Offer?"

"He did make an offer—to buy you out."

"Well not in so many words—he asked if you had made me an offer—like if you had, he would beat it, like paying for what he'd stolen made it Faustian."

"So he raped you and then proposed—that's what he does!"

"I guess—metaphorically."

He stared furiously, said, "A novel lives, it's not a goddam metaphor!"

"That's what he did to you," Sam said.

"Everybody—it's what he does to everybody!"

"But with you it was more personal," she said. Toledo said nothing, walked away like someone she'd never met, someone defeated. "Then how can we bring him into the movie?" she said.

He came back, "We have to—he's already in it, besides, I should've met him head-on years ago."

"Isn't that going to be too personal?"

"Isn't this movie—your novel—too personal? Look, you're

right where Flannery is in the movie, she's surviving but she thinks she sold out."

"But I didn't sell out to Richard."

"Not in a personal way but he's funding it, you knew he would because he told you. And isn't the novel your survival? I mean how important is making this movie to you? Maybe you could go back to psych nursing, you could survive in that sense, but what about your soul? You can give up art but it doesn't give you up."

Sam was shocked by his words, eyes blurry she said, "You're feeling now because you gave up the coke."

"Is that your professional opinion?"

"I mean no one ever said that to me—I never said that to me."

"I know what it's like to live with the terrible need to make something out there that lives." They were squatting in the sand, he sat back, tear-bright eyes.

Sam said, "Let's do it then."

They had a short discussion about whether to hold this documentary footage, not feed it into Playback, if they did, they would start having secrets, what would stop them from doing that with each other, it would change everything, if they didn't Richard would know everything. "It won't matter," Toledo said, "he doesn't believe in anything he doesn't define, he'll just think we're acting, he won't believe anything we say."

Sam's costume was a corporate chic adaptation of Victorian elegance in peacock blue velvet, lilac silk, black lace boots, and the hair Toledo wanted—he had won that battle too—honey brown with streaks, "I look like I stepped out of Sigmund Freud's bordello," she said, Toledo laughed, she laughed, but truth—she barely recognized her face, Toledo liked it that way—the surprise in her eyes when she looked in the Ferrari's rearview mirror, a kind of cross between a paranoid runaway and a Vogue model.

The opening sequence would be a montage—aerial shots of the Ferrari on the Santa Monica intercut with Toledo's blood-camouflage jungle-hopper overhead—he in his usual costume of cutoffs and leather vest impeccably styled, hopelessly worn, dusted with coke—except it was baking powder, Cheekbones tasted. The two sequences would be edited with a jumpcut—car and chopper moving in opposite directions, towards each other, closer with each frame, a bow to Hitchcock's opening of *Strangers on a Train.*

The stuntman hired to drive the Ferrari called from his car on the Hollywood Freeway, it was grid-lock back there too, Cheekbones would sub, she'd stunted for stock car flicks one year while trying to land a studio gig, the CHP cleared the freeway for the Ferrari, Jesus commandeered a CHP helicopter and shot Toledo's jungle-hopper—Toledo piloting and doing coke, Sam riding in the police chopper, shooting documentary video, "Am I going to be sorry I gave you that?" Jesus said.

Sam said, "You don't like the other side of the lens?"

"It breaks my concentration."

"The camera or the photographer?" the CHP said.

Jesus said, "Quiet on the set!"

Cheekbones jigged and jagged through the traffic, from the chopper they could see the freeway clearing, Jesus finished shooting the exteriors of Toledo's chopper, the CHP pilot put down on the same penthouse in Beverly Hills Cheekbones had that first night, Toledo put down there too, Cheekbones met them, they all climbed into a limo Cheekbones said belonged to The We, "Do they know what they're funding?" Sam said.

"Money is money," Cheekbones said.

"So how does this work?"

"Meaning?"

Sam said, "Well if Richard's part of the funding, doesn't he have the script?"

"Huh-uh—nobody outside us."

"They're funding a movie when they haven't seen the script?"

"Listen, chickie-chick, those boys don't read. You know what they funded."

"I do?"

"Think about it."

Sam thought, "Not the improv?"

Cheekbones laughed. "Now I see that innocent."

"Maybe it's spelled stupid."

"No, no—what you don't get, what you'll never get, is most people have no idea what could be in your mind."

Sam said, "Unless Richard has the novel."

"Not to worry—he can't read either—no idea what you're up to."

"But do we?"

"We'll work it out."

"Why do you have so much faith?" Sam said.

"Always did, then life burned me and I filled the hole with coke. You came along and I'm back to the dumb believer."

"I guess we all are," Sam said, "—into the valley of death road the six hundred."

"Uh-huh—or, yea though I walk through the valley…"

Sam said, "You're Catholic—that's why you stayed pregnant—tried, I mean?"

"That and feeling like a goddess."

"And when you lost it—"

"One of the holes," Cheekbones said.

"So this is a baby we won't lose."

Police escort complete with sirens accompanied them to the Santa Monica, Jesus assigned a crew to do the aerial shots of the Ferrari, he directed the ground crew, there wasn't time for him to shoot it all, he watched the sun like a jealous lover, "Jesus hates montage sequences with different light qualities," Toledo said, "the picture will jump where it shouldn't—he doesn't know he's the only one who'll see it."

Sam said, "Image isn't fantasy to a cinematographer."

"Maybe not intellectually," Toledo said, "but visual fantasy is still fantasy."

"What do you mean?"

"What we see is as much determined by myth as what we think."

"But isn't that what you said about Richard?" Sam said, "He doesn't believe in anything he doesn't define?"

"The difference is, he thinks his interpretation of myth is the correct one—like a self-appointed biblical court—like he was at the Victims Vigilant show."

"So his interpretation is wrong, but there's still no reality, I don't mean absolute reality but something that goes beyond current myth, consensual reality—like advancement in science. I mean, if what we think—and write—lives, doesn't what we see—help me out, Chuy."

Toledo said, "Chuy?"

"Nickname for Jesus—is it okay?" she said to Jesus.

Jesus said, "Shall we shoot before the next millennium?"

They shot the first script sequence from the chopper, Cheekbones in the Ferrari, charging in and out of the traffic, also stunted, no real travelers permitted, funny how that word, real, moves around, creating all questions, there were near crashes, honking, sirens, finally a black-and-white catching her.

Then it was Sam's turn for the interiors and close exteriors.

Script Sequence

I glance at my image in the rearview mirror—perfectly made up Medialennium property, the driving not mine either, Flannery the agent they bought, maybe suicidal, maybe just drunk with despair at being theirs but what if it's the transfer of power, am I really so pure, so ethical, so good, what a tragedy this power, the Ferrari careens, horns go off, drivers scream out their windows, I straighten the wheel, switch the radio on—Coltrane playing Billy Strayhorn's *Lush Life,* I hum along, wild honking and curses bring me back, I ignore, reach across to the passenger's seat, my camera, run fingers along its edges, make sure it's there, real—the only familiarity left— these clothes, for instance, feel like a high-priced whore—who else would wear nouveau Victorian for work? I'm a doll, skin crawling like hives, whirl of color flashing in the rearview—CHP patrol car, hellbent for the Ferrari—I pull over and stop, the cop gets out, swaggers through the dust, says, "License and registration, Miss," I fumble with the handbag, glovebox, "Are you Samantha Flannery?" he says.

For a moment the name sounds strange yet familiar like someone you used to know.

"Are you on something?" the cop says.

"Consciousness," I say.

"Is that like Ecstasy?"

I laugh, say, "Just tired—Sam Flannery—yes."

"Do you know how fast you were going?"

"Emergency call—no excuse, I know."

He ogles me, says, "You're going to work?"

I reach into the handbag again for a leather badge wallet— Medialennium ID, legitimacy, baptism, confirmation, all of it— open it in his face, say, "Special assignment."

He pales, steps back, salutes. "Sorry, ma'am—I didn't know."

"No problem."

"Escort you?"

"Thanks but it would blow my cover."

"Right," he says, "please Ms. Flannery—call if you ever need anything," he salutes, says, "sorry for the delay."

I laugh furiously, as if this shit is his fault, what is he but Medialennium's lackey, but what am I, I should be over these little airs, some would say prima donna stuff, after six weeks of orientation—boot camp, the image agents call it—yet I still can't believe it, I keep thinking the curtain will fall, someone will yell cut, something real, I drive like hell again—like my insides, the running that used to be for something—to something—the need to create, even when I lost, I won—making the mistakes to learn, doing the work I was here for, so I thought, what a crock, now Flannery's just like everybody else—a shell obsessed with the armor—clothes, make-up, cars, home of dreams—lighthouse on Malibu—Medialennium's final offer—hard bargain, they said—as if I'd been bargaining instead of just too dense to get being owned. Before boot camp I used to tell myself I wouldn't lose my art, just put it in storage—Flannery hasn't sold out, just faced the realities of survival, even Shakespeare worked for the Man. Only when I look inside to check the storage I can't see anyone, nothing, not even the gnawing that drove me, now it's just hating them, hating me hating.

The car phone is ringing, I prolong the moment as if answering the phone will make Flannery of Medialennium final, the ringing stops, starts again, I pick up and say, "Alice in Wonderland—what?"

Sardonic male laughter comes over the line, "I thought your name was Flannery."

"On the tip of my tongue—what's yours?"

"Griff—the Image Center?"

"Griff as in gift or grift—or God forbid, grief?"

He laughs, innocent tone, "God?"

"Oh-oh, reference to forbidden myths—heresy in our midst?"

"You're going to be a gas," Griff says, "long as you last."

"Don't tell me—I'm already suicidal."

"Better let me brief you on your scene—or can you guess?"

"I'm late—"

"For the Governor—remember that part?" Griff says, "—and from what I hear, he's not laughing."

"How many times has he called?"

"Called you—or your boss?"

"How many times did he call me before he called her?"

"Hey, don't tell me you're doing this on purpose?"

"Call it strategy," I say, hoping I can sell that to her.

"That's right, I hear you're into some kind of drama..?"

"Some kind."

"I'm into improv," Griff says, "is it like that?"

"Sort of—bastardized."

"No shit—well, you better have a good line for Toledo—not to mention Soledad."

"Will I feel any pain," I say, "or will death be instantaneous?"

"You'll feel it like your skin."

I groan. "Be sweet and tell Soledad it's strategy?"

"Tell Soledad—anything?"

"I'll explain when I talk to her."

In a hushed voice, Griff says, "This means you're re-imaging the Governor!"

"I didn't tell you that."

"Fuck!"

"Give Cheekbones my love!"

"Cheekbones?" he says.

"I didn't say that, either."

I drive the Ferrari off US 1, onto the beach.

End of Script Sequence

They did retakes, Sam didn't count how many, Toledo gave her pep talks before each, hugs, kisses, she felt less sensation from him than from the camera, but of course that wasn't sensation, lack of it, desensitization tank, something else—that inside rising.

"You okay," Toledo said, "want a break?"

She felt weightless, as if no longer attached to her body—that now existed only on camera.

"Sam—you okay?"

"I don't know—different."

"Being on camera?"

"I don't know—something."

"Talk to me."

"Like an out of body thing."

"What do you mean?"

"Like in the country."

"Birds, bugs?"

Sam laughed. "More like silence."

"Silence—here?" He swept the scene of equipment, cacophony of noise.

"It's crazy—inside—like none of this matters anymore."

He thought for a minute. "So you're either suicidal or in some Zen space. Come to think of it, that's the way I always feel when I'm acting—I just never tried to express it."

"Acting?"

"Yeah, acting—as in the movie—the script."

"But it feels real—that word again. I mean it feels like it's all there is."

"That's acting—the incredible freedom—like your Grotowski—freedom from not doing it."

"From not doing what?"

Toledo paced, said, "Well it's about art but, say, being there, doing it, just as it is—no caveats, no as-ifs, no later."

She craned her neck and kissed his, he shook his head and stopped, she kissed his mouth—still no sensation—she wouldn't even have been sure she'd touched him except for the pressure of his tongue between her lips, she wanted to make love, to sense, but no time, they had to get the next take while there was still light, it was supposed to be sunset so Jesus would use filters, "You're there now, go with it," Toledo said, "make it real."

She said, "Funny how we say that."

"Real is in the mind," Toledo said.

"I thought you said it was in the act."

"Which is in the mind—right?"

"Maybe I need some absolute form..."

He put his arms around her. "Your form feels pretty absolute."

"It feels like I've lost it."

Toledo said, "What do you mean?"

"I can't feel it."

Toledo hugged her so tight she could barely breathe, "Feel that?" he said.

"The pressure."

He looked more closely at her, "You're not kidding—are you okay to shoot?"

"Maybe I'm still in the movie."

"During the takes, what are you thinking about?"

"It's not really me, I'm just playing this role, but what if it is really me? What if it is reality, I just have this fantasy of being an artist."

"So you're not thinking about the governor?"

"No—not—no. Well, I'm humming this love song, wondering why the hell a love song—"

"Love song—*Lush Life*?"

"Well, lost love—what's the difference? Aren't love songs the medium of fantasy—of cultural hype—Hollywood?"

"Except when they're art."

She ignored him, said, "A whore singing love—?"

"Wait," Toledo said, put his arm around her, "who did you lose?"

"Is this going to be Stanislavski?"

"No, Grotowski—do you know you're shaking?"

She didn't, if they hadn't been outside she would've been looking for exits.

"Who," he said, "that shrink you lived with?"

"I'm not like that," she said, "all that mawkish lost love."

He was mercifully silent, they got coffee, he talked to Jesus, Cheekbones, the crew, Sam kept not thinking about his question, ridiculous, she'd stomped out of the shrink thing, never thought about it—well, except the power stuff, how he'd fucked with her head. Toledo came back, said, "What about the lost you? You— Flannery—thinking about selling out, reducing the hope of art to a fantasy."

Lost me, he was right but they did countless takes before she got there, mascara-mud streaming down her face. That was it, they were on to the next scene, she was wrung out—which of course was exactly right. The boat was ready for the surf shots, Toledo would go with that crew. Jesus was in a wet suit with the underwater camera.

Script Sequence

Mascara face, I snap off the radio, drive the Ferrari off US 1 onto the beach, almost to the water then stop with the engine still running, reapply make-up, think how of course I can do this, I've been doing it, going on all my life, what's so different about this, there's the governor, I've seen his movies, love his movies, even the bad ones, something about them, something lost, like me, well isn't that why we go to the movies, to see ourselves, find ourselves, some company in the terror of reality, I walk towards the water, pan the horizon with my eyes as if the answer is somewhere in the dying sun, I run across the sand as if I could reach it—is this who I am, the one who, having lost art, hopes for romance? The Victorian boots sink in the sand, I pull them off, toss them at the fiery sky and take off again towards the sun, into the surf, the peacock velvet skirt floating out in a circle around me, the sky on fire, I wonder has the governor ordered some special effects from his filmmaking days? The fire seems to move towards me as I towards it, tentatively, as to an old lover I haven't seen in too many years to recall his face, only the waves of heat emanating from his body as if *he* were the sun and I gone, my vestige the velvet circle floating out where nothing impedes the sea, not even mortal danger—what is danger to the bodiless mind? I can't imagine why I haven't seen this before, why others haven't—they who still love and anguish—when this takes nothing but vision—mind—this freedom enfolding me like the sea, carrying all to its vastness, where the sun flashes and goes out.

My head seems to break, I hear the pieces fall and see the sky jump crazily while I speed along as if propelled by dolphins.

Shouting, "Cut—goddamn it, cut!"

Script Scene cut

More shouting then the sound stopped, started, stopped like a broken record, bursts of light the same way—light, dark, light, dark, Sam wasn't sure whether she was asleep or awake, face zooming in and out, in, out. Something bobbed in the water—Toledo, his face screwed up with fury—sweetly comical, laughter bubbled up and took Sam over, voices surrounded her—Toledo's mostly—swearing. Jesus said something low she didn't understand but the sound of his voice was nice, she reached towards it—into cold so fierce she couldn't catch her breath, then something landed on her, she had an image of a small dog's legs, puppy legs jumping up and down up and down.

"You all right?"

She heard the words but could not make sense of them, she was coughing and choking, Jesus' voice, his face came into focus—the shadows under his eyes. He was leaning over her with his hands on her chest like CPR. "Your eyes, Chuy," she said, "You should get more sleep."

"I should break your neck!" Toledo said, his face over her now, red as the fire sun, she laughed, started coughing again, Toledo lifted her by the shoulders, said, "What the fuck do you think you're doing?"

She was lying on the sand and they all seemed to be wearing it, "I didn't do it on purpose," she said, "but I wouldn't have missed it."

"I'm fining you," Toledo said, his face white now, "—it's a goddamn fine—you can pay the stunt artist who was supposed to do that scene—out of your own paycheck!"

"My what?" she said.

"You heard me."

"What paycheck?"

"Don't change the subject," Toledo said, "just tell me why. You want to blow the movie—fear of success—is that it?"

She said, "I can't think with you shouting at me."

Toledo's eyes were ice, he spun away, strangled sound, his body squeezing, shaking out sobs, Sam got up with half the beach in the velvet skirt and went to him—he half walking, half running, Jesus reappeared with his camera, more cameras and a monitor arrived on a Jeep. Were the lenses recording them or were they acting for them, did she nearly drown for the camera? She put her arms around Toledo and his sobs, he coughed and said, "Christ-all-fucking-mighty, you scared the shit out of me!"

She noticed he was wearing a wet suit, said, "You were going down, too?"

"What the fuck do you think I am—some Hollywood director who'd kill his grandmother to make a flick?"

"What do you mean—kill?"

"You think I'd let you go down there alone?"

"I wasn't alone—I just didn't know—you were supposed to be in the boat. You couldn't have put on a wet suit in that amount of time."

"What does this mean?" Toledo said.

"Who was the stunt artist?"

"What difference does that make?"

"Cheekbones?"

From behind me Cheekbones said, "She means you expected me to drown."

Toledo laughed—a deep, ugly sound, "You're practically an Olympic swimmer," he said.

Sam said, "Logic has nothing to do with it."

"What in hell are you talking about?" Toledo said.

Cheekbones said, "The way you always know when one of these little incidents will happen to me."

"Incidents?"

"The so-called suicide attempts."

Toledo stared coldly, "You think I'm trying to kill you?"

Cheekbones said, "Trying—no."

"Oh, so I don't have to try—it just comes naturally?"

"No," Cheekbones said, "I don't know, there's just some connection."

Toledo glared at Sam, said. "Something to add?"

Sam said, "Maybe you know—or worry or something."

She took his hand—cold as his eyes, "We had an agreement," he said, "I let you go down and you agreed to come right back up—remember?"

"Down there I didn't—it was different—everything was different."

"How?"

"I don't know—suspended—like stoptime."

"Your eyes have changed," Toledo said, "—maybe you were right to do it—maybe we needed it in a way I can't see yet. But I'm still the director—I'm responsible—okay?"

Sam said, "You're not responsible for this."

"I am—a director is a professional!" Toledo said, "when are you going to get that?"

He ran up the beach, a hovercraft video crew tracked him, Jesus appeared in a jeep, Sam got in feeling even lighter, as if she'd left something in the sea.

"What's the connection?" Jesus said.

"You mean what Cheekbones said? I don't know."

"We need to find out."

"Sorry—"

"Don't confuse things with guilt," he said, "what's that about?"

"Nothing—it was just stupid."

"Naming is power," he said, "don't name yourself—ask why. Every act has a reason."

"It sounds crazy but it was like going home."

"Then the worst has happened," Jesus said.

"You mean I died back there—and I'd rather do it again than remember?"

"It's over," Jesus said, "no matter how bad it was and how bad it feels now, it's over."

"So I'm free?"

"Yes."

"And you?"

"I don't know," he said, "but whatever happens, I'll get back to you."

Sam didn't know what he meant, felt a rushing in her, they set up to shoot the lighthouse scene, sun had long since set, even the afterglow was gone, they'd shoot night-for-night. The house and surrounding area had to be cordoned off with security guards— in addition to the road blocks, the mob came by boat, air, and foot—with portable TVs so they could see Playback and the live shooting at the same time. They decided to do something human with the audience, some interaction that would move them from a fire-chasing mob to an audience—rap sessions at the end of each day that would also be fed into Playback, they'd have a call-in component too—members of the audience would be considered bit actors—which was in Sam's novel, characters acting in a play, the audience as a role. "Perfect," Toledo said, "even in science there's no pure observation. The observer changes what's observed."

"So there's really no control," Sam said, "only the illusion of controlling or being controlled."

"Illusion or delusion?" Cheekbones said.

Script Sequence

The shot opens with a silhouette of the lighthouse against waves climbing the beach, running out over me—Flannery, lying washed up on the sand only a few hundred feet from where I left the Ferrari, bumper-deep in seafoam—coughing, heaving, shaking, the Victorian velvet plastered to me, I roll over and look at the sky—this far from LA you can see the stars, even the Milky Way. An image flashes in my mind—a man pointing up to the sky—for some reason it panics me, I squeeze my eyes to dispel it, roll over again and look towards the lighthouse—my dream home—for the price of my work, my self. Hysteria rises in me, I laugh and cry— back and forth—as I half crawl, half drag myself up the sand and stumble to the Ferrari.

End of Script Sequence

Jesus wanted to shoot the next part mise en scène—one shot of the entire sequence—as opposed to the short takes of montage editing, Toledo didn't see it, Jesus insisted on trying a video preview—he on a dolly with track laid all along Sam's path from the Ferrari in the surf—up the beach to the lighthouse, "Do it the way you think of it," he said to her.

"Toledo said, "I believe I'm still the director?""

They all bowed to him, he laughed.

Video Preview of Script Sequence

I reach the Ferrari, surf foam licking the front bumper, I can't get in it with the wet velvet on, I take the keys from the ignition, go to the back of the car, open the trunk, pull a tee shirt from my valise, shaking, teeth chattering, strip and throw the clothes up on the beach. I don't know whether I'll be able to get the Ferrari out but somehow it matters less, my body has the new lightness, I think every moment is the last—first and last, only, I'm inside—whatever that means. I dry myself and brush off the sand with the tee shirt, pull it on, get in the Ferrari and back it out of the surf, all the way up to the lighthouse, park near the spiral staircase, climb, feel weird, as if I'm breaking in, top of the stairs, small etched sign— FLANNERY—charges through me, I walk the balcony circling the lighthouse, shadows of sea and sky meet and fall away, meet and fall, clouds move and the moon is stripped, its reflection dancing along waves to the beat of gull wings. I want it to be ours—mine and the gulls', sea, sky, clouds, moon—ours, I want to belong to them—belong to someone, somewhere in the universe.

Electronic beep sounds from inside the glass door, I hesitate— everything will change when I go in, the sea will never be this vast, the moon never so high—loneliness never so gentle. The beep gets louder, through the glass walls a videophone monitor flashes violently—MESSAGE—URGENT! MESSAGE—FLANNERY! I close my eyes and concentrate on the after-image of the night, wait for the sliding of the glass door—activated in response to my image read by the electric eye—go to the computer and key in NO PASSWORD. The words on the screen dissolve to Cheekbones' face, surrounded by a cocoon of black hair, "Choose your password and key it in," she says.

I key in FAUST.

Cheekbones smiles, "You're on—why Faust?"

"Too many literary courses. Why do I have a password if you can see it?"

"You're not a unit, you're part of mine."

"That makes me feel so much better."

Cheekbones raises her left eyebrow, "Is this your first morality play?"

"That I remember."

"Ah yes, the amnesiac," she says, "that was your first."

"Depends on what you call a morality play."

"And what did you call that swimming bit?"

Cheekbones' video image dissolves to one of Flannery in the water with the Victorian billowing around her like the leaves of a water lily, she fights the current, is pulled under, her face close-up seems to burst, she floats as if dead, the shot cuts to her body lying on the beach, her face grey and streaked with hair, terrible eyes, not-there eyes—the whole image unlike any reflection of mine I've ever seen, yet I know it as the sculptor knows the form within the stone.

"Ever see yourself on TV?" Cheekbones says.

"Not like this."

"What was it about?"

"I was working something out for the scenario," I say, "—to get a feel for how to play it with Toledo."

Cheekbones smiles sardonically. "Artistic—why don't you come over?"

"Now?"

"I work in the middle of the night—insomniac."

"I don't sleep much either," I say.

"Good—we'll talk."

The videophone screen fades to black and mirror-like, reflects my image, then the video comes back up—a child's face, and a voice-over says, "The program you are about to see was taped live in a neighborhood in Los Angeles—it could be yours. The people are real, the events real—it could be you."

The child stands at a bus stop, her eyes are huge, sunk in their sockets, one infected and tearing down her cheek, dirty white between the green streaks, hair the color of dead daisies, crusted clumps, arms and legs bruised and scabbed, she leaves the light of the bus stop, limps into an alley, cats shriek, rats knock over trash cans, she doesn't react or look, doesn't seem to notice, watches her feet in shoes too big, her limp a kind of shuffle to keep the shoes on but she looks as if she's been doing it so long, she would do it even if the shoes fit or she was barefoot. Other footsteps sound on the brick, I want to call out, warn her, but by a minute change in her own pace, the tilt of her head, I know she's aware, her steps hesitate, she looks up, a shadow moves around a corner only a few feet away, a kind of wheezing sound, as if the other is trying to breathe through water, at the sound the girl turns on a dime, takes off running, stumbling in the shoes, falls on the brick, kicks off the shoes, scrambles up, but the other—a shadow, hat covering face—blocks the way, the girl strikes out with her fists and head, the man laughs himself into a coughing fit, gets her left arm behind her back in breaking spot and pulls up, I see her face turn into tics and twitches then harden into deathmask not changing when she screams, "Come on," he says in a sing-song voice, almost a croon, "come on slut, witch, whore, come on bitch—do what you were born for—" The girl's free fist hits his groin, he shrieks, pulls up on the arm he holds till it breaks and the girl falls limp, deathmask fading to white, "Have to make me do it, don't you, dolly?" the shadow man says, yanks the girl onto his knees and begins to slap her rhythmically, the blows throw her back and forth till she comes to and begins to make anguished, animal sounds. The voice-over says, "The people and events in this taped-live program are real. The man is not yet forty years old yet he has a fatal venereal disease contacted in this or some other alley. This sex addict, this pervert, this *dead man* could be you!"

The image goes to black, I feel suspended, the system has gone down but I stare at the black monitor, waiting for deliverance the way the lover watches the door with helpless fascination after the beloved has gone. I try to figure out what it means, like a TV ad you never get, you just remember the brand. Medialennium. Shorts like this had started the first night of boot camp, there were monitors in every room, always on, the shorts came on anytime, even the middle of other programs, we recruits thought they were just part of the training, our conditioning process, but then we had a class called Production of Approved Myth, the control of crime through "educational TV." We learned that far from being "real" and "taped live," they are highly produced, we learned to make them—shorts like this as well as longer programs—we had to write them, act in them, direct, shoot and edit them. The shows are scheduled to begin airing on general broadcast and cable channels with the fall season, the gun-jumpers could be starting now—this one, for instance, could be airing already on one or more channels—or all of them as, say, a presidential speech that preempts any other show. The only channels Medialennium doesn't control, the very small, hokey locals will be also connected by the new technology that patches into any system.

Fear-hate and pleasure fused—horror flicks, late night "adult" sex-and-violence—taped live, the screen says, delivered to your own home by the cable network you can't turn off—when you work for Medialennium—even if you don't, you can't turn on anything else. Each program begins with the announcement that the following program was taped live, some even have a list of the "real names" of participants, themes include busts for drugs and guns, rape and child molestation, domestic sex-and-violence, all varieties of street crime including murder, assassination, terrorist attacks—complete with taking hostages, prison breaks, gang war, riot, urban siege. All Medialennium employees are required to take a regular part in their making, agents have to participate in the production of at least one educational show per quarter.

But this one is different, I tell myself it's not, it's Medialennium propaganda like the others, I tell myself, stare transfixed at the black glass, arms heavy as if holding something, maybe that child, who repulses me even as I want to run after her, I try to turn the monitor off, remember I can't, think of running. Cheekbones' voice says, "Log on, Flannery," and her image comes back up on the monitor, "Did you get lost?" she says.

For a moment I can't remember my password, I fumble with the keys till it comes back—I key in FAUST, say "Can we meet tomorrow?"

"Something come up?"

"Yes—I forgot I have to meet someone."

"I know—his ego is very bruised," Cheekbones says and laughs, a soft warm rush of mirth, "I like your style."

I say, "I have to meet someone else."

"Who?"

I freeze—what have I been thinking—that Cheekbones could understand—be a friend?

"I'm going to send a car for you," she says, "I think it's TLC time."

"Oh—thanks," I say, hating the gratitude in my voice.

End of Video Preview

Toledo walked into the set, Jesus following with a documentary crew.

"What happened?" Toledo said.

Sam could see them, hear them, but no words formed in her mind, only the image of the child, the feel of her weight, her dying face—Sam's own face sweaty from the lights—must look like hell, she tried to say it was so hot but the words wouldn't come out, she wondered if she was having a stroke—everything seemed to be breaking.

"Come on, baby," Toledo said, "you can cry with us."

Sam wondered why women were always supposed to cry but all she could say was, "The girl—" and the words turned into hiccoughs then sobbing, she had an image of a seawall leaking through cracks, the water driving the cracks wider till it rushed through like a falls, music humming her ear, ear rocking—more than ear, head, arms, body not as much, legs—she felt the parts of her flow into each other as if they were all one piece—Toledo's arms around her, his chest and legs, rocking. "What's that music," she said.

Toledo stopped humming and said, "Mozart."

"I've never heard it before."

"You have—I hum it all the time," he said, "it's the *Jupiter*."

"The one you dream about."

"The first music I ever heard."

Sam said, "Me too," meaning she'd never heard music this way, the way it moved through her from one part to another—connecting everything—like the sea.

"What happened in the scene?" Toledo said.

The girl—Sam had almost forgotten her, sat bolt upright, said, "How did you shoot the scene with the girl?"

"You were brilliant—watching her you were watching yourself," he said, "like a metaphor for what Medialennium has done to you. You must know that's why I didn't tell you about it."

"I don't care about that—how did you shoot it?"

"You still don't trust me,"

Sam stood up and looked for Jesus, said, "Who is she?"

Jesus said, "She wasn't hurt."

Sam was trembling now, so much she had to sit back down to listen, they'd used a double, a dwarf for the rape sequence, even though very little of her was shown in those shots, it was the angles and the editing that gave the effect of seeing more, they said, Sam said, "What about her face?"

"It was two faces—the girl's and the dwarf's," Jesus said.

Toledo said, "What did you think of the editing?"

"Who was the dwarf?" Sam said.

Toledo said, "An actress."

"What's she acted in?"

"Why—what is this?"

"I need to know," Sam said.

"I'll give you her resume."

"Porn?"

"That wasn't on her resume."

"I'm asking you," Sam said, "what kind of work does a dwarf get?"

Toledo said, "What if she has done porn?"

"I want to meet her," Sam said, "I want to meet both of them."

"Why?"

"I don't know."

"Isn't it just that the scene worked?" Toledo said.

"You did it because of the girl at the bus stop I told you about?"

"I thought the image was powerful for you—yes," Toledo said, "are you all right?"

Sam said, "No," then laughed to make a joke of it, but the sobbing started again, when it stopped Toledo picked her up, carried her, she lost track of where, she must have slept, when she opened her eyes she could see the stars through the skylight, though the sky was already grey with dawn, everyone had left the glass house except Toledo and Sam, on the circular bed surrounded by the jungle of equipment. One of Toledo's arms, under her neck, gripping, twitching, the other arm across her breasts, his weight lifting, falling, lifting, her own arms rigid as if straight-jacketed, she tried to relax, sensation rushed through her veins, her muscles burned with fatigue as if holding that child yet straining to get away.

It occurred to her that this was new—allowing herself to be fucked up. She'd never dared before—that she could remember.

Seven

Toledo was ecstatic, he barely ate or slept anymore, the rap sessions with the crowds after each day's shoot were like a drug to him, better than coke, though hardly cheaper, the cable audience could call in, too. One night a cable audience caller asked when he slept and ate, he always seemed to be on, "This is my food and rest," Toledo said, "don't you get tired of not doing something fantastic?"

"My god—you're brilliant," the caller said, "I hate my life."

"Boredom can kill you. Real work takes complete concentration—it's Zen—ask any guru."

Someone in the shooting crowd said, "Are you a guru?"

"Only in the sense that everyone has something to teach."

"What are you teaching?" another crowd voice said.

"I don't know—maybe just my own bullshit."

"What do you mean?"

"This movie has made me question all my assumptions," Toledo said, "even who I am."

All the media talk shows wanted him, the crew had a pool on which one would call that day, Toledo said they should write this into the script—Medialennium gives Governor Toledo a talk show as part of the re-election campaign.

Cheekbones got Richard Toledo and his Victims Vigilant organization for the movie, the contract stipulated that Richard would recognize production authority including Toledo as director, Sam was afraid of it but she thought that's what got Toledo, directing his father, Cheekbones didn't think Richard would do it, neither did Sam, Jesus said whether he would or wouldn't, it was the movie. The day the negotiations were complete and the contract drawn, Toledo was so charged he decided to have the signing take place after the shoot that night at a celebration that would also be Richard's debut into the documentary—except for the footage Jesus and Sam had shot at the Bowl.

"Who'd've thought this movie would bring me closer to the old bastard?" Toledo said.

Sam said, "It feels like the movie brings everything closer."

"Close as Freud."

"Desire for the mother is really passion for the father's power?"

Toledo said, "Maybe it's kill or be killed."

Now that Richard was in the movie, he increased his funding, money no object, they could shoot all the scenes in the same sequence that would be used for the final edit—an unheard of extravagance, what Toledo had always wanted to do, his realistic style would be expressed not only in the images but in the real-time development of plot and character—especially vital to this movie because of the documentary aspect.

The day's location was a Beverly Hills mansion complete with marble columns, Toledo and Cheekbones had owned and lived in it during their marriage, after the divorce Richard had bought it as an investment and was renting it to a Hollywood director who was away on location in Greece, "It's perfect for Cheekbones' house," Toledo said and grinned the way he always did when he called her Cheekbones, "It *is* hers—her art," he said, "she remodeled it and decorated it—you'll see her the way she was back then—perfect for the part."

They used Richard's grey Jag for the car Cheekbones sends to pick Flannery up for the meeting. The chauffeur was Griff, the Medialennium location operator played by a Black actor and playwright who'd had character roles in several of Toledo's movies. The shoot started on Rodeo Drive as Griff is driving Flannery to Cheekbones' house after her second call. Actual time was 9 pm and the crowd was the biggest yet, Rodeo Drive was cordoned off by the National Guard, the crowd pacified by large monitors situated so everyone could see—and for the promised postshoot rap session.

Broadcast media arrived and complained that no press area had been reserved, they were treated the same as the crowd, Toledo promised them an exclusive after the shoot, there would be an event at San Toledo complete with a critical press release, they would be inside—front row center.

They started shooting the exteriors of the Jag, the traffic so slow Griff and Flannery could be seen through the windows, they had to be in the car for every shot, during the exteriors they couldn't even talk—moving lips might show in the frame, "You don't want to talk anyway," Toledo said to Sam, "you're still back in the lighthouse, the video of that child—give me that Flannery." Sam didn't know which was worse, the light and free Flannery or the one ripped between disgust and pity for that child. Yet something else, something she had seen in the sea.

The Jag interiors they did right there in the middle of Rodeo with National Guardsmen pushing the Jag to get the motion while camera operators shot from dollies rolling on track beside the car doors. Jesus shot from the back seat.

Script Sequence

Shadows on my white linen suit remind me of her bruises, everywhere I look I see some part of her—even my own reflection in the window—her eyes. It's not as though this is the first "educational short" I've seen, the ones in boot camp surely had violence against children—I can't remember exactly, I didn't really watch them—learned to keep my eyes open without seeing, to hear the sound tracks as cacophonous voice rhythms without words, the ones I made didn't have children in them, "Do it like a horror flick," another agent said, it turned out to be the perfect answer, we laughed all the way through production, once I played a hooker who got syphilis, went bonkers and started killing her tricks, the moral—stick with Medialennium call girls. What was the moral of this one—stick with Medialennium kids? How do I know it wasn't real? Who was the child? Not only my art but my mind is in storage—all meaning locked up.

"I caught the video of you on the beach today," Griff says.

"Was it on the evening news?"

"Closed circuit—very exclusive audience."

I say, "Yes?"

"Imaging agents are a select group."

"How did I get in?"

Griff smiles. "There are reasons and reasons."

"The dossier on me must go way back," I say, "are they hard up for hitmen with tits?"

"There are reasons," Griff says.

"You use the same cliché for every occasion?"

This time he glances at me in the rearview, says, "You could play an important role."

"I'm a quick study but could you give me a hint?"

"All in good time," he says, "—a new cliché."

We're up in the Hills now, the streets wind and climb, farther and farther from reality, "Where's the Griff I talked to this afternoon?" I say.

"I'm shocking you?"

"You're Blacker than anyone I've seen so far," I say.

"That's because you've only seen the actors—in front of the curtain."

"Am I shocking you?"

Griff says, "Only your recklessness."

"What do you mean?"

"If you want to die, you will," he says, "there's more than one path."

"Cliché number 3—I liked you better on the phone today."

Griff stops the Jag and takes it out of gear, "I'm more than one person—like you."

"How do you think you know what I'm like?"

"I've read your dossier."

"Fantasy's your trip too?"

We get out of the car, Griff stands and watches over the top of the Jag as I pull at the wrinkled white linen skirt and try to stuff the blue silk blouse back down in the wasteband, "Look fine," he says.

"I shouldn't have worn white."

"The white's good," he says, "especially with the blue."

"Are you going to run in the side door and turn into yet another character in this circus?"

Griff says, "I'll be around."

I turn to the house, the marble columns feel like centuries descending on me, the steps are marble too, so white I wonder who scrubs them, whether they have to watch the videotapes, Griff hinted at a way out—didn't he? Was it another test? The door is oak with a brass knocker in a triangular design—the Medialennium logo—three points abstract calligraphy-like slashes representing the individual's past or personality, the "work" that transforms the individual, and the community of the transformed—Medialennium. The door opens and I walk into the foyer—more scrubbed white marble—to an anteroom of glass—a greenhouse filled with orchids and cactus, in the center a palm so tall it reaches through the open skylight. Soledad appears dressed in an orange bikini, her hipbones as elegant as her cheeks, she smiles and offers her hand, "What a gorgeous suit," she says, "but you shouldn't have dressed up—I should've told you," her handshake is strong, she leads the way into a hexagonal room with a breathtaking view.

"All LA at your feet!" I say.

"Perks are perks."

"Ah yes—my kingdom for a view."

"Is that what you paid for the lighthouse," Cheekbones says, "—your kingdom?"

"What was left of it."

Cheekbones laughs, I follow her across the room, past a huge fireplace surrounded by pillows, to a glass door that opens on a butterfly-shaped pool with colored lights rippling across the water and in the center a black marble woman, delicate yet strong—even her bones almost visible—her face the picture of—what?—struggle? Freedom? On top of her head a video monitor she carries like a basket, "We women always carry something on our heads," I say.

Cheekbones says, "When I moved in here all that white marble nearly sent me running."

"Where did you find this beauty?"

"In the marble."

"It's wonderful," I say, "I didn't know you were an artist—sorry to be so ignorant..."

Cheekbones smiles, "It's not exactly what I'm known for," she says, "—we're all handmaidens. You're an artist too."

"Was," I say.

"In some cultures artists are more organic," Cheekbones says. "—ritual drama, for instance, teaches survival roles."

I study Cheekbones—the black cocoon of hair, the amazing cheekbones—as if they could tell me who she is, I say, "That sounds like some of Moreno's ideas about psychodrama."

"It's because you've studied psychodrama that you're here," she says.

"But I don't know whether I'm ready to use it—this way."

"My job is to understand your concerns and help you work through them."

I turn back to the Black sculpture and wonder how the woman who made her could work through anything for Medialennium, Cheekbones says, "what do you think of the colored lights?"

"Nice action," I say, "—butterfly in flight—" break off, embarrassed.

Cheekbones says, "But—"

"The sculpture is so important—I'd like to see it in a more natural setting—like the room where the tree grows through the skylight."

"That's what I told Toledo when we lived here together," Cheekbones says, "lose the colored lights."

"What is it with men that they have to put women in water?"

"Symbol of the womb—regeneration."

"And feeling—maybe contained by the water?"

"That's the psych nurse," Cheekbones says and looks at me as if to see all the way into my core, "—something to drink?"

"Thanks—whatever you're having."

Cheekbones seems to glide towards a bar at the far end of the pool, takes two bottles of Guinness from a refrigerator, "Beer is going to make me fat but I can't help myself," she says.

"Sure you could drink that much?"

"You don't have to flatter me."

"I'll remember that—if I'm ever tempted."

Cheekbones laughs. "You're going to be a match for that man," she says, "—swim?" and leads the way to a dressing room with a huge wall of closets and drawers, dressing tables, exercise equipment, weights, another wall covered with glass pieces—stained glass, sea glass, mirrored glass—some framed, others bare, several with broken edges—a collage of colored shards joined in a bullet hole. The third wall is covered with steel mesh over vertical bars—prison bars.

"You should be doing this fulltime," I say.

"I just wanted you to know you're not the only one."

"I never expected to meet a kindred soul."

"In Medialennium—vampire of artists—wasn't that what your Governor wrote?"

"Right," I say, "—in a *Macho* interview—the only thing intellectuals buy it for."

"Right—they abhor the skintrade," Cheekbones says and pulls a black bikini out of a drawer, "and if that vampire remark were Toledo's only indiscretion we might be able to save his ass."

"I wondered about that," I say, "—who owns *Macho* now? I thought Medialennium owned everything with circulation."

"You mean why wasn't it censored?"

"Do you think it slipped through?"

Cheekbones laughs, "Maybe so—sometimes the simplest answer is the right one," she says.

"I figure one thing they haven't learned to control is incompetence," I say, "—even among censors."

"But there's still a major difference between you and me—you think you sold out."

"I didn't?"

"Talent can be sold," Cheekbones says, "but talent doesn't make the artist."

"But doesn't the artist's use of talent make art—or propaganda?"

"Put this on your skintrade," Cheekbones says and tosses the bikini to me then swings out the French doors, to the pool.

I turn back to the dressing room, my eye caught by the glass wall sculpture—a section with a surface like the fine cross-hatch of video screen—now lighting up with an image of Toledo, talking into a mike, I lean my head out the door and say, "Is this closed circuit—can Toledo see me?"

"He can't see his own nose—come out here, he's prettier with the pool lights—I knew they were good for something."

I laugh, realize I like her, she's disarming me—anyone who does work like hers can't be vamped out, I believe in art the way some people believe in God—you can't fake the real thing and all that, I look again at the wall—the prison collage—before going out to the pool.

Cheekbones studies me in the black bikini, "Made for you," she says.

"When did you do the dressing room wall?"

"It's in progress."

"It's Medialennium."

"Is it?" she says and glances at the monitor atop the Black Woman's head, "I ordered a dramatist and got an art critic?"

I follow her eyes again to the monitor—which doubles as a bug? "I'm a hopeless rebel," I say.

"Is that why you stood Toledo up?"

Toledo's image fills the monitor screen, his eyes like black ice, "You're asking if I was stood up," he says, "—by the maskmaker?"

The interviewer says, "You mean Sam Flannery— Medialennium's newest acquisition?"

Toledo grins coldly at the camera and waves in a caricature of the home movie subject, "The same—Ms. Maskmaker—maybe even Doctor—God help me. But liberated or not, the lady is a vamp."

I say, "When was this taped?"

"It wasn't."

"Isn't that the Circus—he's not still there?"

"He lives there—upstairs—don't you read *Fame* magazine?"

"Only in the dentist's office—I haven't had my teeth cleaned this year," I say, "—is he on TV all the time—or did something happen?"

"Something happened."

"You don't mean he's on because of me?" I say, "—oh shit!"

"Your little tryst was supposed to be the pre-campaign launch event—what happened to you?"

"I wanted to get his attention."

"By drowning?"

"I didn't do that on purpose."

"How did you do it?"

"I was wading and got out too far."

"Your dossier says you're an advanced swimmer," Cheekbones says, "I have to know if you're suicidal."

I walk to the edge of the pool and say, "I just never sold myself before."

Cheekbones laughs, "I'm not laughing at you—well, maybe a little," she says, "White ladies kill me sometimes—never sold yourself before!"

I dive into the pool and want it to be the sea, to continue fathoms deep where the current rules and all bodies are the same—nothing unique, no more nor less than clumps of sea grass being carried by the vastness. The worse part is I suspect Cheekbones is right—I have sold myself before, I just don't remember, maybe that's the whole amnesia bit. I swim underwater, ahead a shadow image reminds me of the girl in the video short—craning her neck, looking for someone, watching like an ambusher, checking her reflection, trying to be a chameleon and change the mask of her face to look like the one she waits for, the enemy she fears but fears more that he won't come, that the part of her he has will be forever lost.

My head breaks the pool surface, "Now I get it," Cheekbones says, "you're a dolphin. You just go down there to play while us dumb humanoids run around getting into diving gear—because we can't do it!"

I laugh and say, "I wish you weren't so nice—"

"Don't worry, I'm not."

"When do we get to that part?"

"Coming up," Cheekbones says and points to the monitor on the Black Woman's head—Toledo again.

"Playing his usual role," I say, "the Dostoyevskian character with a compulsion to tell the truth?"

"His truth," Cheekbones says.

The video picture moves into a close-up as the off-screen interviewer says, "Governor, why did you give up making movies?"

"I got tired of artistic failures that made money—mostly for my father—I especially couldn't forgive them for that."

The interviewer says, "Have you ever tried making one that wouldn't be big box office?"

"I don't seem to have the knack—otherwise known as genius."

"Who was your greatest influence?"

"Hemingway," Toledo says, "when he couldn't write—which was most of the time—he turned to great White hunting—where he could fail at macho and have something to write about. My great White hunt is politics."

The video picture flashpans to the Circus crowd—now Toledo's audience—laughing, clapping, making animal grunts and cries.

"Are you going to fail at it and make a movie? Is the Third World Party candidate—Jesus Cahero—going to beat you?" the interviewer says, using the English pronunciation, Jeezus.

Cheekbones says, "Like we're running Toledo against the son of God—I told them to use bilingual interviewers!"

Microphones proliferate around Toledo, who says, "If the voters had any sense he would—but no danger of that."

"Takes a White man to raise a lantern to his inferiors," I say, "think he writes his own stuff?"

"What I am wondering," Cheekbones says, "is who writes yours? But your man here has too damn much ego to let anyone write for him—which is why fixing the fool's image is going to make or break you." Cheekbones snaps her fingers and the picture goes to black, she watches me swim over and pull out of the pool, "The only problem with having a dolphin," she says and hands me a Guinness, "is that we could lose the camera operator."

"Do you have a camera on me all the time?"

"Only when we can find you."

"Why?"

"You've been to boot camp—this is OCS."

"What about you," I say, "are you always on someone's monitor too?"

"Token Black—are you kidding?"

"What about now—are we entertaining some security don's dinner guests?"

"If we are—want to up the ratings?" Cheekbones gets into a racing crouch on the pool edge, "—on your mark!"

I crouch, Cheekbones calls it and we dive in, both of us fast but I win by a hand, Cheekbones shakes the water out of her eyes, "Didn't you ever hear you're supposed to let the boss win?" she says.

"Double or nothing?"

"This time I take no prisoners," Cheekbones says, she gets out of the pool and strips her bikini.

I follow and jettison mine, we make the dive and I torpedo down to the other end but when I hit and come up, Cheekbones is there—laughing, "How do you think I did that?" she says.

"Token Blacks have to be better."

"You're a better swimmer—you know it." She pulls up out of the water and plops on the pool edge—easy in her nakedness, reaching for the beer, "I beat you because I'm a killer," she says, "the difference between us—motivation. I don't intend to be poor again. I know you hear I passed for White till I married big bad Ray Soledad, but I came up Black—the lightest with the best hair sure, but that was Black enough for Ray Soledad," Cheekbones says, "Black is color, but it's also experience."

I'm still treading water, wondering if I can get out naked with passable ease, "How is Toledo about the Black—or Third World—experience?" I say, "The way he talked about his political game..."

Cheekbones says, "Arrogant and patronizing—like most White liberals."

"The fantasy that if a worthy opponent appeared, he'd be gentleman enough—even happy—to lose gracefully—heroically—to the better man," I say.

Cheekbones says, "*Tale of Two Cities*—what's the word—?"

"Renunciation. *Casablanca*, too."

"Yes—he even imagines he'll be vindicated for holding his corrupt office," Cheekbones says, "as if the only reason he's there is to save the seat for the angels of regeneration."

"The Black angels he's always dreaming about," I say, "who of course will recognize him as the Archangel."

"You do know something about White fantasy."

I feel the warmth of her approval then a charge of fear, I wonder how far into the web I've already come, "It's the only history I have," I say and pull myself up not too close to where she sits on the pool edge.

"At least you know it."

"I suppose it's only because I'm amnesiac about my personal past."

"Medialennium has some concerns about that," Cheekbones says, "you're the first image agent we've brought in who didn't get a unanimous endorsement."

I nod and say, "The unknown—I'm afraid of it too. In fact, I was wondering if the background check turned up anything."

"On the other hand, you have a security advantage—no one else knows who you are, either," Cheekbones says, "Medialennium can create an identity for you—and no one can dispute it."

"The one who didn't vote for me," I say, "was that the reason?"

"See how you assume there was only one," Cheekbones says and laughs, "you know the men voted for you—think there must be a woman who didn't want the competition?"

"Maybe—I'm afraid I'm not that conscious."

"Well, you better think about how you're going to get that way," Cheekbones says, "your no-vote means to find that shrink you lived with."

"Now I see how I got the job—they couldn't find him."

"What would he say about you?" Cheekbones says.

"Anything that's ever been said about women."

"Shit, you're lucky he didn't scramble your frontal lobes," Cheekbones says, "let's hope he doesn't turn up—Toledo could just about get you burned at the stake—without help."

I comfort myself with a feeling that Cheekbones seems to be on my side, I am trusting her again, admiring the way she walks, forgetting her nakedness, she gets more beer and a cigarette case, brings it all back and opens the case, takes out a hand-rolled cigarette, lights it, sweet smell of marijuana. "Tell me how you're going to bag your man," Cheekbones says, and passes the joint.

I shake my head and say, "Thanks."

"It's not heavy—just chill you."

I see she needs this, I take the weed, inhale and cough.

Cheekbones pats my back and says, "Don't tell me you're a virgin, too?"

"Not recently."

Cheekbones laughs and takes the weed again, "You think I'm trying to catch you off guard," she says.

"You're not?"

"I'm just trying to get to know you."

"When you do, will you introduce me?"

Cheekbones passes the weed back, watches me toke, "You know about jokes," she says, "what have you done to find out who you are?"

I feel the grass now, like entering a familiar room. "I traced the route of the bus I arrived in New York on, went to every stop from Chicago—the missing persons bureaus, the office of birth records, the schools, even churches—"

"Why churches?" Cheekbones says.

"Every once in awhile I hear music in my mind that sounds religious—once for two years I did practically nothing but listen to religious music hoping it would jog my memory."

"Do you play anything?"

"I tried piano and picked up some—guitar too—but no breakthroughs."

"What about singing?"

"Not like you."

Cheekbones says, "Then like who?"

"Oh—a kid walking in the rain..."

"Why?"

"Where no one will hear," I say.

"Hear what?"

"The untrained voice."

"Because of what isn't there," Cheekbones says, "or of what is?"

"What do you mean?"

"Sing."

"Now?"

"The oldest song you can remember—a lullaby, maybe—or hymn."

My body begins to tremble, Cheekbones passes the joint back and I inhale deeply, feel the sweet putrid smoke slide around my throat and move into the air pockets of my lungs, feel them open like flowers, exhale, feel myself fly out with the smoke, up where the low clouds wait for what will happen below, wait and listen to Flannery half sing, half hum *Body and Soul*—I don't know where it comes from, it nauseates me, I stumble blindly, "Where's the toilet?" I say.

Cheekbones takes my hand and leads me to the bathroom where I throw up the beer, "I don't always make such a sensational first impression," I say.

Cheekbones sits on the steps of a tub the size of a small swimming pool, "What's it about?" she says.

"I don't know—nerves."

"Were you in love young?"

I hear the words but somehow can't put them together logically,

I think it must be a joke I'm too fucked up to understand, I laugh as if I do.

"Take another toke," Cheekbones says, and holds the joint to my lips—vomit lips—as if that doesn't matter.

"I think it's making me sick."

"Are you in love now?"

I laugh again, feel again the sting of vomit in my throat, shake my head and say, "I'm sitting this dance out."

"What dance?"

"I don't know," I say, "—life?"

"Were you raped?"

She has to repeat it for me to understand, "On the contrary, I'm into sex," I say, feeling the lie.

"I thought you said you were sitting this dance out."

"I was talking about love not sex?" Too late I realize I made it a question. "It's a test, right?" I say.

Cheekbones says nothing, runs water over a wash cloth and gives it to me, then shows me the medicine cabinet where she has mouthwash, toothpaste—even a brush I can use, "Do all your agents throw up?" I say.

"I throw up when I'm upset."

"I don't—I can't remember ever throwing up," I say, then as if it follows logically, "what was it like when people thought you were White?"

Cheekbones doesn't miss a beat, "Like lying," she says.

"I always feel like I'm lying."

"Not knowing who you are is a kind of lie."

I have an image of myself in a mirror, my head begins to float like a balloon, I ride it, follow Cheekbones out of the bathroom, "Does Toledo smoke weed?" I say.

"Toledo does everything but he doesn't get away with it anymore," Cheekbones says, "—that's where you come in. He's got to give up everything he wouldn't do in church."

"Church?" Flannery says, "what's that got to do with me?"

"He's going to do it for you."

"Do what?"

Cheekbones laughs, "That's enough weed for you, girl," she says, "that man's going to give up his evil liberal ways and marry you."

My voice comes out like a croak, "Marry?"

Cheekbones laughs, You make it sound like a death sentence."

"You mean like a psychodrama thing?"

"Like a life thing."

"I thought it was just a re-imaging gig."

"There's no just in re-imaging."

"Wouldn't it be better if you remarried," I say, "—for the Third World component?"

"That's not where Medialennium is going."

"You mean because—was Ray Soledad assassinated by the CIA?"

For a moment, Cheekbones looks as if she'll crack, I can't imagine what Flannery is up to, "Sorry," I say, "sometimes this raving maniac comes out in me."

"You make a better witch than a madwoman," Cheekbones says, "if Soledad had been assassinated by the CIA—do you think I'd be here?"

Yet there had been speculation about whether he was delivered by his own people, "Please," I say, "consider me brain dead."

"Oh no, you don't" Cheekbones says, "—finish what you started."

"I suppose I've always wondered what happened—like some series I missed the end of—sorry."

"You think I'd be dead if I hadn't been part of the hit," Cheekbones says.

"Your suicide attempt back then—I've wondered whether it was a hit that missed."

"I think I'll let you wonder about that," Cheekbones says, she's recovered now, her smile glows enigmatically, "So—you stood up Toledo to get his attention?"

"I've found men like to be curious."

"About you?"

"Any woman."

"That's your problem," Cheekbones says, "Toledo's got to be interested in you—not some abstraction. He hasn't even seen you, all he knows is you're some bitch agent who can make trouble. Rule number 1: don't stand a man up till he's made an investment."

"Same old same old?"

"Just be glad you've had twenty years to learn liberation so you know when you lose it," Cheekbones says

"The slave loves the master—the wife loves her husband," I say, "imagine looking that 'love' straight in the eye?"

"Can you take it?"

"I honestly don't know."

"Are you too nice for this work," Cheekbones says, "do you want to change them for their own good instead of yours?"

"Moi?"

Cheekbones offers the weed again, I shake my head, "See what I mean?" she says, "you're tied in knots this weed can cure but you can't let it happen because you're afraid you'd fall apart."

"Maybe all I am is the knots."

"You have to learn how to use control instead of being used by it."

"Control freak," I say, "is that my diagnosis?"

"Don't even joke about words like diagnosis—labels create their own justification."

Cheekbones offers the weed again, this time I take it, inhale deeply, say, "I hope I won't get too paranoid—but I'm not sure what that means anymore—where the perspective is—whether it even exists."

"Picasso lost it," Cheekbones says, "and found his genius."

"Others have found madness."

"What am I going to do with this psych nurse?" Cheekbones says.

"Vision or madness—that's the question, isn't it?"

Cheekbones inhales, holds the smoke so long I think she must be breathing through her ears, "Quit sitting at my feet," she says, "—you tell me."

I jump into the pool and swim to the Black Woman, I think she's been in my dreams—exactly this way, every detail of her body, the flow of her lines, the solidity—the mass of her, her face looks different as I move around her, once I think she's smiling, even laughing, laughter of goddesses, I race in circles around her, each one closer, the water deeper till I can't stand, must swim—for some reason, faster and faster, finally underwater, she is there too—her feet stand on the shoulders of another Black woman whose arms stretch up and around her legs. I surface to breathe and say, "Why didn't you tell me," but don't wait for an answer, plunge again and face the underwater woman, who has no eyes, her hands—her body—is her vision, I stand behind her and lay my arms and hands on hers, move around to feel every line of her, the warm marble, she's alive with something, I stay down so long Cheekbones comes diving after me, she takes my hand and pulls me up to the surface.

"You going to make a habit of this?" she says.

"Why didn't you tell me about her?"

"Tell you what?"

"That she's there," I say, "—alive!"

Cheekbones laughs so infectiously I follow, "You're not a killer," I say.

"Better not speak too soon."

"Are you doing any sculpting now?"

"Only with flesh and blood."

"Image agents?" I say, "you shape us and we shape the targets?"

Cheekbones gets out of the pool, walks into the dressing room and returns with towels as I pull myself onto the pool edge. We dry ourselves and each other's backs, "Where did you get that term—target," Cheekbones says.

"It just came out."

"Always this cynical?"

"I didn't mean it in the pejorative," I say, "sometimes words come out wrong."

"When you least expect it?"

"I suppose I haven't really thought about it—but yes, because what I was thinking about was the underwater woman—I think I fell in love with her."

Cheekbones laughs and says, "Start thinking about the cynicism—we can use it for Toledo."

"Who could be more cynical than he is?"

"The woman he'll fall for."

"You think he'll play Faust to my Marguerite?"

"The old myths are the deepest."

"I just remembered though, he has seen me," I say, "he told me on the phone this morning—said he saw my job interview, the tape of it was run as a filler in some local newscast. I thought he was drunk."

"He probably was," Cheekbones says, "he was also lying. What he saw was your psychodrama tapes."

"Toledo?"

"Those tapes made the sale."

I say, "Those tapes are confidential! Anyway, where did you get them? Everything I had was stolen from my apartment."

"You haven't figured that out yet?"

I'm stunned. "You don't mean Toledo?"

"I'm going to let you wonder about that, too," Cheekbones says.

"Can I get them back?"

"Deliver Toledo."

Hysteria rises with new waves of nausea, my skin feels as if it belongs to someone else—her agent cynique, who is Flannery, of course—who knows all this talk about art and kindred soul has been pure pragmatism.

Cheekbones says, "Brandy?" and without waiting for an answer, unwinds her arms and legs from the pool edge, walks away with the fluidity of cat, "Talk strategy," she says over her shoulder.

"Why did you say he hadn't seen me?".

"He's seen the psych nurse—the therapist—not the agent."

"Neither have I."

"You're getting there."

I'm burning with the thought of him robbing me, I say, "You want me to vamp him?"

"So he'll never know what hit him."

"Then I can't contact him—we'll have to run into each other."

"That's easy. What you have to focus on is the goal."

"That's what bothers me—how can he beat the Chicano Martin Luther King—with an issue like secession?"

"You think that's going to be carried by any channel except the Spanish-speaking locals? Besides, they'll carry Toledo's wedding, too."

"I wish you'd stop talking about that."

Cheekbones studies me, nods, "The cynicism is good," she says and walks around me, "but try a sweeter delivery—innocence—drive him but not over the edge," she circles again, "the same with your body—I'll talk to Wardrobe."

"Innocence," I say, "now I know I've flipped."

"You are innocent, in a way."

"Sure it's not stupidity?"

"Isn't that the one thing you've never been accused of?" Cheekbones says, "By the way, if you're on the pill, go off."

"Around Toledo?"

"It'll keep you from temptation—as they say."

"Innocence."

"That's what we're selling."

"I think I've been in this play before."

"Was that when you lost your nerve," Cheekbones says, "and forgot the difference between your vision and madness?"

End of Script Sequence

After the shooting was over, Cheekbones said, "Double or nothing," ran and jumped in the pool, she beat Sam to the Black Woman, where they treaded water and talked while the video crew shot from the pool edge.

"You were fantastic," Sam said, "but are you okay?"

"I'll never be the same—but that's no loss."

"I felt like the cockroach in *The Metamorphosis.*"

"You were beautiful."

Sam laughed, her head ached as if she'd been hit, then Cheekbones blurred in front of her eyes, she couldn't do tears now so got ready to dive down to the underwater woman, "Wait," Cheekbones said, "—tonight—be careful."

"What do you mean?" Sam said, but it was too late, Toledo was diving into the pool with his clothes on, he had champagne brought to toast his two stars, we got the bottle and poured it on his head— just as Jesus showed up with the underwater camera. He wanted to retake some of the shots with the underwater woman.

Script Retake

This time as my hands trace her form, I see through the surface of her, into the black marble, the image of the child who was raped in the video short, my hands feel her face—the deathmask—my fingers rub it, try to warm it, as my arms hold the Black woman's legs—and feel the child's broken body. My self.

End of Script Retake

Sam stood up and still saw through water, Jesus turned the camera off and just stayed with her, not touching or talking, she couldn't have explained why she was crying for that child, if that was it, but down there she understood it, there she was Flannery—but where was there and who was she?

"I was into it down there," Jesus said, "like always when I shoot you—but this was the first time I was alone with you."

"What are you saying?"

"I don't know if I'm violating you."

"I don't feel that from you."

"Maybe you do," Jesus said, "and what happens to the film after I shoot it—who's going to edit it?"

"We've said we'd all be there."

"I don't know if I believe that."

"You don't trust Toledo?"

"Maybe it's myself I don't trust."

"Don't leave me with this," she said, he was so tall her arms only reached around his waist, his arms folded around her, they leaned together, rocking like children quieting each other, "Those men won't feel what you do," Sam said.

"There are obstacles."

"What obstacles?"

"You don't know what you feel," he said.

He was right, Sam didn't say anything, his arms tightened then released, "I tend to disappear—but don't worry," he said, "I'm never far away."

There was a driver for the Toledo Productions van to take them back to San Toledo, Sam lay exhausted on the floor with the snarl of equipment and watched the back of Jesus' head, even with her eyes closed she could see him, wanted to ask about the Flannery he shot under water, as if he'd know, she'd forgotten that the contract with Richard would be signed tonight, with the celebration following, she thought of not going back, of leaving—but that was impossible—which was new, leaving had always been the default, now she was naked.

By the time they arrived at San Toledo there were National Guard roadblocks, detours, a corridor of "safe space" separating the villa from the crowd that followed them everywhere, now joined by the unmistakable members of Victims Vigilant, the villa would be a mob scene too—investors, guests, media. Before they left the van, Jesus and Sam sat still for a minute. His eyes were blacker as he disappeared into the crowd, something of her disappeared with him, maybe that Flannery she was under water. But she didn't feel lost.

The contract signing was already taking place in the courtyard, Toledo paced as he talked at media and Playback mikes, Courvoisier dangling from his fingers, the other hand raking his hair, "Nobody could have told me I'd be working with my father," he said, "I'm not even sure how it happened—something about this movie."

"Peace that surpasseth understanding," Richard said, Sam heard his voice before she saw him—sitting on one of those tall director's chairs, wearing the white tux of that night at the Hollywood Bowl.

Toledo started to smile—doubtless at the spectacle of Richard in white, waxing religious—raised his Courvoisier in salute to the small table, complete with papers being carried in by production assistants. Cheekbones carried the signing pen, "Age before beauty," Toledo said, "—my father first." Richard stood up to meet Cheekbones, who seemed to change as she approached him, she gave him the pen then stood as if confused—not the Cheekbones Sam knew.

Richard gave her a charming smile, went to the table, said, "As a representative of Victims Vigilant, I sign our agreement to join this remarkable venture, *American Movie!*"

Toledo went to the table and took the pen from Richard, "My father has probably never said so little about so much," he said and signed then offered his hand to Richard who took it and put his other arm around Toledo, they embraced awkwardly, Toledo's face was purple as he pulled away, called for champagne, no mention made of the movie's co-producers, who apparently weren't required to sign the contract, they let it go, whether because they were worried about Toledo or because they were all under the spell of the Man. Or The Man's money.

Sam drank champagne, reeled through the crowd—too thick for her to get to the lighthouse room so she walked out on the beach, the crowd so dense she managed to evade the documentary cameras, the beach empty except for security guards, who told her to turn back, she too tired to answer and somehow stumbled on till the sound of the waves embraced her mind, she sat on the sand, forgot everything but the feel of it, the sound of the breaking surf, the reflection of moonlight on gleaming foam. The not feeling lost.

Even before she saw the figure walking along the surf, she felt him, his coming was as inevitable as her waiting, "When I arrived tonight and you weren't here, I lost my mind," Richard said.

She knew she should say something—tell him not to talk like that—but her tongue was paralyzed, her body too, she waited barely breathing, watching, "Please," Richard said, "don't pretend I don't exist."

"Are you really a Victims Vigilant believer?"

"Is that what you think of me?"

"I don't know."

"I'm playing a role—undercover, you might say," Richard said, "—the movie will expose the hate-mongers."

"What if we hadn't brought you into the movie?"

"I didn't let myself contemplate that."

"You planned it all, then?"

"When I met you everything changed—"

"You were already with Victims Vigilant," Sam said, "your speech at the Bowl was fascistic!"

"It was a script—yours—"

"My script?"

Richard said, "I was thinking about your novel."

"So you were the one who cleaned out my apartment."

"I didn't know you were that paranoid."

"Sometimes paranoia is true."

"That's ridiculous, it was the way you talked about it, I thought this would fit in. Victims Vigilant—its funders—had contacted me in the past, they needed someone to play the role—someone rich. I admit I wanted to be near you—but had I known you would hate me—"

"It's fascism I hate," Sam said, "anyway, who are its funders?"

"Friends of mine for years—I'm sorry to say—financiers—I didn't know they were taking this direction until I saw the script—and then I wanted to get to the bottom of it," Richard said, "do you believe me?"

"The script?"

"They actually had someone write a script for the Bowl affair. I didn't know—still don't—what it's about, but I wanted to find out—and what better way than to play their part."

Sam said, "And the woman who was attacked?"

"Not in the script."

"What happened to her?"

"I'm afraid I don't know. There was so much confusion, and they had people get me out."

"What people?"

"Aides—guards—I don't know, exactly. Everything happened so fast."

"And now—this contract?"

"I told you, I'm undercover," Richard said. "But you really don't believe me, do you?"

"Undercover—on your own?"

"Of course not, but I'm not at liberty to discuss it."

Sam laughed, somehow the idea of Richard as an undercover operative was too much.

"You think I'm too old?" he said.

She laughed again, waves of hysteria, spilling.

"You are cruel," Richard said, "you've thought of me though—not just the hate-mongers?"

She managed to say, "Of course."

"Thank God. I'm staying on my yacht—moored out there, you can see her lights. I have the amphibious car—"

"You're Toledo's father—that's how I've thought of you."

"I know it's hard for you," Richard said, he came closer, she thought he was someone else, someone she knew, she was somewhere else, somewhere she didn't know, he grabbed her hair, pulled, snaked his tongue at her mouth, her mind went crazy thinking it was the first real thing, he yanked her hand to his crotch, perfect aim for her knee, something she never thought she would do, his shriek was surprised, furious, she was running, running, finally dropping at love beach, rolling in the dunes as if she'd lost them forever, dreaming an old man in a monk's robe—couldn't see his face, just the shadows of the hood but wherever she ran he met her, she'd turn and run the other way but he was there too, when she woke her arms were over her head, she was sweating, her sex throbbed and ached, she ran into the surf to get numb with the cold. she was home now, down deep where the evil was. A documentary crew shot her from the beach, she wondered if they'd been here all the time. Richard.

Eight

Sam decided to never again be alone with Richard, he wouldn't let anyone else know about his obsession with her, she was sure of that, besides maybe he was that way with all women—doubtless counting on their discretion—and shame—to protect him, what bothered her most was how obsessively she thought about him—why had he done it, why didn't she see it coming—as if she were arguing with his disrespect, she was nauseated a lot too, at first she thought she might be pregnant but then realized it went with thinking about Richard, she knew she should tell the others but couldn't, she thought she knew what rape victims felt but that was ridiculous, this was just a hit she got away from, the worst part about it was waking up with her sex burning, something had happened before, somewhere in that sea of lost time, she was paranoid about it, the way Jesus looked at her she wondered if he suspected, Cheekbones seemed to have something on her mind too, and Toledo said, "You're in love—I see it in your eyes."

"What about my eyes?" she said.

"They're bluer and too bright—almost feverish."

"What makes you think it's love—instead of infection?"

"You're tormenting me the way you do in the movie."

"You're telling me that's what you want—the way you do in the movie."

"What do you mean?"

"You know what I mean—you just want to fight."

"Well fighting is something."

"Meaning?"

"You're blowing me off."

Toledo was sweet even in his anger, she *was* blowing him off, she couldn't stand the idea of sex since Richard, it was as if he possessed her in spite of the knee jab, every day father and son had more plans for the movie, the latest was flying the whole crew to Washington, DC, to shoot the meeting of Flannery and Toledo at the Kennedy Center Opera House—where by coincidence Richard was funding a new opera, *Faust,* by an unknown, with a diva he said could rival Callas, they would shoot live at the opening and do the pick-up work later. Faust—by coincidence! Sam wondered how far this would go before one of them said no. Before she said no.

On the same day as the opera, there would be a national rally of Victims Vigilant on the steps of the Lincoln Memorial, since they were in the movie, there were video crews with them constantly, the edited movie would cut back and forth between the scripted scene at the opera and documentary footage of the rally, scripted media coverage would talk about the California gubernatorial campaign—a warm-up for the next presidential race—against the background of growing political unrest and rising fanaticism.

Both in and out of the movie, the opening of the new *Faust* was a Veteran's benefit, *American Movie* was pledging box office receipts, the whole Kennedy Center was involved, entertainment in every theater—one act plays, comedy, dancing, music from symphonic to jazz to Rap, the blood red hallways and the opera house somehow evoked scenes of prerevolutionary Russia, even France—people in diamonds and furs squeezed next to postbeat, posthip junkies in jeans and suede.

The day they started shooting, the entire Watergate-Kennedy Center corridor had to be roped off—the crowd was larger than in LA, traffic was at standstill everywhere, federal government closed for the day, and the National Guard was out in force.

Script Sequence

I'm in the Medialennium box with a few of the inner circle, I've been everywhere with them lately introduced by them, photographed with them, asked for interviews I refuse, all of it for the sole purpose of media coverage Toledo is sure to see, I always have an escort, I'm always demure, dressed in a style Cheekbones created and dubbed Le Sorcièr Innocent—pale soft fabrics, flowing lines—the picture of alluring mystery, for some reason I feel at home this way, as if bewitchment is my true calling. It nauseates me.

The opera scene is where Faust has Marguerite, my escort is called to the phone, Toledo enters the box and takes the escort's seat, I resist looking at him, Faust sings of his love for Marguerite, she must not fear him, he has had everything and now only wants her to accept his devotion, I feel Toledo leaning, feel warm with it, like an ingenue noticed for the first time, "I never understood this before you stood me up," he says.

A voice says, "Shhssh," I give Toledo a sidelong glance, hint of smile, feel a thrill inside, think this is going to be hard, what if I fall for him, what about the strategy, it must be the clothes, I focus on Marguerite singing her dilemma—if she surrenders, he'll despise her soul, if she doesn't he'll despise her heart, either way she dies.

"Is the diva flat," Toledo says, "or is that opera should never be sung in English?"

"Shhhsh!" the voice says.

I lean imperceptibly towards Toledo, "Flat," I say.

Toledo takes a quick breath and says, "Golden ears—I sensed as much. Forgive me, but I can't let you sit through this—please!"

I give the smile hint, as we leave the box I notice Cheekbones isn't in her seat, in the hall Toledo says, "I must remember to thank my father for his wretched taste in music. For weeks I've been following you."

"Me?"

Toledo grins then formally kisses my hand. "Your witchcraft is a turn-on."

"The governor flatters himself."

"You're right—it's my consuming desire to be summoned by you," Toledo says, "we men always project our desires—as you know—we're too weak for moral truth."

"And we women uphold the lie."

"All this and honesty, too?"

"All in a day's work."

"The sweeter the lips the harder the sting."

An usher runs up, "There's a message from the Lincoln Memorial," he says, "—urgent!"

Script Sequence cut

In the script, Cheekbones was to have slipped out of the opera and gone to the Victims Vigilant rally to meet with Richard in his role as a Medialennium executive who was bringing Victims Vigilant into the fold both to show that protest is accepted as a sign of healthy democratic government, and when it gets out of hand, to justify repressive police tactics. Their activities and propaganda would be entirely controlled by Medialennium.

However, the urgent message changed things, it had been relayed from Jesus, the messenger didn't know the details but we were to come to the rally immediately, we all piled into a Toledo Productions van, I got Playback on the monitor, they were showing the rally, the crowd looked much bigger than the one at the Hollywood Bowl— and the Victims Vigilant members in polyester and tennis shoes were outnumbered by toughs, some with long hair wearing Sixties jeans, some with Goth hair, all with the sweat-streaked, sooty look of postapocalyptic movies. This too was scripted, the crowd was to have been salted with mercenary terrorists by Medialennium, whose economic control—and the political control being the only viable source of survival for candidates—destroyed the middle class and what remained of representative political process, and created the pandemonium symbolized by the rally. So far they didn't see anything wrong.

Then the Playback picture went to the speaker's podium on the steps of the Lincoln, Richard and Cheekbones stood talking with some men they didn't know, Jesus appeared with a megaphone, film and video crew looked as if things were going according to schedule, a band recruited from local high schools struck up the National Anthem, the picture showed the audience, Victims Vigilant members standing with hands over their hearts, singing earnestly, while the crowd mercenaries chanted, "Medialennium sellout—hell no!"

Toledo said, "What are they jumping the gun for?" The mercenaries were of course supposed to wait for their cue—to come after Richard introduced Jesus as location director and Cheekbones as assistant, the sequence of action had been explained and the shooting begun with scenes of Richard's speech, Victims Vigilant testimonials, the passing of the hat. The crowd action was scheduled as the last sequence, and the shooting was to wait till they had finished at the opera and joined the crew at the rally.

"We went over this a hundred times!" Toledo said.

Sam tried other channels, most were carrying the rally, messages ran at the bottom of the picture on all the channels: The events you are witnessing are real...taped live only minutes ago at the Lincoln Memorial in the nation's capitol... The action on your screen is not a movie or fictional program...the scenes are actual events still taking place in the midst of national monuments and memorials to the fallen heroes of the United States of America...

It made no sense. Sam turned back to Playback just as The National Anthem ended but the chanting continued, Richard went to the mike, raised his hands, said, "Welcome, members of Victims Vigilant!" The band struck up again, the chanting grew louder, "Welcome Nam Vets!" Richard said, and the chanting grew into pandemonium.

Sam said, "He's going right into the scene."

"Bastard—why isn't he stopping it?" Toledo said, "I'll get him for breach of contract!"

Richard was still talking into the mike, "Wait," he said, "Vietnam Veterans are victims—maybe the first victims of the international reign of terrorism!" Again the band went at it, the chanting rose like a hell howl, National Guard uniforms seemed to multiply in the crowd, Richard raised his arms again, said, "Let me introduce one of your own—" The crowd cut him off with cheers, whistles, and the chanting.

"Thank Christ," Toledo said, "at least he's turning it over to Jesus—not a moment too soon."

Sam said, "I don't see Jesus."

Richard was speaking again, "Let me introduce a Black American who lost her husband to your revolution—"

There was a moment of dead silence reverberating with the echo of the word, revolution, then the pandemonium returned.

"The fool is starting a real riot!" Toledo said.

The van was stopped in traffic, there were National Guardsmen all over the streets, the car phone was jammed, the Playback picture showed Cheekbones at the podium, her lips were moving but there was no sound.

Toledo said, "Sabotage!"

The picture flashpanned from place to place in the crowd, at times swung crazily, as if itself in the center of the free-for-all—Victims Vigilant extras shouting, "Terrorist bastards!" seconds before being pummeled by mercenaries—just as Toledo was to direct it. There were no uniforms in any of these shots.

Sam said, "Where's the National Guard?"

They had scripted a sequence of a child being trampled, the actor came from Central Casting—complete with a mother who was going to be the hardest part of the shoot, now as they watched the runaway scene, they saw the child actor in the crowd, disheveled mother swinging at a mercenary, her backward thrust hit the child clutching her from behind, he went down without her noticing, there were shots of his head being stepped on.

"Who's shooting that?" Toledo said.

Sam said, "Not Jesus."

"He's taken over Playback!" Toledo said, "how could I be so dumb?"

Suddenly white uniforms were all over the screen—the Citizens in full riot gear, M-16s ready—the brown uniforms of the Sentry nowhere to be seen. The Citizens moved in formation through the crowd—paralyzed by the sight of them, some with hands on top of their heads like POWs, some dropping to their knees, Citizens stationing themselves in Vformation, flanks marching straight up the Lincoln steps to the podium, surrounding it.

Richard said into the microphone, "Would you like to tell us what's going on?"

"He's in with them or he wouldn't have known the speaker system was back on," Toledo said.

The Citizens didn't respond, two of them flanked Cheekbones and marched her off, the TV picture cut to a shot of the Lincoln steps—empty, a voice-over we didn't recognize said, "The event you just saw was taped only minutes ago at the location shooting of Stephen Toledo's new film, *American Movie*. Andrea Soledad, widow of Black activist, Raymond Soledad—whose death is still shrouded in mystery—Andrea Soledad, also ex-wife of Stephen Toledo, well-known maker of super-realistic films—Andrea Soledad has disappeared!"

"It was scripted," Toledo said, "—so what?"

The voice-over said, "In an incredible example of life imitating art, Ms. Soledad—who according to the script was to be kidnapped from the scene of a national rally—has actually disappeared!"

Toledo said, "What are they talking about?"

"Cheekbones," Sam said.

"That's bullshit—some media—"

Toledo broke off as the voice-over said, "The rally, called by

Victims Vigilant—a self-styled grassroots movement to protest the rise of crime and terrorism—was scheduled to gain national recognition for the group, but was also written into the script of Toledo's film. This development is not surprising since the leader of Victims Vigilant is Richard Toledo, billionaire father of the filmmaker and principal investor in all his son's films. Richard Toledo is making his acting debut in the new film—unique because of its development of character from the real lives of the actors. The senior Toledo, a psychoanalyst who practiced for years before making his fortune in investments, has been quoted as saying, 'American Movie is both brilliant and dangerous'—considering today's events, a characterization turned prophecy."

"It's all about him!" Toledo said.

The voice-over said, "In a further development, it is rumored—though unconfirmed—that a ransom note exists and speculation is running high about the amount of ransom that might be demanded from the filmmaker—or his father."

"Christ," Toledo said, "what have I done to her—and my son?"

Sam said, "Your son?"

"She's pregnant."

Nothing could have surprised Sam more, both of them had lied, she couldn't think of anything except moving, she picked up a camera, said, "I'm going to try it on foot."

"Running again?" Toledo said.

"I just have to move."

"You're the one she's in love with."

"Men don't get the friendship of women, the connection, it's probably biologic, why women take care of children and each other instead of just fight or flight—" Sam broke off, laughing painfully at her lecture on gender developmental differences, "I guess I don't get it either."

"It was before you and me."

"You said she had a miscarriage."

"That was before. I just found out about this."

"Then how do you know it's a son?"

"I don't know—I don't even know it's mine, if it's even real. I was trying to hurt you."

"Touché."

Toledo took another camera and came with Sam, they left the van and hiked through the gridlock, "Feels like I'm back in the Nam," Toledo said, "—all the rules suspended—reality is the call of the ranking man."

Sam said nothing, focused on the gridlocked streets, more uniforms than cars, more Army than National Guard—it looked like postwar occupation. "Where were you when she was kidnapped?" Toledo said to the sergeant who refused to let them through, they had to wait nearly 30 minutes till Richard appeared with a lieutenant, "Et tu, Bruté," Toledo said, his face younger, the betrayed son.

"Don't be absurd," Richard said, and looking at Sam, "—are you all right?"

Sam said, "Where's Chuy?"

"He was hit on the head—presumably by the terrorists—to get control of the equipment, no doubt—it's not serious."

"Terrorists?" Toledo said, "—your contribution to the script?"

"Army Intelligence believes this is an act of international terrorists," Richard said, "—they left a note in Andy's trailer."

The lieutenant took a folded paper from his breast pocket and read from it, "Toledo, if you want to see your wife again, don't tell anyone about this. Continue your shooting schedule. You will be contacted at the Vietnam Memorial." The lieutenant looked up from the paper and said, "it's signed The Real Director."

Toledo turned to Richard, "What bullshit," he said, "the way you acted, you had to be in with them!"

"I was acting under orders from Army Intelligence," Richard said, "we had a bomb threat before we even started shooting."

"Why in hell didn't I know about this?"

The lieutenant said, "Intelligence is in charge here, sir. Your father was under orders—just as he said."

"Does my father know his grandchild was kidnapped too?"

Richard looked stunned. "She didn't tell me—are you sure?" he said, "—it's not as though we haven't been through this..."

Once we were inside the cordon, Sam left them to search for Jesus and found him setting up for the Viet Nam Memorial sequence, he looked ten years older, they went to one of the trailers to talk. "You're hurt," Sam said.

"Just freaked out."

"Toledo thinks it's connected to Richard."

"That would be the simple answer."

Sam couldn't hold it any longer, she told Jesus about Richard hitting on her.

"Toledo told me once Richard did that with his first girl friend."

"So that's all it is?"

"Something else happened," Jesus said.

Sam was mortified, she'd thought this was something, it was just Richard, maybe just men, she was being a victim. "Just Princess and Pea stuff," she said, walked away fast.

They had to start shooting again, feeding it to Playback so the kidnappers would see them complying, Richard seemed to be everywhere, Sam couldn't stay away from him, when they were rehearsing the scene he stood so close she thought Toledo would kick him out but he didn't. Sam remembered when she'd wondered how long they were going to go on with this, with Richard, when one of them would say no. Now they couldn't stop, they didn't even know who had Cheekbones—who the enemy was.

Scripted Sequence

The action starts as Toledo and I arrive at the rally grounds and walk along the Reflecting Pool after Cheekbones is kidnapped— according to Medialennium, by terrorists. A sea of uniforms—Army,

National Guard, DC police—covers the Mall, otherwise deserted except for the litter left by the Victims Vigilant marchers and the mercenaries, now gone. "Looks like Normandy," Toledo says, "—the morning after."

I say, "What do you think happened?"

"Beats me. Since Medialennium—after the honeymoon was over—I found out it wasn't my intelligence and integrity they were after—I try not to think."

"I'm beginning to understand that."

"Used to live here among the monuments, didn't you?" Toledo says.

"In DC—yes. Are we going to trade dossier stories?"

"Why did you leave?"

"To go west and make great movies—like Toledo."

"All this and flattery, too?"

"It's true—sort of," I say, "—give or take a bit of narcissism."

Toledo laughs then abruptly stops, grabs my arms and lifts me up to his face, "I don't make film anymore—narcissistic or not—I make money," he says, "—for the Big M—remember?"

"Do you have copies of your movies?"

"My movies don't exist!"

"They'll always exist," I say, "nothing can change that."

"Except Medialennium—don't you know they've all been re-edited—just the way you're going to re-image me?"

"Re-edited?"

"Sound so innocent—part of the act, isn't it," Toledo says, "the worst part is, I almost believe it—you've got talent, Ms. Maskmaker. If I were still making flicks, I'd sign you on!"

"You think I'm a whore."

"Do I?"

"What about you?"

"Company man."

"What's the difference?"

"Anatomy," Toledo says, "and judging from what I can see of yours, the difference is qualitative." He says the last over his shoulder as he runs ahead, towards the Lincoln Memorial.

"Oh—I got my job with my body and you got yours with your mind?"

Toledo runs in a circle, "Elementary, my dear," he says and continues running towards the pillars that house the Lincoln and cast long shadows from spotlights trained on the marble figure.

I watch him disappear in the shadows, I hardly know what to do or what the point of anything is—if it ends the way it has for Cheekbones. I can hear her voice saying, "I'm a killer." Where's the killer now, I wonder—and how long will I care? How long before her memory is no sharper than the hours of those long, hungry days I spent writing stuff no one read? I watch the litter float in the Reflecting Pool and vow not to forget—Cheekbones or writing—no matter what Medialennium does.

Toledo's laughter wafts across the grass from the Vietnam Memorial, I move towards it, say, "I know you don't trust me—I don't know who to trust, either." No answer except wind in leaves, I walk closer to the black marble slab etched with the names of the dead, bathed in moonlight nearly bright enough to read them, plastic flags and wilting flowers on the grass beneath, "They look almost real," I say.

Toledo says, "So do you."

His voice comes from the direction of the three sculpted Vietnam soldiers, commissioned because the black slab with the names was too stark, the gravestone too real. I move towards the sound, say, "I keep hoping there's a way to wake up."

Toledo claps hollowly. "Once more—with feeling."

"Does everyone in Medialennium read Hollywood lines as if they were written by Nietzsche?"

I see Toledo's face now, he's walking the distance between us and stops just close enough to touch me, I feel his breath, "You're asking for trust," he says and laughs coldly, "—trust a maskmaker?"

"What do you have to lose?"

Toledo leans down and smacks my mouth with his, I step back reeling, his arms make a vice around me, he roots for my mouth, I twist away and run, his laughter lunges after me, wraps around me and the Vietnam, the slab with its names and dead flowers and flags, the sculpted soldiers that fail to recall Iwa Gima. Toledo doesn't fail, he's a triathlete I remember reading, he tackles my legs, I turn violently, nearly get loose but my heel sinks, we go down and roll in the wilted flowers and wrinkled paper flags, I shout till he smacks my mouth again. "I'm crazy about you," he says, softly now.

"Crazy is the word."

"Who's side are you on?"

"Is there more than one?"

"You know there is. We could be a team."

"Us against Medialennium? Modern Romeo and Juliet?"

He laughs, says, "It's not that bad," kisses me sweetly, I start to go with it, his face so earnest, eyes searching me, disappearing now, like a mask falling away, dissolving to another face, the focus isn't sharp but there's something so familiar it's on the tip of my tongue—fighting with his, trying to warn him about the explosion in my guts, the hot lava rising to my throat.

Toledo makes a sound in his throat then pulls away, staggers off retching, my mouth tastes like bile, I try to move and feel something tear inside—animal in a trap.

Script Sequence Cut

Sam had thrown up in Toledo's mouth, she lay wondering what in hell she was doing here.

"Take some water," Jesus said.

"Sorry I ruined the shot," she said.

"You didn't."

"I threw up."

"Take some water."

Richard was with Toledo, giving him water, talking to him like a prizefighter's coach, "What's he saying?" Sam said.

Jesus said, "Don't worry about him."

"I should've thrown up in Richard's mouth."

Jesus grinned. "No justice," he said.

Toledo decided not to talk about the incident, "Let's stay with it," he said, "—take it from where Flannery vomits."

Scripted Sequence

Toledo retches against the Vietnam marble, pulls a flask from his pocket, gargles and spits, drinks and reads from the etched names of the dead, drinks again and crawls back to where Flannery lies in the littered grass, "Drink?" he says and holds the flask over her head.

"I'll get vomit on it."

"It's already done."

"Oh shit—sorry."

Toledo leans down close to my face. "Don't be—it's made you believable," he says, "—in another life you'd be a great actress."

I laugh. "You think I threw up on cue?"

"What else can I think—that my style made you sick?"

I laugh again, he offers the flask, I take it and gargle, the Courvoisier is so warm I swallow some, "Good," Toledo says, "I go down easier with booze." He touches my hair, his face petitions, "See, I need to."

"Sounds a little Fifties."

"You don't understand."

"What?"

He looks around as if someone might hear, "Lately with all this about the election—how I could lose—I haven't been able to ah, perform—as they say."

"How irresistible."

"You really know how to make a guy feel special."

I check my watch.

"Oh now I do feel special."

"I just have to check in with my supervisor."

"You have a supervisor?"

"Everyone in Medialennium has a supervisor."

"Do all the women have this kind of dominatrix thing?"

I laugh, say, "So I'm the problem?"

"No problem—it's a turn-on."

He reaches for me sweetly, kisses sweetly, touches, I start to get into it, think this is what I've always wanted, can't imagine how it could happen here, now, I always leave by now, spin off somewhere away from the sex, it strikes me as funny, I'm in love with this beautiful, hopeless man—in the movie, I'm in love in the movie!

"Cut!"

Script Sequence cut

Toledo kept saying cut but Sam couldn't stop laughing, even when he lifted her by the shoulders and put his arms around, said, "Talk to me," hugged gently—his usual hard arms of desperate passion gone, still she couldn't stop or breathe, finally gasped and the laughter turned to sobs, she tried even harder to stop those but it went on like a broken pipe.

When it was over Toledo said, "Have you been raped?"

For a moment there was a silence like none Sam could remember, as if time stopped, everything stopped, then she laughed again—not that rape was funny, just Toledo and his coaching—so Grotowski, then she thought about Richard, maybe that was it, she wasn't in love in the movie, she was just over the edge, "No," she said, "I'm just cracking—have we heard anything about Cheekbones?"

Toledo's face softened, "I'd tell you—don't you know that?" he said.

"Don't I trust you—you mean?"

"That's right."

"Wrong—I mean I don't know.

"Baby, come on—"

"Don't call me baby!"

"What are you mad about?"

"Baby," she said, "—you naming me—any woman—your doll."

"That doesn't follow," Toledo said, "you aren't making sense."

"Nothing makes any sense when you don't feel."

"You don't feel—like that thing of being out of your body?"

"Actually I meant you—" Sam broke off laughing again, "you know, men don't feel. But you're right, it was me and I think I just crashed back in."

"And?"

"I don't know how to tell you."

"Just do it."

"In the scene—where I was supposed to be Flannery manipulating the governor—I was in love with you."

He scowled, trying to figure it out, muttered, "In the scene, in the scene, in the scene—you were in love with me?"

"Well…"

"Well?"

"Yeah."

"In the scene—" He got up, pulled Sam up, started dancing her around, singing, "In the scene, in the scene, in the scene she was in love, in the scene she's in love, she's in love, she loves me!" He was insane dancing her, singing, she thought oh God, he thinks it's true, he thinks acting is real, he said that, the Grotowski freedom to stop not doing it, to do it, to be, to be in love, dancing, singing, like children playing in the streets of war.

Nine

The kidnappers didn't make contact until the crew returned to Malibu, every morning they received a phone call from a new voice with a new accent asking questions about the day's shoot, then a message recorded in Cheekbones' voice, giving the date and time and some curse. Toledo made a daily announcement of his readiness to pay ransom at postshoot rap sessions with the crowd and Playback audience. Richard spoke for Victims Vigilant, each day with increasing militancy, "Are we ready to stop terrorist acts such as this kidnapping? Are we ready to concern ourselves less with the civil rights of criminals and more with the right of law-abiding Americans to be protected from anarchy?" VV members who followed them on location were transforming from the invisible victims of street crime to young men and women with intense eyes, drawn faces and rigid bodies, dressed in Army and Navy surplus, who did everything in formation, clapped, chanted and cheered in unison.

"They're one step away from a Brave New Army—maybe closer," Toledo said to Richard in a rap session.

"You wrote the script," Richard said.

"We brought you and Victims Vigilant into the script as one more example of how in Medialennium all politics are co-opted because the political structure is fused with the economic."

"And in the script the membership of Victims is the recruiting ground for the elite police," Richard said, "—the members start to dress for the part."

"In the script, yes, but these uniformed zombies follow our shooting schedule when they aren't in the scenes," Toledo said.

"They're in the documentary too, aren't they?"

Toledo was stunned, "No," he said, "our contract is for extras in certain scenes."

"But the crowd that follows the shoot is in the documentary," Richard said.

"Only incidentally—not by design."

"So if members of Victims are here incidentally...?"

Toledo said, "You're twisting my words to blur essential distinctions—implying there is no real difference between reality and art."

Richard said, "Isn't that what this movie is about?"

"Yes—and what we're about is making that artistic statement— not promoting the deterioration of distinctions—the co-opting of culture and values to political ends."

"Can art really maintain such a comfortable distance today?" Richard said, "—or is it possible that you're playing poor little rich boy here—thinking your father controls the world and is responsible for everything—like the disappearance of Andrea Soledad?"

"This isn't about you!" Toledo said.

Call-ins from the Playback audience jammed the lines and the session went on half the night—most of the callers supporting Richard, who also heard from a Hollywood agent that he would be nominated for best supporting actor. A senior citizens group called during the rap session to say they had named Richard their honorary president, it started a trend and Richard became the man of the hour—magazines wanted interviews, publishers wanted his memoirs, colleges wanted him to speak at their graduations and accept honorary doctorates, Hollywood wanted him for a picture about his life, "It's all because of *American Movie*," Richard said, he was working on the distribution already—including advanced ticket sales, personal appearances and gala openings—to be taped live and produced for sale with the movie's release on video.

The actors and production crew were assigned agents of the Security and Intelligence Bureau (SIB), an agency they didn't know existed, couldn't find out anything about them, functionaries reached by phone alluded to special investigations of kidnappings and other possible terrorist-related activities, the agents were everywhere outside the villa, even inside, they turned up all over, during the night they were on the balcony of the glass house, they set up camp in the room Cheekbones had slept in, brought in a truck-load of equipment and endlessly watched every foot of film and tape, Jesus had daily packages of the originals transported to a friend at the University of Mexico.

Sam suspected the SIB had tapped into the closed circuit television at San Toledo, it might be on even when controls were off. It was Medialennium—as Richard had said. In the middle of this, Toledo and Sam were happy, absurdly, they talked about being in character even when they weren't shooting the script scenes, a joke because there never had been a difference in who they were, what they felt, it just took the movie to get there, they were prisoners yet existentially free, their smallest intimacies laid bare, their favorite fantasy was that Cheekbones was doing an improv act like picking Sam up in the jungle-hopper that time, she would turn up, yet as the hours turned into days they knew that was a wish-fulfillment dream, a dream they were living with each other, how could they ask for more, where the hell was she anyway—and what was Richard's real role? Sam was starting to feel maybe she knew him from before. She and Jesus decided Toledo should know about Richard's hitting on her.

"It'll freak him," Jesus said, "but his not knowing could be worse."

The beach was the only place they couldn't be bugged, one night they managed to meet there, just the three of them, and there in the surf with Richard's yacht lights twinkling from their mooring, Jesus keeping watch for the SIB hovercraft with its search beam that every night swept the dunes, to protect us, they said. Sam held Toledo's hand while she told him, at first he didn't understand, as if the surf was too loud for him to get her words, he sat still as death saying nothing, then charged up running, she with him, Jesus a few paces behind, Toledo ran so fast he finally stumbled just as a wave broke and swept him out till they yanked him back and he coughed the sea out of his lungs.

His eyes were cold. "What else haven't you told me about him?"

"Only that I might have known him before."

"Before?"

"In the part I can't remember."

"What?"

"I don't know—he just seems familiar. Didn't he have a practice in New York? Maybe I ran into him there."

"Don't you think that's too much of a coincidence?"

Sam was relieved, said, "Yes—maybe it's just paranoia."

Toledo nodded. "Paranoia—that's what he used to say about my mother, Rachel too."

"It's what he said about me."

"You told him you thought you knew him?"

"No—first he said he was undercover and it was scripted, he got the idea from my novel, that's when I said he must be the one who cleaned out my apartment, he said I was paranoid, it was when we had dinner that time, the way I talked about the novel that gave him the idea of playing the head of VV, the movie would expose the hate-mongers, but I didn't talk about it, the only way it makes sense is he got the novel."

Toledo shook his head. "He didn't know you before that night, how would he know to steal the novel?"

"He saw the audition tape—I guess I mentioned being a writer."

"It's thin. What about the undercover story?"

Sam said, "His story depends on it."

"So what else is there?"

"Obsession."

"With you? He hit on my first girl friend."

"Maybe that's his obsession? What about Cheekbones?"

Toledo stared, gave Sam a now-I-know-you're-crazy look, said, "She never said anything."

"Neither did I."

He started pacing. "Why do women do this—doesn't silence just perpetuate it? Why?"

"Shame."

He didn't hear, went on, "It's like you think all men are the same, maybe in the past no one believed it, mostly men, but now it's different."

"Shame isn't about thinking, it's beyond thinking, even feeling, it's more like being taken over—like possession."

Toledo stopped, looked in a way Sam couldn't read, rushed over and covered her with his arms. "Now I'm doing it—shaming you."

"No—"

"Don't try to protect me! I should've killed him," he was pacing again, "Didn't Freud say somewhere that the original patriarch of the primal horde was so terrible his sons had to kill him? If they didn't, he might've killed them—but he did, see, by making them murderers."

Sam said, "And they were so afraid of it happening again, of their murderousness, they created the ideal father and his law—"

"Yahweh!"

"The divine director! I had a dream once, me, another woman, and a man chained together. The chains turned to light. Later I read Jessica Benjamin's *The Bonds of Love*—it's all there."

Toledo stopped pacing, laughed, hugged Sam, "I can't imagine how I've lived without you."

"Repression," she said, "the core of civilization—birth of the

Oedipal complex—making the son's aggression incestuous instead of reaction to the real terrible acts of the father?"

"So the myth is gone."

"Revealed—the masks are gone."

They clung together trembling, that night made love and cried till the tears turned to love and the love to tears, love and tears, through the night.

In the script, Flannery's meeting with Cahero, the Third World challenger in the gubernatorial race, takes place when Cahero is to speak at an anticrime workshop at the City of Angels University, known as The Angels, an enclave in Watts. The day of the shoot there, the campus and neighborhood were covered with Army battle fatigues, there were rumors of tanks housed in old airplane hanger at LAX, of an aircraft carrier at Long Beach detailed to the operation, of summit meetings, presidential envoys, rumors of a mass to be said for Cheekbones by the Pope. FBI agents arrived to take over the case of her abduction.

The day they shot on The Angels campus, Victims Vigilant held a recruitment meeting in a tent outside the gates. The scene was supposed to begin with a conversation between Sam and Cheekbones who assigns Sam to take a video crew to The Angels where Cahero is to appear. The morning of the shoot a UPS truck delivered a package for Toledo to the location, a video of Cheekbones holding a copy of the morning edition of the LA Times. She looked like hell—eyes dull and sunken with deep red circles, cheeks hollow, "Shoot the scene around me today," she said, "—give 'em hell and fuck the pigs!"

Toledo watched the video over and over until an FBI agent took it to be examined in a crime lab. The crew had a motorcycle escort through the crowd there to see the shoot, cordoned off by Army troops, the Victims Vigilant crowd was positioned in formation outside the recruitment tent equipped with loud speakers that carried Richard's voice chanting, "Are you ready to say no to terrorism? To pay freedom's price?" It wasn't scripted.

"He can't handle the competition," Toledo said.

Sam said, "He'd say he's just playing the role—to expose them—and you're supporting that by having a video crew cover everything he does."

"He's gotten so addicted to the camera, he has to perform whenever there's one around—he's bound to give himself away."

"So while he pretends to be exposing Victims, we pretend to expose him—isn't it naive to think it's only his ego trip?"

Hate radiated from Toledo, he said, "You don't know his ego. Did he tell you he paid a Mexican whore $200 for my fourteenth birthday? Did he mention the whore flunked me—and he spent the night with her to get his money's worth?"

She didn't say Richard told her, except for the last part. Toledo's hatred for his father somehow relieved her obsession with Richard, as if he were carrying it for her now, her knight, her job to be his goddess, keep his patricide symbolic.

Script Sequence

As I drive the Ferrari to the main Angels gate I hear on the radio that The Angels is under siege by Blacks and Latinos who during the night sneaked on campus and pitched tents all over the grounds as a symbol of their contention that The Angels—which recently bought up a five-mile radius of real estate for its planned expansion—robbed them of their homes and jobs in the shops and small businesses that rent space in the affected area, now re-zoned, owners will be paid at or above market value, or given space in another neighborhood and moved at The Angels expense. All offers, however, have been refused.

The anticrime workshop is being conducted by the Angels to educate students in conflict resolution and self-defense techniques, as a response to the sharply rising rate of personal crime reported by them, and the resulting parental concern. A minority student organization, SAVE ONE—for Save the First Amendment—contends that the anticrime campaign is really a racist move against the neighborhood and the minority student body, that part of The Angels' reorganization strategy involves weeding out student liberalism and making The Angels into a West Point of the New Right. SAVE ONE sources claim that Jesus Cahero, Third World Party candidate for governor, will speak at the workshop. University sources, however, deny that an invitation has been issued to Mr. Cahero, and say that no one outside the University will be speaking, the event is for students only.

I arrive at The Angels gate, the guard looks at my Medialennium press card and salutes, an Angels cop in dress uniform awaits me in a golf cart, a second cart for my crew. We turn the camera on the campus buildings—showcase of Spanish Mission architecture mixed with Victorian and Anglo-modern—students wearing the latest and priciest walk or ride expensive bikes, parking lots filled with sports cars, the campus mall where a battalion of Angels Security line up in dress uniform, as if for a parade, the center of the mall, a sculptured fountain—water shooting from the mouth and tail of Quetzalcoatl, the Aztec sun god, a marble serpent with stained glass plumes—the statue rotating at the base, lights around the fountain edge constantly changing the angles and colors. The sculpture seems to laugh and dance, even spring to attack.

"Where are the tents?" I say.

The cops drive us to the athletic field—a jungle of tents, people making music, singing, dancing, children chasing each other and dogs. I heard somewhere Mexico is full of stray dogs, they must have been recruited for this scene. We get out of the chariots, approach a young Latino man, start to speak but are interrupted by a siren—Angels Security van approaching—behind it other vehicles, all filled with cops, they shriek up to the tent area, cops spill out and rush the people around the tents. A cop with a megaphone says, "You are trespassing on University property, if you don't leave immediately you'll be arrested," the people sit down, the cop says, "Leave the area immediately or face arrest," the people stay seated, children too, even the dogs, the cops take out their clubs.

In the midst of this, a tall brown man in a white suit emerges from one of the tents, he has a megaphone too, stands facing the cop who gave the orders and says, "Good afternoon, Captain, my name is Jesus Cahero." The people cheer till Jesus holds up his hand.

"Leave the area immediately or face arrest," the captain says.

Jesus says, "I'd like to propose an alternative."

"No alternatives," the captain says into his megaphone, "— you'll be treated the same as the rest."

"What you're proposing will result in police violence—captured in living color by Medialennium's documentarist, Ms. Flannery," Jesus says, "—are you sure that's wise?"

The captain says, "This is your last chance to get in the police vans," he looks towards the cops with their clubs ready and nods, the cops sweep the seated group, clubs raised, a gun is fired in the air.

"Stop!" Jesus says into his megaphone, "I warn you every one who uses a club or fires a gun will be prosecuted along with the captain who issued the orders!"

The cops hesitate, "Arrest these perpetrators!" the captain says.

Jesus says, "Put away your clubs or face charges of felonious assault!"

"Arrest this man!" the captain says.

The cops stand with poised clubs as if frozen, Jesus walks closer to them and says without the megaphone, "Put away your clubs and abide by the principles of nonviolence and I will personally nominate this entire outfit for the Medialennium Peace Prize."

"Bullshit—arrest this man or I will personally nominate the lot of you for suspension without pay!" the captain says, his phone goes off at the same time as several phones in the police vehicles start ringing, he turns towards them and says, "Answer the goddamn phones!"

"These people are unarmed," Jesus says to the cops, "put the clubs away."

The driver of one of the police vehicles runs up to the captain with a phone, "The governor!" he says.

"Yes sir, Governor," the captain says. The cops put away their clubs and begin to carry the people to the vans.

Jesus says into the megaphone, "Governor, I am prepared to represent these people in negotiations designed to incorporate community participation in The Angels development plans."

"I'll be goddamned—sir," the captain says into the phone, looks at me, says "—on satellite?" Says to me, "Governor wants to talk to you."

"Ms. Flannery," Toledo's phone voice says, "I'd like to request that you stay with this event all the way through—with your camera on."

"Of course, Governor," I say.

"You'll be included in the nomination for the Medialennium Peace Prize."

"What is that—sir?"

"I intend to introduce co-sponsorship in the State Assembly tomorrow."

"Does this prize actually exist, Governor?"

"It does now."

"Does this cooperative effort between you and Jesus Cahero constitute a model of negotiation to be followed with disenfranchised minorities on other issues?"

"It certainly is a precedent," Toledo says, "let me speak to Cahero."

Jesus is sitting down, waiting to be arrested, I give him the phone and he puts it to his ear just as two cops begin to lift him, he says into the phone, "Yes, Governor—"

Jesus' voice is cut off by the sound of an explosion.

Script Sequence cut

It was not part of the scene, the script called for an explosion but later, at the end of this sequence, and only a smoke bomb on location, the sound track and the fire would be done in the studio. Yet from the athletic field they could see smoke pouring out the windows of a campus building, sirens screamed constantly, they clambered into the police vehicles and raced to the building with flame licking out its windows, the crowd must have broken through the cordon, people ran screaming in every direction, reached dead ends, trampled back on each other like a gigantic beast.

Jesus kept talking through the megaphone, telling the people to stop running, be calm, panic was the enemy, the crew tried forming human chains to lead people out but some of the crowd were new, they looked like the mercenary extras who had appeared at the Lincoln Memorial in Washington—the same postapocalyptic dress, the same mob-inciting behavior—grabbing at people, shouting and pushing, several of them rushed Sam, grabbed her camera, the next thing she knew, she was jolted to consciousness in one of the production vans, Jesus driving, he must've been behind, seen her get hit, she looked out the window, fire engines and more police cars—that is, they were white with whirlybirds and screaming sirens but no police identification, Citizens poured from car doors in full riot regalia, it was the Hollywood Bowl and Lincoln Memorial all over again.

Sam got up to the roof-mounted camera, Jesus maneuvered the van into the fire area where Citizens were surrounding groups of people, shoving them together like cattle, herding them out of the mall, the media arriving—video crews from broadcast and cable channels—in vans that must have gotten through the Army cordon outside the campus, all traffic now blockaded by Angels Security, the line broke for a group of Citizens dragging three production

195

assistants who looked unconscious, Toledo drove up in an Angels cart, "Get the bastards!" he said, and Sam shot the Citizens as they hog-tied the PAs and threw them in the Angels Security van, Toledo said, "You are all on candid camera being fed live to cable TV!"

A group of Citizens charged the van, Sam shot them climbing up—to destroy the camera, she thought—but one said, "We found three men with grenades—enough to fight a war—stationed on top of a building near the one that caught fire. We know they were employed by Toledo Productions. One of them was a Vietnam Veteran of a demolition crew—"

Sam said, "Is this another crazed Vietnam Vet story?"

"They had live grenades!"

"Can you prove that?"

"Witnesses saw it!"

"What witnesses," Sam said, they didn't answer, she pressed on, "Who are the Citizens?"

They jumped off the van and were gone, all the crew could do was continue recording the scene, there was amazingly little equipment damage, almost as though the Citizens wanted the scene recorded, Toledo was interviewed by the media crowd, they went through their art-imitating-life rap, repeated Citizen allegations that Toledo had ordered the fire to create realism and live up to his reputation.

Jesus discovered technical problems with the Playback transmission, it hadn't been on the air at least since the fire started but when the Citizens were gone, Playback was up again, the point had been made, they—whoever that meant—were in control.

During the rap session callers asked how they could go on with the movie, would someone have to be killed before they called it off? "For compelling reasons we can't divulge, the shooting must continue," Toledo said.

Richard appeared in the rap crowd, flanked by his VV brigade. "Andrea Soledad's life is at stake," he said.

Someone from the crowd said, "You mean the movie is the ransom?"

Toledo flew at Richard, tackled him, said, "You know fucking well we weren't supposed to tell anyone!"

"I received a phone call a few minutes ago instructing us to make it public."

"Phone call my ass!" Toledo said, "you're *them*—and this is about getting control of the movie!"

Richard said, "If you think that, why don't you kill me?"

"Only one reason—my mother."

"Your mother is dead."

"To you," Toledo said, "but her body still lives in that hellhole of a hospital you bought to lock her—"

Toledo's words were cut off by Angels Security, they dragged him off Richard who shouted at them, "Let him go—this is a family matter!"

Later Toledo told Sam that his mother had given up when Rachel died, she would just sit in her room and stare at nothing, Richard had given her all the drugs, shocked her brain, lobotomy, everything to put her away.

"What happened to her?" Sam said.

"In a way he's right, she died—all but the flesh—rotting in a first class prison."

"Because Rachel killed herself—did she feel responsible?"

"I used to think that," Toledo said, "now I wonder whether she wanted to kill him—he was the reason Rachel was so afraid of men."

"Did he abuse her?"

"I would have killed him!"

So it did happen, Sam thought, that's what he hates—that he couldn't stop it.

Toledo began to dream of it—killing Richard—in the middle of the night he'd thrash around the bed shouting curses, he started walking in his sleep, one night Sam followed him out to the beach where he shadow-boxed with Richard, knocked out his imaginary body then dragged it back up the beach to the courtyard, dropped it and said, "Live or die, murderer!" stepped over it and went back to bed.

Sam told Jesus how worried she was, "Stay with him," he said, He meant not just for now, she thought, not just for the movie. Yes, she thought. So it's decided. That night she dreamed of the blue light, Toledo and Jesus.

The crew were always together now, they faced the fact that the Citizens would show up wherever they were shooting, Richard claimed to be meeting with presidential aides, Cheekbones would be located, there were breakthroughs in the case, they must keep going—trust—no one had been killed or even seriously wounded, although he wasn't free to provide details, this was a direct result of security and intelligence activity, he had well-placed friends working on it.

Sam wanted to stop, to get out of this hell, Toledo said they had to trust that Cheekbones would be found, Jesus said, "It's the movie—the way out is the way through."

The next script scene involved Cheekbones, who comes to see Flannery as a result of receiving an anonymous video of the tryst between Flannery and Toledo—the Vietnam Memorial scene— which apparently someone taped, and which certainly compromised the Medialennium plan for their chaste courtship and wedding. Cheekbones sends Flannery on a mission—ostensibly to find out whether Jesus knows about the tape and if so, to get the original— but her real agenda is to test Flannery for the resistance movement in which both Cheekbones and Jesus are involved. They had to shoot around the scene with Cheekbones to the one where Flannery is to meet Jesus at a bar in Watts called Café Negro. They used Toledo's Circus bar, dressed down to make it look like a neighborhood place, had a storefront built onto a side door. The sequence would start with mise en scène footage of a street deep in Watts, where few Whites would go.

Script Sequence

The street is poorly lighted, buildings need repair, some with boarded windows and doors, too late I realize I shouldn't have driven the Ferrari here, it's gauche, reminds me of my prostituted condition, my presence even without the car could be provocative, I remember hearing some White guy talk about keeping a copy of *Ebony* in his car when he drives through Black neighborhoods, remember thinking how pragmatic—even utilitarian—the remark was, how it changed the way I thought about him, I remember this without the slightest memory of him—well, a smile perhaps, more sly than sheepish, as if getting along in the world were simply a matter of learning to tell the right joke or make the ironic remark that precisely expresses the requisite regret—class act of White privilege—that things are as they are. Each block looks the same as the one before till I see the storefront with the neon sign, Café Negro, flanked by one for Coors and another for Bud, no problem parking, the street is empty except for some kids chasing each other, I pull alongside the curb and look into the open door, music and voices spilling out, people dancing, leaning across tables, watching the band, through the window I see their backs moving rhythmically to the sound of blues—a guitar I think could stand up to B.B. King's—I sit listening, unable to get out of the car, to imagine being the one White in the place—even on the street—something Blacks feel every day a Black woman once told me—the piano takes over now and I wonder what it would cost to get this close to a White band that could make such music, if there were one.

I get out of the Ferrari, reach for the camera then consider, I shouldn't take it in, it might be damaged—like crossing a night street to avoid a Black who could be a mugger—but don't do it of course, I'm a progressive, on the other hand, they might think I'm there for the usual ripoff of Black music, still I need something, some way to let them know I'm here on business, not just some White girl looking for deliverance, I sit with the Ferrari door open, listening, watching people go in, hearing the greetings, wishing I had some place to belong, wondering whether I'd give up the Ferrari for it—yes and more, I think, yet I've never successfully joined anything, finally I heave myself out of the car, hoist the camera, march up to the door and walk in, all without breathing.

The piano goes on but everything else seems to stop—the laughter, talk, dancing, even the leaning across tables—it must be the camera, what can they think but that it's one more piece of White media-fuck, I consider turning around and taking it back to the car.

"Looking for someone?"

I can't tell where the voice came from, no one seems to be looking at me, maybe it's a game? The voice speaks again—low, close—behind me, I whirl around and nearly collide with a dark brown man, slightly taller than I, shoulders so broad they look like a yoke as he turns them and tosses his black hair—Mexican, Native, maybe African too—even some Anglo, judging from his green-flecked eyes.

"I am—yes," I say, "—looking for someone."

"So am I."

"Oh—I mean, I'm here to meet—I have an appointment with Jesus Cahero."

"Appointment," the man says.

"Yes—I'm Flannery—Sam Flannery."

"A man's name."

"Samantha—the nicknames are the same," I say, like a fool.

The man smiles, one tooth is missing but his face radiates. "Nothing between men and women is the same," he says.

"Separate but equal?"

"A mixed metaphor—but deserved, perhaps."

"Thank you."

"Dance?"

"Thanks—but my appointment..."

"Jesus Cahero is busy."

"You know him?"

The man laughs, opens his arms and begins to move to the music.

"I guess everybody knows him," I say, "actually, I'm doing a documentary on his campaign."

The man moves closer, reaches for my free hand, "Are you afraid to put the camera down?" he says.

"You should be making the documentary," I say—just like some bullshit White, "but I don't know your name."

"Shaman."

"Shaman is your name?"

I think he's playing with me—White girl with appointment and camera—but I let him take the camera and put it on a table, "No one will touch it," he says and opens his arms.

I say, "It's all right—media belongs to the people."

"Guerilla television?"

"You're laughing at me—and I deserve it."

He smiles, shakes his head, he and the music take me over, I've never danced like this, the other dancers move back to open the floor for Shaman and this White girl he's doing his magic on—faster now, with turns and lifts only pro's pull off, I the rag doll, no one else is dancing now, all eyes watch—one woman's are riveted to us, burning.

I say, "Are you here with anyone?"

"You."

"But did you come with that woman?"

"I'm free," he says, dances me all around the others, as if proving he's with me, I belong—at least while the music lasts—the other women stare angrily, talk too fast for me to understand—except that it's time to go, "They think you're the French whore from the Cave," Shaman says.

"The cave?"

"The bar—you know it?"

"No," I say, "but listen, I have to go."

"It's just neighborhood business," Shaman says.

I can barely breathe, music frenetic, people crowding the dance floor, I try to pull away but my head hits something, I reel and sink to my knees, then drag my feet under me and rocket up, "You lied to me," I say, "said you were here alone—free—liars aren't free!"

The music cuts off, everything stops, eyes stare at me, I walk backwards, each step could be my last, I glance towards my left—could I turn and run? Jesus Cahero stands at the piano, I vaguely remember hearing that he plays—why hadn't I seen him?

"You'll have to excuse us, Ms. Flannery," he says, "we only act this way when grandma comes."

"Grandma?"

His look says grandma means me, I say, "Sorry."

His eyes express something I can't identify—but don't mind, the raging in me stops, as if listening, "It's not personal," he says.

My skin burns, "I'd forgotten where I was—am. I guess Whites do that," I say.

He says, "You're all right."

"Do you know I was sent here to meet you?"

Almost imperceptibly, Jesus nods, "You're looking to shoot a documentary?"

"But I feel ridiculous—like it's all racist."

"We're all that."

I start to speak again but Jesus holds up his hand, listens, I can hear it too, a sound of engines, growing louder now—motorcycles, squealing up to the storefront—through the door, into the people—knocking them down, riding over them, straight into the walls, back and into the people again.

Script Sequence cut

The cyclists were supposed to be our Sentry but instead of the brown uniforms, these riders were in postapocalyptic dress like the mercenaries from the VV rally in DC and The Angels campus—but they were Black—and real, people bleeding, sirens screaming in the distance, Sam went to the bar to call 911, something flew over her head and shattered the bar mirror into a million shards—each one reflecting something she finally saw, she couldn't imagine why she hadn't seen it before, there was real madness behind this—like the psychotic whose rampage is carefully planned, complete with brilliant clues—the story of his own tragic life. As she moved among the wounded she wondered if she could be the insane one— beneath the amnesia—Mr. Hyde occupying her soul.

Half a dozen people were taken away in ambulances— concussions, cuts and bruises, possible fractures, one who might be having a heart attack.

In the rap session Toledo was confronted on whether this was one more gimmick to get his super-realistic style in the scene, again there was minimal equipment damage, Toledo himself had been shooting video fed into Playback, callers insisted it looked too good to be unplanned, he tried to explain that although the motorcycle attack was in the script, these weren't his stuntmen—they had planned to shoot that part of the scene in the studio, just like the fire—crew phones were jammed, callers wanted to see the footage over again, the media and shooting crowd demanded it too, Richard appeared and argued that it would only inflame things, the LAPD wanted the tape for evidence, Jesus was already shipping the day's originals out, for the police he produced a copy from a camera that had been knocked out.

Later at San Toledo they looked at the undamaged tapes, in

one close-up of a stuntman's face, they could see he wasn't Black, it was make-up—blackface. "This is too much," Sam said, "we have to stop it."

"Stop the movie," Richard said, "and let Cheekbones die?"

It was the first time Richard had called her Cheekbones—to manipulate, Sam thought. Toledo noticed it too, but said nothing till Richard had returned to his boat, "It's him," he said, "what they're saying I'm doing—this super-realism rap—it's him!" He wanted to put Richard under 24-hour surveillance, he couldn't believe he hadn't done it before.

Jesus had though, he'd learned Richard had a computer on board the boat, it was under armed guard, Jesus had an expert who could break into anything but she couldn't get through Richard's security.

"How long have you been watching him?" Toledo said.

"Long enough."

"What does he do?"

"Works at the computer—or goes to Beverly Hills and meets people. We don't have the equipment to pick up the conversations."

"Get it," Toledo said, "find out what he wants and give it to him. When Cheekbones comes back, I'll kill him with my bare hands!"

"Suppose he has what he wants," Sam said, "he or whoever it is—to have us do the movie—his way?"

"With him there was never a family," Toledo said, "we were just his puppets."

Sam said, "What if I go out to the boat?"

"Think you can buy him off?"

Sam raised her hand to slap him, froze, stood like a statue waving, thinking how this was where the other, Flannery, used to take over, in a way she was a statue, moving statue, robot, acting as if alive, as if not a puddle of fear—panic—about what, that was the next question, always what does it mean, what if it doesn't mean anything, just a short in the wiring setting off an alarm no longer connected to whatever it was designed to protect, maybe that's what crazy is, she saw the pain in Toledo's eyes, that's what it meant now, his pain, he was saying something she couldn't hear, didn't know what other madness she might do, started running, he'd follow, he had to, she couldn't leave now, except maybe he was right, maybe she should go out and try to buy Richard off, why not, somewhere she still believed he was obsessed with her, narcissism of the lost, maybe she could end all this, she ran out to the beach, past the inner security cordon formed by Toledo Productions guards, the SIB must be following, any moment she might hear a shot and feel that too, she ran all the way to the outer cordon of troops—now in riot gear—that slowed her down, she asked why, what they expected to happen tonight but they wouldn't answer, she ran all along the cordon to the upper edge of the beach then back to the dunes, something would happen tonight, she knew it, she had to find Cheekbones.

Sam climbed to the highest point in the dunes and found Jesus there with binoculars, "I don't know what I'm doing," she said.

"You're all right."

"What about Toledo?"

"You know he'll come."

"I think I'm out of my mind."

"We all are—let it go."

Sam laughed at how simple it was for him, maybe for anyone who knows who he is, she wanted to be him—that was her, always wanting to be someone she admired—someone.

There was an SIB agent on the boat, when his relief came they would smoke and drink together for half an hour, all along Jesus had refused to say how he managed to ship out the footage daily, now he told Sam that through the same contact, he'd received a riot suit and mask, the same kind worn by the outer cordon troops, who had been wearing this uniform for a week, Jesus would slip into the ranks and when the dinghy went out to Richard's boat to take the

SIB relief, he would be running it, he'd go aboard with the relief agent. Richard had left in a chopper while Sam was running on the beach, they could only hope he stayed away long enough, "What if he took Cheekbones with him?" Sam said.

Jesus said, "He was alone."

"You don't think she's on the boat, do you?"

"No," he said, "but I want to know what is."

Jesus had been slipping coke to the SIB agent assigned to him at night, to cover him while he dressed in the riot uniform, now Sam gave him cover, took coke to his agent and hers, they insisted she do it with them, she knew she had to, was amazed at the feeling of power, of a superbody fueled with a kind of adrenalin that seemed to be in her mind, completely under her control, she was aware of everything—the night, Jesus disappearing in it, the inner and outer security cordons, the SIB agents—Frank and Bob—flanking her, some engine approaching in the distance, a light crawling along the beach, hovercraft, "God, it's hot," she said.

Frank said, "Why don't you take off your clothes?"

"In front of you?"

Bob said, "We've seen you without your clothes."

"Only on camera—that's not really me."

"Let's see," Frank said and lunged towards her.

The hovercraft lights were running along the beach in the direction Jesus had to go to slip into the troops, "Catch me first!" Sam said, jumped up waving her arms and took off running towards the hovercraft light, Frank and Bob roared after, the light turned towards them, tracking, it was Toledo, with camera, Sam ran up the beach in the opposite direction from Richard's boat.

"Where the hell have you been?" Toledo said as he climbed out with a camera.

She wound her arms around him, camera and all, "Remember the day we met?" she said, Frank and Bob arrived and tried to act like agents, "Remember skinny-dipping?" Sam said and ran into the surf, Toledo followed, he'd given the camera to Frank, he and Bob passed it back and forth but stayed far enough away for the surf to cover while she told Toledo where Jesus was.

Next they heard a chopper approaching, Richard coming back, they had to keep him away from the boat, "Put on a show he'll have to watch," Toledo said, they tore each other's clothes off and fake sex-danced in the surf, "The longest erection of my life," Toledo said, "—wasted!" In her mind's eye Sam saw the child from the street at the Circus, from the video in the movie—inside her—still as a freeze-frame, no tears, nothing—as if she were dead, how she controlled the rage, the love too, saw her float then disappear in the deep water.

It worked, Richard's chopper brought him straight to the beach, he took the camera from Frank and Bob, walked out in the surf, said, "Encore!"

Finally they saw the dinghy returning from Richard's boat, gave Jesus time to get back then chased each other to the house, leaving Richard behind. On the boat Jesus had found the kind of computer made for military intelligence use—technically illegal for civilians but not impossible to get for those with the right connections. The news carried a story about a Coast Guard seaplane that had been shot down in a sting operation near Tijuana, police sources said the pilot had been running drugs, his drowned and rock-battered body was recovered. It was Jesus' friend who had been delivering our film and tape to Mexico, they'd gotten the day's run—but who were they?

"The lunatic Right," Toledo said, "—that's Richard."

Sam said, "A conspiracy?"

"For what?"

"Say a military presence."

"In LA?" Toledo said.

"Maybe all of southern California—to the Rio Grande."

"All that to control immigration?"

Sam said, "At one level but really to control culture—the country, maybe more."

They were in the shower that Toledo had built so he knew the space well enough to be confident it hadn't been bugged, he leaned back against the shower wall, "I walked right into Richard's trap—and you knew it."

"No—I was just afraid of it—him."

"Are you attracted to him?"

"I despise him."

"That's not what I asked."

"No, I'm not attracted to him."

"I am—his power," Toledo said, "I was in love with him when I was a kid."

"In love—like obsession?"

"He controlled everything, everyone."

"I felt controlled by him before I told you what he did."

"I thought he got you too—you don't despise someone you're indifferent to. What about now?"

"I think we can beat him," Sam said.

"Why were you crying—on the beach when we were simulating and I had such a hard-on?"

"I didn't know I was, just thinking about the little girl—you know, the one I saw outside the Circus and you put in the movie—I saw her drift away."

"Maybe you don't need her anymore?"

"Then why was I crying?"

"Don't people cry when they're happy?"

Sam laughed, "Oh—I don't know a lot about that."

"I'm happy too," he said.

It was strange, this happiness, in the midst of so much madness, Cheekbones gone, Jesus' friend dying, the movie being out of their control, maybe they had to be happy with each other, maybe happiness only existed in contrast—like art?

The next day they were to shoot the airport scene at LAX. At this point in the script, Jesus has received Medialennium's co-opt offer to join forces and run for lieutenant governor on a platform to be hammered out mutually, so they said. Toledo's re-imaging for the gubernatorial race—ultimately, the presidency—calls for him to switch to Republican and accept a Purple Heart for flying a chopper to evacuate the wounded in Vietnam, the award would be made on national TV by the President, it would be the first such honoring of patriotic service by a civilian—and journalist—equal to military heroism, and would carry with it an honorary commission of colonel in the Army—to be conferred at the same time on the hero. Flannery, now in the resistance, has learned from Cheekbones of the real Medialennium agenda, a plot to assassinate Toledo and frame Jesus for it. Flannery and Toledo decide to leave Medialennium, go off the grid, they meet at LAX, disguised as vacationers bound for Hawaii.

While they were setting up to shoot in LAX, Playback received a thumb drive by messenger, everything stopped as they watched it, Cheekbones—bones sharper than ever, eyes dull, skin almost yellow—seated against a white sheet on which the front page of today's *LA Times* is hung, with a Black in a white coat and stethoscope who talks about her excellent health and spunk, Cheekbones says, "Get out of here, damn fool!" The doctor laughs indulgently, gets up and walks to a door, a shot rings out and his face, close-up, is the picture of shock, more shots sound, his forehead is hit, blood runs from a hole and as he falls, Cheekbones reaches him, picks up his head and rocks it, "I told you," she says, "—fool!"

The sequence ended with a voice saying, "Get it?"

It was weird, the images so real seemed fake, impossible, felt like losing their grip on reality—versus—what?

Richard's Malibu jet was ready for the scene, they'd never talked about flying it out of the movie but maybe it had been in the back of their minds for a while, now they had to do it. "Brilliant bastard," Toledo said.

The airport looked like a ghost town, the troops had cordoned off everything, even the extras were military personnel—down to the mercenaries interspersed in the crowd, in fact they were the same ones. Sam said, "If anything happens—" and her mind went blank, she had no idea what she was going to say. Sadness welled up like a river lying in wait.

Toledo said, "We're going to beat him—remember?"

"Right."

Script Sequence

My hair has more streaks, I'm wearing pink leather pants and vest cut to show, pink jeweled boots, in the restroom I take off the vest and pull the pants down to check my mirror image in black lace lingerie, garter belt and stockings, "So my husband can think about it on the plane," I say to a bug-eyed woman waiting for a stall, "do you think I look too fat?"

The bug-eyed woman says, "If my husband got me anything like that I'd throw it in his face!"

"Yeah?" I say, "I just hope it works," pop a stick of gum in my mouth and go out.

I spot Toledo in a three-piece suit, horn-rims and hat, he's pacing back and forth in front of a news stand, pulls out a flask, drinks furtively, I approach but he doesn't recognize me.

"Looking for a good time?" I say.

Toledo stares.

I say, "Act like we're making a deal."

He pulls a twenty out of his pocket, says, "Keep the change."

"You promised it would be a hundred!"

"That's for the booze."

"Champagne!"

"Let's see the goods first," he says and yanks my vest open, clears his throat, spreads his arms and sings, "You are too beautiful—"

"Fool," I say and try to pull him through the crowd.

"Where's my lai?" he says.

"Not till we get to Hawaii."

"Isn't this Hawaii?"

I find a phone booth and shove him in it, "This isn't burlesque," I say, "do you want to leave or not?"

"I want to fuck you in your black lace cleavage."

"You're drunk!"

"Sus'sposed to be."

"Supposed to *act* drunk," I say.

"I'm a method actor."

"Fuck!"

Toledo starts unzipping his pants, my eyes start tearing, I say, "You know you have a death wish?"

Toledo draws himself up like a drunk and says, "You really believe this cloak-and-dagger assassination bit—look at you—"

"Why would Cheekbones lie about it?"

"Got me," Toledo says, "never could figure out why my dear wife did anything—"

"Wife!"

"*Ex-wife.*"

I say, "You're still in love with her."

"You're jealous," Toledo says, "at least I can get that from you."

"Is that why you keep her on coke?"

"She needs it," he says, "if I had cut her off she would have killed herself."

"Why—what is it she can't face?"

"She wants more than I can give her."

"Has it occurred to you that is what you need is to believe?"

"You've been talking to her," Toledo said, "and it's a damn lie—women lie about things men don't even know exist."

"How do you know we're lying then?"

"On principle," he says, "—women lie on principle!"

"Maybe men can't face the truth and we protect them from it."

"You're saying women don't need men?"

"Not the way you think we do."

"Fine," Toledo says, "see if you can get out of this fire trap alone!"

He opens the phone booth, we can barely get out for the crowd streaming by—much larger now, people seem to pour in from everywhere, they bump into each other, fall and grab others to pull themselves back up, children shriek—it's too real. Toledo begins directing traffic, I grab his hand and push our way through the crowd, he digs his feet in, "How do I know you're not setting me up?" he says, his face white as a clown's—cheeks red too—and his eyes accuse me, "You get me here with a suitcase—some creep photographs us together and smears the pictures all over the state," he says, "who's going to re-elect a chump who pays for it—and gets caught?"

His voice hates me, his eyes hate me, his fly is still open, I can't speak over his hate, the crowd presses in on us, their faces hate too, "You're not running for re-election, you're running for your life," I say, "besides you know because Cheekbones told us and you love her," I say.

"Love is for the movies."

"Oh yeah—seen any lately?"

The crowd is too tight now to move at all, nightmare of feet scrambling over fallen bodies, hands grabbing, mouths agony-wide. "What is it," Toledo says, "—earthquake?" A baggage cart slams into us, the driver jumps out and begins loading from the back, "You drive," Toledo says, "—I'm shotgun," he falls in, I aim the cart straight into the crowd—now one gyrating monster, Toledo pulls out his flask, drunkenly waves it at people who run to catch the cart, grab at it, half climb in, fall, I driving like a maniac, crowd screaming constant now, blending with the weep of a tenor sax on the sound system.

"What the fuck?" Toledo says.

I say, "Guns," and point to the brown-uniformed Sentry with their M-16s, other baggage carts try to cut off the path to the runway where the Hawaii flight is parked—and the Malibu is to meet us—I lead them on a chase back through the airport to another exit, more Sentries pour in, shots sound—and more screams—people fall bleeding, feet trample them, Toledo standing up in the cart, yelling the Declaration of Independence, I drive through the sea of Sentry, through the shots toward the Malibu, a Concord turns into taxiing position, Toledo stands lashing imaginary horses, I reach over and knock him down as the cart slides under the Concord wing, careens past jeeps, trucks, Sentries running and shooting, police cars—the siren war-cries—accompany us to the Malibu, we jump out and take the steps, the shots follow, as we reach the cabin door Toledo spins against the railing.

In that moment of his damned realism so good I could swear the shot was real, the blood, I'm suspended as if time stopped, I grab and push him inside.

Script Sequence cut

"Cut!" Toledo howling, the Sentry actors transformed, surrounding us, Citizens join with weapons, real ones, we're still in the movie, in and out, not in control anymore—if we ever were. Toledo's really shot, they let me help with his wound, which went through the edge of his skull and back out, the problem is the bleeding—not the part I can see, the chance there's more. They ply us with gourmet food, wine, and Courvoisier—I don't let Toledo have anything because of the head wound—they even have coke, I'm sure they've monitored every second of Playback and know he was off, I guess they want him on again—more controllable. He keeps howling orders, they ignore.

They give us everything but information, answer no questions, just fly us to the San Francisco harbor, on to an antiaircraft carrier patrolling out beyond the three-mile limit and put us in a helicopter that takes us to Alcatraz Island, we descend through the fog, the lighthouse seems to rise towards us as if we we're zooming in on it through a camera's eye, I think of Toledo's lighthouse and am filled with nostalgia, this one was history itself, the first lighthouse on the west coast, long edges of concrete climbing to the light, guard towers emerging from the fog, first the one on top of the Rock then others like soldiers circling the king, the closer we get to the ground, the more birds seem to appear, as if to greet us, so many of them I can almost hear their wings, their freedom. Citizens with helmets and face shields, moving synchronously, as if every step, every gesture is choreographed, I wonder if Richard watches our arrival—from the lighthouse? Gone are the National Park signs, replaced by ones reading Institute of Criminal Reeducation. Gone, all the tourist stuff, the Rock has been commandeered for more important business—once again a prison but not for recalcitrant soldiers or intransigent inmates, this time for moviemakers. They march us—Toledo on a stretcher carried by Citizens—down below the prison, the lower level of the old fort—the dungeons—our steps accompanied by the screech of gulls, the foghorn, finally the clanging of iron.

Ten

I haven't seen Toledo or Jesus since the day we arrived, I don't know if Cheekbones is here, don't know how long ago it's been, there's no way to tell time or the passage of days here—no windows, the light is all artificial, recessed in ceiling and walls, ingeniously positioned for shooting video. I put a mark on the wall every time I go to the yard to do the obstacle course but I don't know how often that happens, sometimes I see the fog, sometimes only darkness broken by the sweep of the lighthouse beam, as if here there is no need to block out natural light, when it's fog and the birds break through, I think how this is really their world, was long before the fort or the prison, the impotent cannons supposed to protect San Francisco but even in a mock attack could not hit a stationary target, even the 1969 American Indian Movement occupation ended, apparently so did the National Park Service, the tourists, it all belongs to the birds now—like in ancient times when it was a mountain and valley, slowly sinking into the sea—only the birds live here with impunity, with even the hope of deliverance, they nest on jagged rock ledges, I rename the Rock the Birdnest.

My nest too for the baby I think I'm carrying, hope, strange because I never thought of having a baby, yet this feeling moves me, not like the feeling of writing—well, something like that, bringing something new, but different inside, quieter, softer, like spring when I was child—I remember! Or dream the woods where the usual noise and panic are gone because everything that could happen would be good. If it's memory it must be because of the life inside.

But sometimes I worry that I'm not pregnant, that I don't bleed because of this jail, I hate to think that could be. The cell is only wide enough for the narrow mattress and a foot of walking space, there are no bars, only the steel door, and what used to be the only privacy for an inmate is lost because of closed circuit television, observing all, the cameras are recessed, their eyes invisible though I can hear them move as I move, the monitor is mounted over the toilet with its stains and stench, and the sink with spigots that don't work except to drip, the only sound except the foghorn and the video, the closed circuit system, the heart of the reeducation program, explains the videotaped orientation to the Institute—my Birdnest. Citizen guards monitor the cells from the control room, everything within the cell can be seen and heard, every cell is solitary, company—and privacy—are for the innocent, as it was in the old days, the hole must be temporary, I tell myself, eventually I'll be returned to the population where the cells have bars, you can see other inmates, maybe by then I'll know the crime I must have committed.

As there is no company, no privacy, there is no darkness, lights are kept on for the video observation and to control the level of consciousness with recorded education programs, I begin to lose the distinction between the video monitor and my mind—images and sounds from the monitor become interwoven with images from my mental landscape, I do Tai Chi mentally, I get so I can do it even when I'm watching the video images, I tell myself it counteracts them.

Whenever no other program is being shown, the monitor output is switched to the closed circuit cameras that follow my every move— *Autobiography*—they call it, I see myself constantly—like living in a mirror, nothing I say is responded to, no question answered, as if the world has ended but the cameras still project images on screens in some hell of perpetual reruns, for awhile I'm not sure whether the picture is of me now—in real time—or in my forgotten past, with hypnotic attention I look for signs of reality—what this place is, what the time relationship is to the last thing I remember before this—shooting the escape scene at LAX, then without warning I'm overcome with déjà vu so profound I think I even remember this cell from years ago—an eternity, I wonder whether I had any real existence—or was it all tape-memory? I hear a voice saying, "You're crazy as she is!" "She" being my mother, I suppose, and wonder if this is an insane asylum I've always inhabited, it feels so familiar somehow, I can hear a shrink saying it's my guilt, my need to be punished, but isn't guilt the condition of so-called civilized folk— guilt concealing the killer? So I didn't have to actually do anything to be here..? When I think like this I've forgotten the movie—my actual crime. I get lost in this place then remember then get lost. I try to hang onto the memory like a madwoman clutching at the remnants of her mind. Then I remember the baby, I must stay sane for her, I must get out.

Even when I go to the yard I'm alone, my cell opens only after a remote-controlled cage-car has locked into my door, I enter, the cage locks me in and runs on track to the yard door, opens and lets me out in the yard—empty except for Citizens patrolling up on the tower—neither speaking to each other nor stopping for a smoke, their marching back and forth the only sign they live—but they could still be robots, I envy them being up high enough to see out, to see one of the most beautiful skylines in the world, they don't even notice the birds—the only sign of life, I read somewhere that Alcatraz is a Spanish word for a certain type of waterfowl—how can they not know this?

I'm continually amazed at how terrifying the loneliness is—how much worse it is with them up there, deaf or numb, at first I called to them, tried to bait them—if they came down and attacked, at least I'd know we still exist—my imprisonment would mean something, they didn't, nothing changed, not even the position of their face shields, I suppose I'm obsessed with them, at least they move in some facsimile of humanness.

When I am loneliest I remember the baby and think, if she's real, I'll never be alone again.

If I knew this was all for the movie I'd know it will end, credits will roll, there will be something after this, as it is I go from my cell to the obstacle course—from one monitor screen to the other—I don't know whether I'm any different from the Citizen-robots, suppose I could transform into one of them so slowly the change would be imperceptible?

Instructions for the obstacle course are given over a huge screen, my kill average—the number of targets I make with the various forms of killing the course teaches—karate, knifing, shooting, bomb construction, bomb detonation, piloting a fighter-bomber, pushing the STRIKE button, suicide missions—all the kills are tallied as I do the course, if I maintain it I continue to be in the Kill Unit and eligible for Citizen Recruit, if I don't, my image will appear on the targets of the other members of my Kill Unit and I'll be turned out on the Rock, branded Enemy Agent, the ones hunted for live-kill practice by Citizens and Citizen Recruits, I'm told this over and over on the monitor, I go through the course like doing a kata to the music of the foghorn, iron gates clanging, the birds, my softness the child inside.

I have no idea why I'm here, where Toledo, Jesus and Cheekbones are—even Richard—though of course he's here, he's the only thing that could make sense of this virtual nightmare, in the script we were kidnapped to kill Jesus—his candidacy, the idea of California reunification with Mexico—but there was no Institute of Reeducation, none of this. In the script we do get away, I cling to this.

My greatest torment is the knowledge that it all started with my going to Toledo's Little Hollywood audition—grandiose, inflated, altogether absurd as it sounds—yet I'm haunted by it, then the deal we all made with Richard—for the movie, for his money. The Medialennium of the movie required a Faustian bargain for survival, I remember Toledo saying this was survival for me but that's metaphor, assuming there is a world other than metaphor, we the moviemakers walked into it freely—into Richard's trap, as Toledo put it. The memory of Richard saying he was undercover makes me wonder whether it was the truth, whether he was then, maybe still is, working for the government in one of those jobs they deny the existence of—and deny knowledge of the person if caught. Did this place—and others like it—exist before the movie? Were they afraid the movie would expose it? But what is *it*? Antiterror/terrorism—what the mirror shows? The world would remain more sane if I could believe this was all just Richard, the madman, if Richard went into Victims Vigilant— maybe even started it himself—as a manifestation of his own delusion—which he pulled us into, yes, that would make sense, I cling to this, yet I worry that Richard started VV and got into our movie as part of his agent job, when I think that the paranoia of it overwhelms me, I have to go back to Richard the madman, all this goes on in my mind constantly, especially when I'm doing the courses, when the video is not on *Autobiography*, but even then, it runs in the background.

At night whenever I manage to fall asleep in the intense light I'm instantly in a dream of Richard, a woman who looks like me, and a child—sometimes a baby, sometimes as old as ten or eleven, the three of them naked, frozen in position—Richard standing, the woman sitting on a white iron bed with the child, they're connected by handcuffs, I try to become the director of the dream—to make them move and act but they won't, I touch one of them and realize it's a doll, I know I've done it—turned the person into this mannequin—I try to escape but everywhere I go, people turn into dolls, I run faster but the faster I run the more dolls appear, from behind me I hear a voice—always the same man's voice—I know I know it but can't remember whose it is—always saying the same thing, "You fucked them—they're dead!" Then the handcuffs turn into blue light. At first I'm freaked by it, as if it's some weird special effects, but then I start to feel its softness, enchantment.

Lately I have the dream every time I sleep and when I wake up, the video monitor picture jumps as if with a flashcut—I wonder if the dream is a tape—I'm not really asleep but hypnotized, the worst part of this is thinking I could be existing entirely in a trance— with Richard the hypnotist. Thinking this scares me the most for my child inside, I must get out, we must. I realize she might be a delusion but one I need.

Today when my cage-car takes me to the yard, sunlight seems to radiate from everything, I'm shocked as if the sun can't shine here, it must be artificial, the obstacle course looks more surreal than ever, and as usual the monitor announces I'll be tested on new skills, I finish the physical obstacles and start with the rifle-range, move to hand-guns then the karate house with its four walls of video screen—each wall showing a different camera angle of instructor demonstrating techniques and forms, as I go through the movements, a computerized shadow of my image is superimposed on the instructor's to show exactly where my form needs work, next sparing partners are projected, my counter-moves are scored electronically then I move on to the scenes where I'm ambushed and finally situations in which I have to ambush and strike first.

I'm told that my score is exceptional—I'm a born killer—and am directed to the sabotage hut that teaches small explosives, everything here is taught by computer, it's as though my mind is a digicam making a perfect record without the slightest effort, I learn to make a bomb small enough to put in a disposable lighter, to wire it to the ignition of a car, next is the cockpit of a chopper that radio-activates various sabotage devices as well as operating four high-powered rifles from a computer screen, the computerized cockpit of a fighter jet teaches me antipersonnel targeting with computer technology.

When I emerge from the cockpit, the sun is gone, the video

monitor is dark too, I see the night sky for the first time since I've been here. "Even more beautiful than the memory, isn't it?" a voice says—Richard, he's walking towards me, smiling, holding his arms open like a long-lost friend.

I'm overwhelmed with joy to see another human being even though it's the worst one. I feel dizzy with hope, step back, "So it is you—all of it," I say, careful not to make it a question.

Richard stops a few feet from me, lifts his arms in a gesture of helplessness in the face of my intransigence, his cheeks glowing from the equipment lights, "Paranoia always was your weak spot," he says, "do you know how long you've been working today?"

"Not long enough to miss you."

Richard smiles, "Your anger is pure aphrodisiac—you know that," he says, "you've been working for fourteen hours straight."

"What is the date and time?"

"Time here is success," Richard says, "come, you haven't eaten in too long and I need the company."

"I'm not hungry."

Richard laughs, steps closer to put his arm around me, says, "God, I've missed you!"

I jump away, square off and wind up to hit him, something in his fingers flashes, the yard lights and video monitor come up—and I can't move, I stand like a statue in half-strike position, "Fantastic," he says, "I forget you're a registerable weapon these days—you can see the monitor—wonderful shot, freeze frame—isn't it?" he says, "you can't move but you can talk, it takes higher doses to neutralize mental processes. It's a new development in laser technology—called lazar, after Lazarus—nice touch, don't you think? It's actually a bit like curare, causes paralysis but without relaxation."

"A kind of living death but you can raise us up," I say, "—assuming that life in this place is up?"

"It's very convenient—and noninvasive—don't you see?"

"What's the meaning of noninvasive when transfixion can occur without a visible wound?"

"Transfixion—interesting concept. You were always interesting—sometimes brilliant."

"But this is your brilliant solution to the mess of humanness," I say, "and you're getting this on camera too?"

"Of course, I wouldn't miss a second of your movie."

"Mine?"

"Ours," Richard says and smiles, "I'm having the time of my life."

"And our death."

"Don't worry, lazar treatment doesn't last but a few minutes at this dose."

"What about the guards up on the tower—what's their dose?"

"So observant."

The video monitor shows us in the yard, Richard's face looks older, deathly pale. I say, "Where is Toledo?"

"*I* am Toledo," Richard says.

"Not my Toledo."

"We'll talk about everything—please, let me feed you."

"Do I have a choice?"

"Always."

"So long as I don't mind paralysis," I say.

"Would you rather go back to your cell?"

"Yes."

"It's a lie—but an honorable one."

He's right, I want desperately to talk to him—anyone, just another body, I shake with the desire as the cage-car takes me back to my cell, a tray arrives spilling over with fruit, cheese, wine and a card from Richard, "If you insist on suffering, you have to eat."

All night I lie smelling the fruit and cheese, when my eyes drift shut I immediately see Richard in the dream, wake myself up and wonder whether he's giving me drugs—maybe in the regular food, a nauseating gruel claimed to be super-nutritious by the Birdnest promos shown every seven minutes, just like broadcast commercials, I get off the mattress, prop it against the wall and do the Tai Chi form till I'm ready to drop then I meditate in lotus position, as my body relaxes I see a familiar street and then a child around ten, so the child, the lost me, the one I thought drifted away, she's come back, older now, has a strange walk—a sort of rocking from the balls of her feet up on her toes—dance-like—from a movie, no doubt, I feel the motion of the walk and think her thoughts—leaving here to be on stage and in the movies—the leaving is the point.

I don't know where *here* is for the child—just a street—growing dark, she doesn't mind though, chameleon that she is, night her disguise—even inside the house she enters now on tip-toe—leaving the lights off, taking off her shoes too, climbing the stairs, slow, almost slow-motion, holding her breath, avoiding the steps that creak, the door of her room creaks too, she takes a full minute to get it open far enough to slip inside, her fingers hesitate then turn the lock, she stands looking at the locked door then crawls between the bed sheets—doesn't close her eyes though, that would tempt fate too much, she lies watching the shadows.

It's getting light, the lock doesn't turn until her eyes have dropped shut for several minutes then the knob turns softly—yet at the sound she jumps awake as if with electric shock.

"What do you think you're doing—locking this door?" the man says.

She closes her eyes and pretends to be asleep though she can see him anyway, the way he always stands in the hall light, swaying slightly, reeking, "Get up there, Red Bird," he says, grabs her arm and drags her off the bed, down the hall, up the stairs to the attic where boxes of old clothes and books line the hall, a doll is propped up against the last box, she stops to pick it up, she never goes beyond this point—the other one does, the one who lives only here—the lost one, she watches her disappear with him behind the white door.

It's the dream of Richard, the woman who looks like me, and the baby, now a young girl on the white iron bed—frozen as if with Richard's lazar, now it's—what—hallucination? If it's memory, how can Richard be in it? Created memory—something to fill in the blanks? I do so want Richard to be the madman behind all this, something about that child is too real, though, more than the urchin I saw outside the Circus that time and Toledo put in the movie, the one I saw drift away in the deep water. I was horrified by them, moved by them, but this one fascinates me, I want to see more of her, to know her, maybe she really is hallucination.

I feel my belly where this new child is, I hope.

The trays of fruit, cheese and wine keep arriving, at first I don't look, only the smell haunts me, then I look and notice it's different from the last tray, I realize this always happens, I always look, I don't know how close I am to eating, I even dream of it— no more of Richard and the woman and child, just the food and wine, I meditate and find the child who fascinates me, I ask her what to do, she ignores me—is still frozen with Richard and the woman who looks like me, I begin to analyze the dream, the three projections of my psyche—the madman, the dumbed woman, the innocent—how I want to see the innocent animal—be her, I take exception with Freud, I agree this is the problem of civilization, the son who must kill the father to take his place yet can't so kills his mind, his consciousness, instead, but that's only the condition since written history, I argue, what about the Goddess cultures, agrarian peoples, before the horses and the barbarians, what about the graves with no weapons, no evidence of hierarchy—equality— god, what a dream! But what if it really existed and then the ones on horses destroyed it—but also mated with the women, what if we are all the descendants of lost—raped—humanity? So in our unconsciousness we all know annihilation—and the rapist who did it—inside, they live together in us, and the patriarch is the one we choose to represent it all. *We choose*—I get stuck on that, that whole thing about choice, I want the innocence of no choice but if there is choice, I think, if it's true, we could change—see the barbarian warlord and the goddess too, choose her, I begin to live for that possibility.

Each time they bring a new tray I sit with the frozen three, till the day the child moves, her hand reaches out and we eat, I realize the obvious—that I am she, I was in that room on that bed with someone like Richard and a woman who looks like me, my mother, this is my past, all I have of it—whether fantasy or memory, I think of all the so-called schizophrenics I've known, the theory about their fantasies—what if they are the unconscious of civilization? The sacrificial lambs who transmit truth with their being. And when they're both—fantasy and reality—what then? I think of that line from The Brothers Karamazov—"When all is permitted, what then?"

I want to ask the child—did she try to help her mother by being his sex toy? I think with the child, how to divert his attention from the woman who looks like me, to be the one who could take it, to be the best wind-up doll, the worst—the best worst. I want to ask her, I want to ask her what to do when Richard calls us, ask everything, as if she's separate, when I think this way, the child is still frozen, I want her to trust me—that I won't leave her again, then I realize thinking this way is leaving, the issue isn't her trusting me, it's my trusting her—us—me, I go through all this and know what I will do, forget, go through it all over and know again, I remember what they say about torture—everyone breaks, it's what happened to the woman in the dream who looks like me, the child. We broke. But what about the handcuffs that turned to blue light?

This child in me now will not break.

I still don't drink the wine—each label different, always French and a few years older than the last, it arrives uncorked, standing in ice if white, otherwise alone on the tray, today it's not in ice and I can smell it—a cabernet, I think, it makes me dizzy, it doesn't matter if I drink, it's just something I'm keeping from the brokenness, it's an illusion I know, illusion of control, but I need it.

The monitor flickers, Richard's image comes in, "You're breaking my heart," he says, "at least bring the cabernet and let me drink from your shoe."

I wonder if I refuse will he kill me but I'm not that brave—or that lost. The cage-car arrives—this time with a Citizen—the first person I've seen up close, the first since the kidnapping, except the tower guards and Richard that once, this one looks like Lazarus too—completely covered by the uniform, helmet and face shield, gloves, M-16 shouldered—and says nothing, I think how like them Flannery was, automaton that talked but that was automatic too, the car lets us off onto an elevator that rises and opens on a heliport where a hovercraft waits, the Citizen with me is the pilot, I crane to see San Francisco, even the shadow of it through the fog.

I say, "Do you wear the mask all the time?" The Lazarus doesn't answer, we lift off the building, rise up above its bright lights aimed at the ground, Lazaruses holding rifles, pacing around the outer edge and across a catwalk to the next building—all the buildings we pass are connected by catwalks, as if the ground were unsafe even for the armed, many of the walls and roofs are crumbling, some are patched with jerry-rigged scaffolding, windows are nailed shut with plywood or composition board, the catwalks are connected to each other too, and vines—or maybe ropes—hang down from them—it all looks like the set of a Vietnam movie.

The hovercraft climbs over the ruins, the façade of the old warden's house, lands on top of a building behind the façade, architecture of inelegant expediency, another Lazarus stands guard, the one I'm with leads me down a ramshackle elevator, through halls with huge holes in the walls, some patched crudely with cheap plasterboard—and every few feet a Lazarus holding an M-16, I see how perfect they are—like works of art, frozen in time, except that works of art aren't perfect, I look closer and see a detail that differs—a shoulder, is it trembling? A rifle swaying? Or is it my desire to see life? We stop at a door that opens to a dressing room and bath, I begin shaking, whether from anticipation of the bath or fear of Richard, the Citizen walks around checking the room with a bug-finder, the kind that detects both camera and listening devices—an electronics course cycle I've just started.

"Do Citizens bug each other too?" I say.

The Citizen ignores me, finishes checking the room, walks back to me and pulls off the face shield and helmet—Cheekbones! We stare at each other. I think I must be dreaming or hallucinating, she hugs me, the touch is a shock. "You'll get dirty," I say, "I thought you were dead," and sink to the floor, her arms cushioning me.

She says, "You're sick—what're you eating?"

"Fruit and cheese—lately."

"You're not used to it."

Cheekbones helps me up, we strip off the inmate's uniform, I stand in the shower, the feel of water strange, almost stinging, I think of the Holocaust showers—waters of death—I grasp the spigots and turn them, return to time. "Are you pregnant?" Cheekbones says.

I look down at the slight bulge of my gut, say, "You think so?"

"Of course you are."

"Crazy as it is—in this place—I want her."

"Yes," Cheekbones says, shows me the white jumpsuit I'm to put on, "You're a Recruit now—like me. Everything but the helmet and face shield—verboten except to full-fledged Citizens. These—" she points to the helmet and face shield she just took off, "these are stolen. We steal everything—just as they stole our lives, we're stealing them back."

I say, "The wretched still crawling to Jerusalem."

"They say they're the future and we're the past."

"But what if the past is the future—they're us and we're them—mirror images—video feedback—is that what this place means?"

"It means Richard's on top," Cheekbones says.

I laugh. "You and Chuey—the brilliance of simplicity—while I'm always mucking around trying to figure out what things mean."

"That's what artists do."

"See, you're doing it again—being beautifully simple—and kind."

"If there's one thing none of this is, it's kind."

She told me Jesus escaped and joined the Enemy Agents, they live in the lighthouse—computerized now, no one goes there, at night they ambush Citizens for helmets and face shields, weapons, supplies and information.

I say, "That's why all the catwalks."

"Citizens—and Recruits—are scared shitless of the Enemy— call them devils and vampires—the whole scene is strictly from late night flicks."

"And this is *our* late-night flick?"

Cheekbones says, "More and more Recruits are working with the Enemy in the Transformation—interesting that in Medialennium, we were transformed into conformists. Here we're transformed to resist. The Transformists, we call ourselves—there is no more revolution, that kind of power is past, everything we do now is to communicate the present, we're close to breaking the computer code, when that happens we'll be able to get into the closed circuit system and access the monitors in the cells."

I'm fascinated by the Transformation—hope, when I've almost given up on it. "Toledo?" I say—afraid of the answer.

"We haven't found a way to reach him yet, he's Recruit eligible but Richard won't take him without a confession of conspiracy."

"Is that what he'll want me to do?"

"To Richard, women—or maybe it's Black women—aren't capable of conspiring—just fucking," Cheekbones says.

I tell her about my dream, my confusion about Richard— whether he was the man in the memory, whether it was real.

"You're not crazy," she says.

"So you think it could be real—could be Richard?"

"Could—oh yeah."

There's no time to tell everything about this god-forsaken place, the most important is that Richard runs the Birdnest—I give Cheekbones my name for it—but not the whole show, he's only one member of The We—the financiers who turn out to be the new-old economic elite—fascists. The Nest—Cheekbones adapts my name—is billed as a pilot project, the model solution for the deterioration of inner cities, collapse of the infrastructure and rise of unemployment, crime, political unrest—all the problems of posttechnological society—the training ground for antiterrorist warriors, terrorist defined the way Victims Vigilant did—anyone from a purse-snatcher to a nationstate, a religion—anything not in sync with the goals of The We. The climax of the project will be a mock war between Citizen Recruits and the Enemy, scored by Citizen referees watching on video. Recruits judged as survivors will make full Citizenship. The Enemy will be annihilated. "All for the movie," Cheekbones says.

"Our movie?"

"What used to be. Richard thinks the movie is part of the conspiracy and that he's taken it over—he's the new director. Scenes from the Nest—especially the war—will transform it from the diabolic morass he thinks it is to a story of moral regeneration and social redemption—read conformity."

"Armageddon," I say, "did he get our original footage from Mexico?"

Cheekbones shakes her head, "I've had every truth drug—if I'd known, I would have told where it is," she says.

"What else has he done to you?"

Cheekbones ignores me, says she has to go and hide the helmet and face shield before going to Richard's apartment to do the bug-check that more and more he trusts only her to do.

"He doesn't trust anyone but you?" I say.

"Not me either," Cheekbones says, "he just thinks he has something on me."

"Toledo said you were pregnant—"

Cheekbones stops for a moment—as if blocking on a rehearsed speech. "You're the one who can get to him," she says.

"Why?"

"He has different fantasies about you—the kind men have about White women."

"The baby?"

"There was no baby—Stephen's old fantasy."

"At first he said it was his son."

"Fantasy."

"Talk to me."

"It was always about drugs and Richard." Her eyes seem too bright, she's probably holding back tears but I worry she's telling me another myth, partly what Richard tells her, partly what she tells herself.

I say, "Richard?"

"When I was with Rachel, he raped me. He had a knife—like some crazy. At first I thought he was kidding—I even laughed. That really pissed him. I was wasted or I could have fought him, he would've had to kill me. Afterwards I was afraid to tell anyone, afraid of what Rachel would do—what she did. She took everything out on herself. Maybe on me, too, maybe she thought I should've fought him off."

"She knew?"

"She guessed."

"Had he done it to her?"

"That and more—kiddie porn. I was afraid of what Stephen would do too."

"Kill Richard," I say. I feel heat rising from my stomach, it's vomit, I stagger to the toilet, not much comes up but bile. I keep thinking *kiddie porn*. When I can speak I say, "He's still raping you."

"He tries—even when he makes me go down on him—with the Citizen holding a gun on me—he can't make it. Even when he's watching kiddie porn."

I start to cry, shaking, horrible tears, Cheekbones hugs me and tells me to stop, there isn't time, we have to finish the movie. The thought sends a thrill through me, euphoric hope that it's true, we're in the movie, it will end.

Eleven

Richard is a shock to see—the picture of timeless power, even youthful in the dim light—not what I want, I want him weak and needy the way I imagined him for hours in my cell, he stands in a silk smoking jacket with his arms spread, I let him just touch my shoulders then spin away and walk around the apartment— furnished with antiques, rich wall hangings that almost hide unsightly plasterboard patches, a velvet drape completely covers a window—probably glassless, oriental rugs rise with every step on the broken floorboards, "Beauty among the ruins," Richard says.

"Maybe you've discovered the next architectural period— postapocalyptic," I say, "your antiques are the perfect contrast."

"By beauty, I meant you," Richard says, "I'm the ruins."

I say, "Are you my father?"

Richard isn't shocked, he tells me he met my mother when he owned and ran an upstate New York asylum—The Home, they called it, very innovative, treated psychotics with experimental methods. My mother became an inmate when she was found walking in the street outside the asylum—in her nightgown, she had an envelop with money and a note that she had taken a knife to someone and needed to be locked up—but humanely, the family could have nothing to do with it, she was an embarrassment, however shining with pathos, Richard had asked her about the knife incident, she said it was a family friend, very respectable, who had tried to rape her—something Richard doubted given her sexuality, she was the perfect Eve, he said, perfect evil combined with perfect beauty and sensuality no man could resist, she couldn't resist her own sexuality, no man who had her could be called a rapist. Every month money for her care arrived—anonymously, Red Hell, Richard called her, she fancied herself part Indian—she was primitive all right, and an artist—too talented for marriage, she thought—turned down offers from a score of New England's most respectable fools for beauty, it was said the only proposals she turned down were the ones for marriage, even pregnant she was sex personified, he'd risked his career and marriage by refusing to lobotomize her until after the baby was born.

I say, "Lobotomize her? That was the new method of treatment?"

"She failed everything else."

"Failed—what?"

He sighs and says, "You know you're so like her."

"What do you mean?"

"Uncooperative—dangerous, really."

"What did she do?" I say.

"Tried to escape constantly, made weapons of eating utensils, tried to use them on me—like a prisoner, no ability to trust."

"Well, wasn't she a prisoner?"

Richard shakes his head. "You fail to make distinctions just the way she did. One of her delusions was that she was Persephone."

"But with no Hecate—no mother to rescue her. What was my mother's name?"

"Red Hell."

"Her real name."

"She never said."

I'm too angry to be with him any longer. "I want to go back to my cell," I say.

Richard smiles. "You really make me miss her. You must know you can't go back. The cell or here—you're home now."

"Home—like The Home?"

He says, "It was a beautiful Victorian building—where you were born. I delivered you—just in time."

"For?"

"She got worse toward the end of the pregnancy. Actually I had to induce labor—and when you wouldn't come I had to cut you out—like Caesar—very fitting considering your sense of entitlement."

"Entitlement?" I say.

Richard laughs—strangely, as if he knows I know what he means, he says, "Aren't we all living your script?"

"It wasn't meant to be lived."

"Oh?"

I remember Cheekbones saying he thinks it's a conspiracy, I guess I thought it was an excuse but I see now he's either a great actor or he really does believe it. "Why did you have to induce labor?" I say.

"We didn't know what she would do—maybe to herself, and that would have meant you."

"You're saying you saved my life?"

Richard gives a depreciating smiles. "If you hate me for that you hate yourself—do you, Sam?"

I feel as if something in me is coming apart, I say, "What happened to me then?"

"You lived at The Home—with all the amenities."

"And what exactly are those—in an insane asylum?" I'm stalling for time—not wanting to ask the next question.

"You had the run of the place—and a private school."

I'm stunned. "You sent me to a private school yet you say she was pregnant by another man?"

Richard says, "It could have been any man."

"Even you?"

"I'm touched at your fantasy," Richard says, "but no, I met her pregnant."

"And you were married at the time?"

"Yes—I had a family, a professional life—Red Hell cost me

all of it. I couldn't stay away from her—I suppose my colleagues were right, I should have operated before the delivery, afterwards was too late, I was obsessed. I developed a research project on schizophrenic and psychopathic mothers and their children—spent years following them."

"Research project," I say, "is that what I ran away from?"

"You know, when I found you and you pretended not to know me, I knew I was right about you."

I hold my breath and say, "Meaning?"

"You set the fire that killed your mother— and most of the people in The Home. I'm fascinated to know what that experience was like."

Richard goes on, I barely hear him, he talks about a fire that started in the attic—I realize that was the white door, the white iron bed, he says I was found playing with matches several times before that, I was getting more defiant every year, this happened on my thirteenth birthday, no one ever saw me again—until Richard saw the audition at the Parthenon.

"It was ironic," he says, "all those years searching for you—and you don't know me! Of course I realized quickly it was your delusion or lie—the innocent amnesiac." Richard smiles as he talks, his eyes constantly seek mine—insist on my attention, he tells me that although he's been looking for me for years—the other children of his experiment are all in hospitals—he didn't find me at all, I found him.

I say, "You think I found you?"

"You did."

"But if I did what you say, why would I want to find you?"

"You know the old cliché about returning to the scene of the crime," he says.

I'm suddenly dizzy, transported somewhere, a brightly lit room—so bright there must be camera lights, I blink trying to see more clearly, the iron bed is there—then it's all gone, I hear my voice as if someone else is speaking. "The research project—it was kiddie porn, wasn't it?" I say.

Richard raises his glass, says, "You never mince words—Red Bird—remember that name?" he says, "the first time you climbed in my bed—"

I strike—surprising him, he staggers back, drops his wine, rubs his face, red from my slap, laughs louder. "I rest my case!"

I run to the door but it's locked. "Yes," he says, "every precaution has been taken against the escape of a psychotic wanted for arson murder for—how many years now?"

"I'm not psychotic—you know damn well."

"Perhaps you're right," Richard says, "after today—though it will cost me a twenty-year bet with a colleague. But now I'm inclined towards a diagnosis of sociopath—Antisocial Personality Disorder—Conduct Disorder before the age of 18. All that manipulation, intellect—without conscience or feeling."

"Are you going to turn me over to the police?"

"I am the police."

I say, "Right—your undercover story."

Richard laughs, "If it was a story, why are we here? Why would they let me have you for my research."

"They—who?"

"That information is need-to-know," Richard says.

"What are you going to do?"

"What should I do, Red—give you up?"

"I thought you said it was my mother you were obsessed with."

"It was—until you took her from me and left me. I couldn't stop thinking about you."

Suddenly I see her face as if in a dream, she looks angry or—I don't know, completely alone, as if there is no one else in the universe, yet she's standing with me in the bus station, I know it's me standing there, a smaller version of her, but it couldn't be, could not have been, she never went out of that building, she wasn't locked up anymore, she was too afraid to leave, I tried almost daily to get her out, I pleaded with her to come with me, now she's standing there in the bus station beside me—only for an instant, then I see her from the bus, not looking at me, looking down—as if I didn't exist, as if she didn't, I see that when we broke we became all of them—Richard, the woman who looks like me—the mother—and the child—all in me. We don't exist alone, that's why he needs me—why he's right, I found him.

I say, "What happened after she put me on the bus?"

Richard bursts out laughing. "You are delusional," he says.

"She put me on the bus," I say, "and when she came back without me, you set the fire—trying to get her to tell you where I was."

Richard acts as if he didn't hear me, I didn't say those words, the words were not spoken, never existed—like me—he does it beautifully, perfectly, even now, all these years later, I wonder if I do exist, he drinks, walks away from me. "You know," he says, "when I found your novel I thought it was a terrorist plot—disguised as a novel—really a story for a screen play, it read like a film—or a script for real action. All that was left was your motive—or delusion, as the case may be. Now I see your delusion—your mother's psychiatrist, your fantasy father, made you do the things you did—the things he was researching. It's quite perfect, really, I am more and more impressed with your ability to turn everything into a reason to kill—me and everything I stand for."

I see how it turns, how in his position—his part of us—he's right. "What was the kiddie porn for?" I say.

"Kiddie porn is your fantasy. I was researching sexuality in children—I was and am a known authority on it."

"Forcing children to do sex acts and filming it—how is that research?"

"Forcing?" he says, laughs, drinks. "you believe you were being forced?"

"Any child who has sex with an adult is forced."

This time Richard howls with laughter, he says, "How politically correct!" The room goes dark and on the monitor I see myself and Toledo in his bath. That he should have our intimacy infuriates me.

"Who is forcing you here?" Richard says, his voice rage-filled, yet something terribly sad about it—about him, drinking, shaking with pain he doesn't even get, I understand something or it's at the tip of my mind, something about aloneness so profound he doesn't have a clue. What about his father? What about his mother? How far back does it go? Are the civilized so wounded the only memory we have is the official story? Are we like the Citizen guards—only no lazar needed, so wounded yet convinced by the most elegant language, art forms—and of course the amenities, as Richard calls them.

"Tears!" Richard says, "Well, you are a woman after all." He stares at me, his eyes soften, become almost sweet, he says, "You see, after the lobotomy, your mother touched herself all the time, they all do for awhile but some more than others, some longer than others. When you were with her, she touched you," he nearly gasps, goes on, "it was so moving the way your eyes deepened, as if she was touching your essence. And I realized what was missing from psychoanalytic theory—the demonstration of child sexuality in real time! That's when my research started—imagine inspiring my research!"

I say, "So you filmed my mother and me—and other children?"

"Of course—I had to replicate," he stops, his face darkens again, he says, "So now you know what you stole from me."

"What I stole?"

"What you burned!"

I see it now, "The fire," I say, "your movies burned in the fire. I left and you tried to get it out of her where I was. You forgot you made her stupid, all she could do was put me on a bus, she didn't know where it was going. Maybe you were in a rage and killed her

238

trying to get it out of her and burned everything to hide it. But you tell yourself it was me—or maybe you just tell me it was me."

He doesn't respond, walks away as if I am not there, no one is there but him, he's right about one thing, I would have killed him if I'd been able to shoot, I didn't plan it—even the child didn't know she would pick up his gun, he always carried one—said he never knew when some madwoman's hallucinated God would tell her to kill her doctor. Now I see how pointless that would have been, would be now—even though I know it's still there, the boiling, know without feeling it, at other times I'm so sorry for him I could pray for him if I believed in prayer, but I sold all that to Richard—not as a child, that was only the foundation, the movie was the sale, even the idea of the movie—any movie—seems so odd now that everything is the movie, and it's not even Richard I sold it to, it's the him in me—the killer, the taker, the rapist. The would-be God.

I make three marks on the wall before the next time the cage arrives to take me to him, looks different, smaller—maybe it's his clothes—an old leather jacket and jeans—like my Toledo would wear, a chill goes through me at the thought, Richard says, "I'm beginning to understand that I brought you here because I need your help. I can understand how you misread the past, I can give you that. But the present is extremely urgent. I told you I'm undercover, I know that's hard for you to believe. But consider it for a moment. With your help, I could change the way this turns out."

"This?"

"The graduation exercise—and the movie."

"Change it how?"

"I've learned that the ammunition for the exercise is live," he says, "—I was told we were using blanks. Of course I've suspected something was wrong I just couldn't prove it."

"So you're saying you really thought all this was just to train so-called counterterrorists—aren't the methods a bit realistic—not to say violations of human rights?"

"Of course—that's what made me suspect to begin with—but it's not the first time such methods have been used, otherwise why would you write a novel about it?"

My head is spinning. "I wrote the novel years ago—as allegory. All this is an enactment of your bastardization of it. You just told me the other day you thought the novel was a terrorist plot—and you kidnapped us."

"I admit I got involved in the movie because I—The We— wanted to use it—take what looked like a plot and turn it into a counter-operation. Counterterrorist camps have been around for years too—not exactly like this but your novel is a takeoff on reality—right? The kidnapping was—call it an expression of my ambivalence—I could always say I was using surprise as part of the documentary movie and at the same time, be in control in case it really was a plot. Ever since I started getting to know you I began to wonder if thinking the movie was a plot could be a function of my anger at your desertion—maybe everything I thought about you in the past was colored by that. Then talking to you the other day, hearing your memory of your mother putting you on the bus—it had a profound effect on me."

I'm flabbergasted, I think he must be desperate to try this. "Everything you said—now it's all projection?"

"I know it sounds like a quick 180—but I'm trying to tell you it was a gradual realization—and thinking about the other day broke through my defenses—the aha of insight. Maybe the fact that the stakes are so high helped."

"What about the fire?"

"That could've started a lot of ways—you know that. I always knew it but I guess I needed to believe it was you to deal with the loss—to protect me from my love for you."

"Love."

"I know what you think. Tell me what I can do to convince you."

"Give me a gun."

He opens a drawer, pulls out a 38 and hands to me, I check that it's loaded, think very seriously of shooting him, he gets a pillow from the bed, says, "Use it as a silencer."

"Are you asking me to shoot you?"

"I'm giving you the power—that's what you want, isn't it?"

"And what do you want?"

"You still don't believe me."

He's right, he's done the only thing I never expected and I don't believe it, I also don't know what to do, how to play this, "Apologize," I say.

It's his turn to look flabbergasted, even disconcerted. "I said I could have been wrong about you—was, I'm sure of that now."

"You stole my self."

"That's how you saw it—I do apologize for that."

"It's not how I saw it, it's what you did."

"Everything is a question of interpretation."

"You mean spin," I say, "—if one doesn't work, you try another. That's what this is, isn't it—a different spin. For what? What is it you want from me?"

"Your trust."

"No—you made me evil but not dumb. Why not? Why didn't you cut out my brain the way you did my mother's?"

"I was wrong to do that. I thought it was right then but now I see it was wrong—what it did to you. I apologize."

"I want to go back to my cell."

He looks freaked, as if there's someone behind me about to shoot him—or me, of course he's afraid I'll really do it, I put the 38 in my belt but his look doesn't change, "What're you afraid of?" I say.

"Losing you."

"You never had me."

"Of course—I just thought so—at least as your—how did I put

it?—fantasy father." Next he freaks me, he drops to his knees, goes on, "I'm sorry, Sam—I know I ruined your life."

"Stole my self."

"Yes—stole your self—more important than your life." His voice shakes, eyes are moist.

"Well you are good—I give you that."

"No—I'm evil, I know that—I just want to do something good before it's too late—please." Voice still shaking, even his shoulder, hands covering face, he tells about the graduation ceremony, how Citizens and Recruits will have to kill the Enemy or be killed, "You've only simulated it so far—you don't know what happens to your soul."

"Is that what happened to you?"

"What I did to your mother—we did it to a lot of women, even some men. We thought we were protecting others from them, even them from themselves—like in war when you kill the enemy. Some of them didn't live through it. When Vietnam happened, I knew what they went through—Stephen's movie, he never knew how well I understood."

"Why didn't you tell him?"

"It would've blown my cover."

"What cover?"

"Intel."

"Speak English."

"I was hired to provide forensic psychiatric consultation on terrorists and terrorist organizations."

"By?"

"I thought the government—now I'm not sure."

"Why you?"

"I knew some people."

I say, "The We?"

"We the People—an investment group with a think tank—so

they told me. The next thing I knew I was involved in this counter-terrorist education project."

"Sure it's not government?"

"I've asked, they've denied."

"And the movie?"

"I'm afraid I needed to give them something—and I wanted to know."

"What?"

"About you," he says, "—and Stephen—maybe about myself. I knew everyone I've loved hated me—even if I didn't know why."

"Christ."

"A lot of people—yourself included—will be crucified if you don't help. I know there's a kind of resistance—there always is."

"And if there is?"

"I want to join."

Twelve

I deny knowing anything about a "resistance" even though it's possible, even probable, that Richard knows Cheekbones told me, now we pretend—that I don't know about the Transformation and that he wants to join it, to redeem himself, I believe him—it's oddly like one of those nice relationships, people pretending everything is as it should be, the pretense is what's important, some might call it trust—Richard does, he seems actually happy, I'm to see Toledo and Cheekbones as soon as he can plan it without any bugs, that's where his paranoia has gone, they are always watching, listening, we have to be careful, the Citizen guards are always there, I even forget them the way you forget cameras, mikes, sometimes I even forget Richard—the way I used to think of him, the obsession, now he's just this aging lech trying to stem the loneliness, he has a whole mythology about Jesus and the "resistance"—but it feels like nothing so much as a child saying, "Tell me a story."

"Tell me about Zapata," he says.

I pretend he means the historic Zapata, I say, "The revolutionary?"

"Alias Jesus Cahero—intelligence sources have spent two years investigating his cadre of international terrorists—in the brilliant disguise of *American Movie!*"

"What do you mean—terrorists?"

"You tell me—what is he like?"

"An artist."

"Could he be devoted to a cause?"

"The cause of truth."

"Is it political?"

"It?"

"The idea of truth."

"Sounds like a philosophical question. What do you think?"

"Tell me about him."

"All I know is he met Toledo in Mexico and worked as cinematographer for the Vietnam movie. Why don't you tell me about him—where he is now?"

"All I know is he's classified an Enemy Agent thought to be organizing a resistance to the Camp and planning to take it over."

"And this theoretical resistance—you want to join—how does that involve me?"

"If you could talk to him… I mean The We are convinced about him. You see my problem?"

Richard tells me The We has been following this movement Jesus is supposed to be head of since its conception in the Thirties by international communists, who by the Fifties had infiltrated the American political system, the entertainment industry, the educational system—as manifested in the Sixties and rejected by patriotic Americans, it went underground and now is surfacing in organized terror—the code name for which is *American Movie*—to lay the groundwork for political take-overs of local governments, police departments, military installations, National Guard and state governments, and eventually the federal government and armed forces.

"So the movie isn't just a terrorist plot, it's part of this bigger story about Jesus," I say, "—amazing coincidence."

"It was when he joined the project they became convinced. When people play spy games they become so paranoid they create coincidence."

"They."

"We—yes, I'm one of them."

Like a child playing a guilty parent I say, "Let me see Stephen."

"If you talk about us I'll be exposed and we'll all be killed."

"Us?"

"Our conversations."

"Why don't you bring him here?"

"He wants to kill me."

So the pretense goes on, Richard sends me in full Citizen regalia to convince Toledo he's won me over, there's nothing left to fight for, I suggest taking him to the obstacle course, he'll trust me more there, I can show him how strong I am, how he can be, I go to Toledo's cell in the cage-car, when the door opens I stand motionless, afraid to move, to give myself away, Toledo stares at me ghost-like, I take off the helmet and face shield, for a moment he doesn't change, he's used to controlling his reactions, then he laughs bitterly, says, "So he's won," turns to the monitor as if it's Richard, "congratulations," he says, "you got it all now."

I say, "Don't forget the fat lady."

He glances up, his eyes narrow with distrust but something else in them too—curiosity.

I say, "How could I joke at a time like this?"

He shrugs, I never thought about it before but I can't imagine Toledo shrugging, he comes into the cage car, stands as far away from me as he can, we arrive at the obstacle course, I show him the karate room with the four video walls, he starts to come alive watching me, he moves with me, copying my every move, I'm amazed he can do anything in his condition, he's dancing with me, that's it, but it's a fight dance, he jabs and spins, kicks and spins, jabs, kicks, spins, faster, faster, I don't know how long he can keep it up, each punch and kick comes closer, I start to back off, he comes closer, I see the rage in his eyes, they glisten with hate, it hurts, I say, "Let's stop."

He says, "Uncle?"

"Uncle." I take the chance that the audio isn't great here, no reason for it to be, the monitors talk at you, don't expect verbal response. "It's not what you think. I'm doing what I had to do to see you—what we have to—to get out of here."

He laughs bitterly, says, "So you're doing it but you don't mean it?"

"I'm not sleeping with him."

"What are you doing?"

I tell him about Richard's story.

"He's a brilliant liar."

"We have to keep doing the course," I say, "but listen, will you?"

We go to the rifle range, computer simulation, he's good at this, too. I notice bruises on his chest and arms, he sees me looking, shrugs again, says, "What else is new?"

"What do you mean?"

Toledo laughs. "Worried your new lover might be a sadist?"

It's like icy rain, I see how complacent I've become, how easy it is to believe your own pretense. "I told you he's not my lover. Are you saying he did this?"

"Oh not personally—doesn't get his hands dirty the way he used to."

"Meaning he did when you were a kid?"

"You were always brilliant."

The hatred in his voice shoots through me, I say, "Why?"

"I'm not a chameleon."

"Like me? What wouldn't you do for him?"

"How long have you got?"

"What he did to Rachel?"

I see from his eyes he isn't sure it happened, we move to hand-guns, I tell him about the asylum, my mother, what Richard told me about his research, at first he says nothing, stands like a Lazarus, then starts to shake, "I'll kill him," he says, "I should've done it then—I was a fucking coward."

"You were a boy."

"No—there was a time I could have—he was older, I was strong.

I couldn't do it—couldn't even remember why I was supposed to. He was so powerful—so handsome. Everyone fell in love with him—me too. I don't blame you."

I say, "Some would call it identification with the aggressor, but I always saw how empty he was, how he needed so much. I thought if I was devoted to him he might be able to love my mother—and me."

"You make it sound so sweet."

"Well, that's what I told myself," I say, "now I know he's part of me."

"Part of you?"

"The part I've always hated. He said that to me recently—if you hate me you hate yourself."

"Bullshit," Toledo says, "you just never had anyone come through for you."

"You like the sweet part better? My personal invention of love?"

"Sure that's not what love is—a personal invention?"

"No."

Toledo meets my eyes with his old eyes, I feel him back. "You think, you hope—or you're sure?" he says.

"Sure."

We're in the bomb factory now, he lurches towards me, I put my arms around him, say into his ear, "Richard guessed right about the resistance." I pull away, afraid I'll cry, he'll cry, we'll blow it, we stagger to the next obstacle and the next, I alternate between instructions and, as he does the obstacles, telling him about the scene here, Richard, The Commission, Armageddon, I see life return to him, feel it return to me, at the end of the course, where Richard met me that time, where the audio pickup is probably good so he could get that meeting between him and me for the movie, I give him the confession Richard needs to make him a Citizen Recruit.

"Don't worry, I have a copy," he says.

I see he's playing it, he storms off, looks back at me suspiciously, he's right, he can't capitulate right away, when he goes back to his cell he only glances at me, the cameras are too close here, I put the confession on the floor, "At least look at it," I say for the audio pickup, "His intelligence is really quite amazing." Toledo gives his sardonic laugh. "I'll be back," I say, but neither of us knows whether I will.

When I return Richard looks hurt, suspicious—whether of seeing us on the course or not being able to hear everything I'm not sure—I say, "He's close to signing."

"You looked very convincing—remember The We is getting all the tape."

"How is it they don't get tape from here?"

"I'm still trusted."

I see him squeezed between two pretenses, the one with me and the one with them—even if he's really with them, even if they actually do get tape of our conversations, he has to convince them what he's doing with me is strategic, I see him begin to lose it, I sympathize, sometimes he even has me sleep in his bed, I'm not in my cell so maybe they conclude he's bedding me but he takes the couch, stares at me through a camera, as if that can tell him what his eyes can't—what I'm thinking, whether I've been in touch with Jesus—or as if the camera protects him from my real being—my flesh versus my image, flesh is dangerous, feeling lives in it—I remember he never touched us, not the kids, not even my mother except for a kind of mechanical ejaculation, leaving the camera running as if, like Nixon, in some death wish, I wonder what he might be showing now, how much The We know about his strategy with me, still I understand his not touching, understood it then, became it, his wanting to stay frozen, having a Lazarus self to take over the mess of humanness, the horror of the raging animal inside, so deep most of the time I forget I'm only waiting till the moment it springs—still easier than love.

Richard starts keeping the Citizen guards away, keeps his magnum close, like Toledo he fights sleep—paces, stops to make notes on his computer, sits heavily on the end of the bed, eventually sinks back tensely, passes into a half-consciousness of restless twitching, moaning, snoring, sometimes waking himself, sometimes he's out for a few minutes then longer, I think he might be taking drugs, when he's out I begin to search the apartment, I know where all the weapons are now—the lazar gun, a magnum I empty and hide the shells, knives—what's in every drawer, each closet and cupboard, on every shelf, which key fits each lock—I memorize it all, I read his papers, one night I find a stash of bound letters—from his wife! They date back twenty years—each one almost identical, as a school lesson in penmanship copied from the board—variations on:

I am ready to come home now, I know you're disappointed in me and I can only hope and pray for your forgiveness. I promise to be a better wife to you and mother to our children—who must wish me dead, they never write or answer my letters. I think something is wrong with the mail here, no one ever gets any, though we see a mail truck pass every day. If possible, could you look into what happens to the mail? I hate to ask. I know I'm always asking you for something and you get sick of it. Who could blame you?

The only similarity is the words, the handwriting is different each time—maybe written for her by others. I remember writing notes to my mother—desperate apologies for unnamed crimes I tried to guess at to explain the attic room—her silence. Richard. Maybe Richard had his wife in the Home at the same time my mother and I were there. Did she die in the fire? I wonder how many other women there were, women and children. Again from *The Brothers Karamazov*: "Why are the babes so poor?"

One night in my search I find the footage confiscated from the Coast Guard plane! At first I don't recognize it—I stare at the film and video cans as if they're UFOs, open a can and hold the film up to light—there we are—our memories, our past. Our history, the proof of our existence. I'm ecstatic, as if coming back from the dead.

When Richard wakes he's always scared—as if sleeping means he's losing his mind, he checks the doors, all the locks inside the apartment, the computer, the telephone—even looks out the windows. At first I thought he suspected me but lately I've noticed that when he does this he barely knows I'm here, I wonder if he keeps the Citizen guards away because he's afraid they'll suspect him and tell The We, it's like a ritual—a kind of passage from one state of consciousness to another, the sequence always the same, always ending with the same words, "Did I close my eyes?" He insists I answer—as if he's not sure, looks at the magnum with confusion—did he leave it loaded or not? "Any calls—visitors?" he says, I begin to wonder whether he's as much prisoner as I—maybe The We don't trust him as much as he says, I'm more sure he's on drugs now, when he sleeps he must be crashing—unable to stay awake no matter what he takes, I think how merciful the universe—the frailty of humanness, it begins to occur to me that he really is looking for redemption—maybe has been even back so far as The Home, his research—certainly Victims Vigilant, and now the Nest. So the pretense becomes a premise.

One night as he lies half-conscious I hear a tap on the door—Cheekbones. She has some ether and we keep Richard out with drops of it on gauze, she does a bug-check on the room, I ask if it's possible there are bugs it doesn't recognize, she says of course but we have to risk it, she tells me the Transformation has broken both the computer code and the closed circuit television, they have a tap on the system, I tell her my hunch about Richard's saying he wants to join, my hunch about his being a kind of prisoner.

"We think he's a figurehead," she says.

"Which is the way it started—but for what?"

"Profiteers who believe in nothing, not even fascism," she says, "they play games—war, political movements, terrorist/antiterrorist activities—just like making movies—for money."

"Why am I surprised?"

"You're not—you just didn't expect to wake up in a meta-movie."

I give Cheekbones the confiscated film and video to take to Jesus, she tells me our action—La Inauguración, the opening—will be in a few days. When Richard wakes up he's more paranoid than ever, demands to know what happened, he never sleeps, he doesn't need it, maybe it's in the food, "Get Stephen's confession—now, we have to move!"

When the cage-car opens in Toledo's cell, I take off the mask and helmet, he goes white—as if we hadn't talked, it's good, I wait for him to speak or move, "A real survivor, aren't you?" he says.

"We have to help Richard," I say, "there could be a counterplot."

Toledo studies me, trying to understand, he says, "So he's the one you understand and forgive everything—you're with him now."

It sounds too real, too full of emotion, for a moment I'm lost, the mind-tape blank as after the bus to New York, I hear myself say, "Is that what you have against all of us—me, Cheekbones, Rachel—that we chose life over virgin death?"

Toledo reels, I reach out to steady him and he says, "Well now I'm a survivor too—" breaks off, throws the confession at me.

I go back to the cage-car, he follows, as the bars slide shut, says, "I'm like him—a bastard of my time and experience."

I'm out of camera range, I shake my head, he rushes at the door as if furious, I see he's acting now, I trust him. Act of love. Of life. I feel the baby, one I know I belong with.

Richard's entire appearance has changed—no more youthful debonair—he wears the Citizen uniform—to convince them, he says, has his head shaved, I remember he used to keep his hair short so the gray wouldn't show as much, now some sort of asceticism like the ones on the edge, can't choose between circles of hell, I remember him completely now, almost pity him, one morning an electronic beep begins from the computer, Richard looks as if it's gunshot, runs to the computer, hits his access, a shield fades on—a blue flag with We The People emblazoned across it in red letters on white background—then dissolves to a man in military uniform, seated at a desk, telling Richard to pick up the phone, he reaches for the red receiver in the cabinet below the computer, the monitor audio goes silent, leaves me to study the caller's video image and try to read his lips.

"Goddamn it," Richard says, "on whose authority? This is my exercise—I don't need a field general or any other kind of—" He breaks off and listens again, pacing, trying to break in, finally saying, "I want a conference—yes, all of us—today—and this general of yours had better not arrive before that!" The caller doesn't agree, Richard swears some more and throws the phone at the monitor.

"Can I help?" I say.

"You—you'd love it, wouldn't you?"

I'm silent, he shakes his head, says, "Christ, they're killing me."

"What do they want?"

"Everything—" Richard says then breaks off as if the word slipped out, he gets out a bottle of Courvoisier, swills it, goes on, "They want to send some spaghetti-chested bastard to command the graduation exercise."

"Armageddon?"

He stares paranoically, "Where'd you get that?"

"Revelations—I think. But isn't this graduation exercise a good-and-evil scene?"

He doesn't answer, says, "After I've done the work, some Four Star gets to run the war," he says, "and pretend it's his!" He stops, as if trying to think which pretense he's in, goes on, "The only way we can stop this is to stay in control."

I say nothing, Richard drinks, empties the bottle, his eyes rivet to me—he needs to believe in me, doesn't understand why and it tears him up, the only thing he knows to do is control—me, the Nest—he's too weak though, afraid yet excited by his fear, the chance of a contest he might win by losing, the way he lost to his own father—the hope of punishment enough. Fear of not being in control and the intense desire for it. Buried masochism or buried soul? As Richard paces and drinks I try to think how this affects La Inauguración—Cheekbones must know, they're patched in to all Nest communications—we'll have to move right away, I don't see Richard fall, just hear the thud, the floor shaking like an earthquake, I grab a pillow to stick the corner in his mouth so he won't bite his tongue, suddenly he stops, his eyes shine like a lost child's, mouth moving around the pillow, trying to say something, I tell him not to talk, it could start again, he shakes his head, I take the pillow out, he whispers, "I love you," starts seizing again, I shove the pillow back in, suddenly he stops, only his eyes live, the door breaks open, Toledo charges in, tries to haul Richard up to hit him, "He's stroked out," I say.

Toledo says, "Christ, you might know he'd rob me even of this!"

"Tell him," I say.

Toledo hauls him up again, "I'd kill you if you weren't already dead."

The shining eyes seek.

The intelligence is that the general replacing Richard will arrive just before dawn, they'll bring troops to monitor the event—Citizen Recruits and Enemy Agents fighting to the death. We meet on the cliffs where Citizens don't patrol because no one is fool enough to go there, it's risky enough at low tide, when the tide is high it's sure death, the gulls flutter and shriek around us now, warning, I say, "They know the tide."

"They and electronics," Jesus says, "it'll be low when the troops arrive." They would come in helicopters from the Presidio—nice historic touch—not to mention the back-up troops there. They've even got an aircraft carrier with F-14s—even B57s at the ready."

"Christ," Toledo says, "are we that dangerous?"

"We'd better plan to be," Cheekbones says.

Jesus reports on the computer system. The Nest—the whole island—is bugged for direct international media feed to show the world live coverage of the most advanced US antiterrorist mission— the Institute's graduation exercise.

"Like Vietnam," Toledo says, "they think they're going to win a war on TV. What if we activate it now—show the world our side of it?"

I say, "Wouldn't that bring more troops?"

"The full power of the U.S. military—all for lil' ol' us?" Cheekbones says.

Jesus says, "It's our only chance. Even if we could ambush the ones they're planning to send now, we couldn't get off the Rock, those bombers would level it."

"The Nest," Cheekbones says.

"Some nest."

"Think we'd survive in a nice warm—flat—desert camp?"

Toledo says, "Look, Jesus said it, our only hope is to get back to our movie—out of Richard's—or whoever's. Transformation— like you said. What was supposed to happen after we got captured? They bring us here but to the Rock, not the Nest—this whole closed system. In our script we get away. We can't do that here, we have to open the system—bring the whole damn world in. It's the documentary part of our movie—what we said we'd do."

"Hoping the whole damn world will believe what they see," I say.

"It's all we have," Jesus says, "all we ever had."

Crouched on the cliffs, we listen to the foghorn, the waves, feel the fog, imagine we can do this, and begin.

We extend the closed circuit system, already in the prison and all the other buildings, we set video monitors up at every outside vantage point, our Citizen converts who work in the computer system feed in footage about the "situation" at the Institute, arguments between government officials about the graduation exercise, even some video conference stuff with The We members joking about the new Native uprising on the Rock—echoes of the last stand of the American Indian Movement. When we see it all together, it's clear that Richard's idea of it—Citizen Recruits against Enemy Agents—was never going to happen, too risky. We feed in conversations between military, government officials, sometimes Richard, about the graduation exercise, the New Last Stand excites them, they're almost delirious with the anticipation of slaughter—except theirs will be a sure thing. Finally we put in Richard's phone conversation about his replacement. I realize everything between Richard and me was taped—whether he knew it or not.

When the Citizens and finally the officers, Richard's men, prepare to swat the computer room, we're ready, they find nothing but their own smoke and fire, we moved the equipment, we have them, ambushed, lock them up, leave them to the monitors that first "reeducated" them, to see the documentary, the reality we are creating, they can join us if they want, it's amazing how survival is the mother of perception. We go on the system and talk about how our only chance is to have amnesty on both sides and get together to create a survival plan before the troops arrive. What we don't put on is the plan, we go out and talk to Citizens, officers, whoever is left, we ambush them when necessary, we talk, we show them the monitors if they haven't seen the footage, lock up the ones we have to.

We're ready for the bombers too, we hear them, three of them, even see them on TV from the International News Network—INN—they're feeding back to us, the attack coming, we're about a hundred hiding in the first floor of the old fort dug into the bedrock—our citadel—beneath the prison, we're all together, the handful of Citizens, officers, Richard—lifeless except for the eyes—we have them locked in one of the corridors, we don't know if any of us will survive the bombing, we're hoping for a measured strike plan, tolerable losses, recall the Independence Day celebration in 1876, when all the cannons failed to hit the stationary target—the end of the mythical fortress protecting San Francisco harbor. When the bombing starts, everything shakes, whine of bombs dropping, the prison shattering above us, ceiling cracking but holding, other buildings in the background crumbling, INN shows bombs dropping into the sea, we cheer for the fog, pilot error, human incompetence, the sound of the bombers recedes, on INN we see them leaving, the helicopters lifting off from the Presidio, on their way, there's no time to take it in, we're still alive, no time to embrace, even look at each other, we emerge from our citadel armed with lazars, steal across the rubble, disappear onto the cliffs, into what used to be trees and brush, the rubble of buildings at the outer edges, we don't see INN now, the mikes, direct feed, monitors—all bombed out—the birds are gone, the foghorn silent, the lighthouse a heap of concrete shards, we listen for the technobirds, can't see them through the fog, finally hear the whirring, by the time we see them they're almost on the rubble, six of them, the troops roll out, about a dozen from each chopper, they rush into our circle and freeze like the Citizen guards, like I did when Richard lazared me, Jesus and I shoot with digicams we found in the computer room— emergency equipment—Toledo talks to them through a portable mike, his voice eery after what seems hours of human silence, we take their weapons, lock them all in the citadel with Richard and the others, the troops don't say anything, Richard's men keep giving orders, Richard looks out from the eyes, I say, "I'm leaving," to him, the eyes flinch.

When we emerge again from the bedrock, the scene is lighted like a set, helicopters landing, boats docking, loudspeakers squawking, the media have arrived. Only the birds are silent, the media crews want to hang out and wait for the next military move, they show us broadcasts from all over the world, the choppers landing, the troops surrounded by us, lazared by us, being moved by us towards the citadel, disappearing into the tunnel, all this complete with commentary by military and government officials denying any knowledge of military action on Alcatraz, most of them make jokes about publicity tricks, they all seem to be wearing strange smiles, the kind people use to comment on madness—or to suggest it. "They're gaslighting us," Toledo says and leads the way to the dungeons, the media crews follow into the cracked tunnel and dungeons of the bedrock, we try to talk to the troops, get them to say what happened, they act like POWs and give only name, rank, and serial number.

"Isn't that proof?" Toledo says. "Check their IDs."

Cheekbones says, "They'll be deleted."

An INN reporter everyone calls Annie Oakley has a computer, Cheekbones is right, there's no record of any of the sixty-five men and five women—not in regular service or Special OPs, no record of the choppers, either. INN sets up a teleconference with General Charles "Chuck" Omen, Chair of the Joint Chiefs, for an interview with Annie Oakley here in the Nest.

"General, how could Toledo have all this equipment?" Annie says.

"Have you ever seen a movie where the equipment didn't look like the real thing?"

"Were you a consultant on the movie?"

"Not to my knowledge," Omen says, "but since we're here, I suppose you could assume that in some way, they managed to muster me."

"So you gave permission for the impersonation of military equipment and personnel?"

Omen laughs, says, "I didn't say that."

Annie Oakley says, "What about Alcatraz—how do you explain the destruction?"

"Ask the moviemakers."

"So they were allowed to destroy Alcatraz?"

"That's all I'm at liberty to say."

"Did they buy it? Who did they pay?"

"I'm not at liberty to discuss the matter any further."

Questions are hurled at Omen—how long have you known? How could it happen? Why weren't they stopped? What happened to the National Park Service? Omen waves them all off.

It dawns on us it's a coverup, nothing really happened—just a movie.

The INN crew tries to get the troops to talk, they refuse, now they don't even give name, rank, and serial number—as if they got the new orders from Omen, I see their faces through my digicam, so young, unquestioning, they might have died on this mission, that would be their duty, the media crews start to wrap up, climb back in their choppers, we ask what will happen to the troops, can they send reporters back with them? They agree to take Richard to a hospital.

We take the troops in their helicopters. Annie Oakley agrees to come with us with her camera and sound crew, we split up in the six choppers, clutching our lazars, M-16s trained on the troop pilots, we land at the Presidio, ghost town, the only presence the trucks the troops arrived in, we keep trying to talk to the troops, tell them people were tortured and murdered on the Rock, but it's hopeless, to them it's just a movie, a truck arrives for the INN crew, we all pile in and follow the Army trucks, they lead us up and down the hills of San Francisco, people on the cable cars wave, some call out, "When is it going to be released?" Everyone knows what's real except us, even Annie Oakley begins to doubt, then we hear it on the radio, three Army trucks blown up at the Presidio by Falcons, helicopters with rockets, the troops must have gone back, not knowing what else to do.

Annie Oakley drops us off in Chinatown, she's going back to the Presidio, we split up, Jesus and Cheekbones go to make arrangements for us with Jesus' Mexican friends on their techno-transformed fishing vessel that could down helicopters and low-flying planes but looks like a scruffy working boat, we'll meet at the Fisherman's Wharf, I watch them go, something odd about it, as if we have to stay together. But they'll be looking for four of us—if they are, we're still struggling with what is real.

Toledo and I walk through the tourist-choked streets of Chinatown, across Green Street to Mason, up and down hills, too exhausted and scared to stop but somehow vindicated by the trucks being blown up—if it's just a movie, why would they have to disappear the troops—horribly vindicated by all those young deaths.

"But what's it really about?" I say, "what did they die for?"

Toledo says, "You mean *really*?"

"Okay, so defining *really*—is that all?"

"They who define reality have the power—money, control, the world in their hands. Remember the old man said it's not about love."

"Funny though," I say.

"You mean finding it in this godforsaken hole?"

It is what I mean, Toledo grabs my hand, says, "You're in love with Jesus, yes?"

I'm stunned. "Why do you say that?"

"Because it's true—you should know it—I mean about yourself, you know it. It's okay—you can love more than one person."

I laugh. "So this is an altruistic moment on your part?"

He stops me, very serious now, says, "Yes."

"So that lets you off the hook?"

We walk again, after a while I say, "I love him but no, I'm not in love with him. I don't really know what that means."

"D'you know what *we* mean?"

"Three," I say, "we're three now."

He looks quizzically, I put his hand on my belly, he folds his arms around me—us—dances us around, in and out of the tourists who laugh and clap, I think of our dancing before the Nest, my eyes water, he kisses them, we come to, scan the crowd for anything dangerous, it could be any of them, any guise, we still have the lazars but they'd be useless here, they need strategy and space, we see the boat, the flag torn nearly to shreds by weather, we split up to sneak through the crowd, I can see Jesus now, dressed like a fisherman, he sees me, I squeeze through the rest of the crowd, I'm getting on the boat when I see the media trucks, they shouldn't be here, they're splitting the crowd, practically running over people, Toledo makes it aboard, we're pulling away, one of the media trucks' doors open, Citizens rush out—the movie again.

The shot comes from somewhere else, a high-powered rifle, one shot—Jesus spins and falls. We're racing now, helicopters chasing, shooting, our boat too, and overhead helicopters, someone expected this, we have better guns—for the moment.

Toledo and I beside Jesus, Toledo says, "Why you?"

"He probably thought I had the footage," Jesus says.

Cheekbones says, "He thought you were Zapata."

Jesus' eyes shine at me, he says, "What are you doing here?"

"Trying to save you,"

I stay with him, the others get us just past the three-mile limit where, straight from the script, they make a show of burial at sea, a Mexican flag-draped box, I take minutes away from Jesus to shoot the scene, Toledo speaks just as we scripted it, the sea breaks to the surfacing of an old submarine commandeered through Jesus' companero, we lift him aboard and scramble after just in time to miss the entourage of choppers and planes chasing us.

In the cocoon of the sub we celebrate softly the sadness of freedom and the hope of transformation.

About the Author

Penelope Brindley is a writer and psychologist. American Movie is her first published novel. She began writing it while earning a master's in creative writing. While Dr. Brindley raised three children as a single mother she worked as a psychiatric nurse. Then she put herself through a doctoral program in psychology. She lives and works in Laurel, Maryland.

Printed in the United States
By Bookmasters